Tales from Grace Chapel Inn™

Amazing Gracie

Pam Hanson & Barbara Andrews

Guideposts

CARMEL, NEW YORK

Acknowledgments

All Scripture quotations are taken from
The Holy Bible, New International Version. Copyright © 1973,
1978, 1984 International Bible Society. Used by permission
of Zondervan Bible Publishers.

www.guideposts.org
(800) 431-2344
Guideposts Books & Inspirational Media Division
Series Editors: Regina Hersey and Leo Grant
Cover art by Edgar Jerins
Cover design by Wendy Bass
Interior design by Cindy LaBreacht
Typeset by Nancy Tardi
Printed in the United States of America

 Acknowledgments

With warm thanks to Carolyn Greene.

—Pam Hanson and Barbara Andrews

Chapter ♪ One

"What a perfect rose, and its fragrance is heavenly," someone said behind Jane Howard as she knelt, searching for any tiny weed that dared to sprout in her immaculate garden.

Jane scrambled to her feet, hoping she didn't look as startled as she felt.

"Is it an Amalia?"

The speaker was an older woman, not very tall, slightly plump and pleasant in her manner. Jane felt a little silly for being so absorbed in her gardening that she hadn't heard the crunch of footsteps on the garden path next to Grace Chapel Inn, the bed-and-breakfast she ran with her two sisters.

"No, it's a Mr. Lincoln, one my mother enjoyed when she first planted the garden," Jane said. "I tried to replace some of her favorites when I replanted. I never knew my mother, but I must get my love of gardening from her. The garden was a shambles when my sisters and I inherited the house from our father."

"Red roses are one of my favorite gifts from God," the stranger said, sighing. "Maybe that's because I can't wear red without looking like a clown."

Jane could easily imagine how unsettling a red blouse or sweater might look with the visitor's curly red hair and bright pink cheeks, but the artist in Jane automatically approved of the natural cotton top worn with tan slacks and sandals.

"I'm Gracie Parks," the woman said. "Are you one of the Howard sisters?"

"I'm Jane, and—"

"The youngest," Gracie said. "You're the artist and the decorator, not to mention cook and gardener. Don't look surprised. My friend Byrdie Hutchinson told me all about the three of you. As I recall, she said that Louise is the oldest, musical and a widow. Alice is three years younger, a nurse. She's always been single, and her loving ways make everyone love her." Gracie laughed at her recitation of the information. "I feel as though I should curtsy after that little speech."

"Actually, you deserve an *A* for accuracy." Jane was pleased that their new visitor had such a friendly interest in her family and that she hadn't mentioned Jane's divorced status. Maybe someday she could be casual about it, but she still didn't like to talk about that part of her life. Now, at age fifty, she was happily single. When her father Daniel, the pastor at Grace Chapel for many years, died, she returned to Acorn Hill to help her sisters turn their family home into a bed-and-breakfast. She looked forward to a fulfilling future pursuing all the interests that made her life rewarding.

She gathered her wits, pushed a lock of dark brown hair from the fair skin of her forehead, pulled off her gardening gloves and wiped her palm on her overalls before offering her hand to Gracie.

"We're really happy to have you stay at Grace Chapel Inn while you're visiting in Acorn Hill," Jane said, liking Gracie's firm handshake. "Byrdie has told us a few things about you too. You have quite a reputation as a sleuth."

"Is that what she called me?" Gracie chuckled. "More

likely folks in Willow Bend call me a busybody. But I have been able to help solve a few puzzles, some while working with the police. My neighbor Marge says I have enough curiosity for the whole state of Indiana."

"Well, that all sounds quite interesting." Jane would have liked to hear more about Gracie's sleuthing, but she changed the subject in accordance with the sisters' policy of not prying into their guests' affairs: "Have you been inside yet?" Jane asked. "I thought Louise was watching for you, but perhaps she was distracted."

"No, I saw you in the garden first and just had to have a closer look at what you're doing. I wasn't expecting to find the Garden of Eden in Pennsylvania."

"Hardly that," Jane said, her blue eyes showing her delight at the compliment. "But I have been putting a lot of time into it lately. I'm entering our local botanical society's garden competition this month, and their standards are high. The judges come armed with measuring tapes and lots of expertise."

"I love the way you've made a background of red azaleas and pink rhododendron along the back fence. Your climbing roses are marvelous." Gracie admired the three trellises heavy with red, pink and white blooms. "And these roses are just spectacular."

"They're my best hope for winning the competition. I worked on the plan all winter," Jane admitted. "The garden was my favorite place to play when I was a child. My mother died when I was a baby, so it made me feel closer to her. I was able to duplicate many of the things she had planted, a few roses, the peony bushes and the Japanese snowballs, but I had to totally redo most of the plot. The rock garden was a mess, and even the grass along the path had to be replaced by turf. Oh dear, I could keep you out here talking about my garden, but you must want to see your room. Can I help you bring in your things?"

"No, thank you, dear. There's nothing that can't wait, but where is that cat?" She looked around, bending to check under the snowball plants beside the house. "Gooseberry! Whatever you've found, leave it right there."

Jane spotted a fat orange tail, then the rest of the cat. He looked so smug that she suspected he was smiling.

"He likes to bring me presents," Gracie explained. "I'm afraid I'm not appreciative sometimes. Little mice and snakes are not my idea of welcome gifts."

Jane couldn't help smiling. She'd heard of dogs resembling their masters, but this was the first time she'd seen a feline version of a person. Gracie and Gooseberry shared a similarity in coloring, and both were a tad plump with happy demeanors.

"I did talk on the phone to one of your sisters, Louise, I think, about keeping Gooseberry with me. She said it was fine since you're all cat lovers. But if Gooseberry has any trouble getting along with your cat—"

"Wendell," Jane said.

"With Wendell, then I can leave him at Byrdie's. I only hesitate to give her that responsibility for the same reason that I'm not staying at her place while I'm in town. She really is terribly upset about the renovations at her house."

"I heard that she's had some difficulty," Jane said, "but I don't know exactly what went wrong."

"She's already done a lot of work sprucing up the place, but mostly she's concerned about the insulation in the attic."

"Wasn't it done right?" Jane asked.

"I'm not sure," Gracie said, distress for her friend's situation obvious in her voice. "She didn't want to talk about it on the phone, but I've known Byrdie a long time. I could tell she's upset. I should check in and get to her house."

"Of course," Jane said. "I'm sorry I kept you standing here so long. You're probably tired after your drive."

"Not too tired," Gracie said. "I visited a friend in eastern

Ohio on the way and stayed overnight at her house. It's my nature to get up early and avoid as much traffic as possible. I could stand here all day inhaling the fragrance of your garden if I wasn't worried about Byrdie. You'll surely win first prize on scent alone."

"I'm so glad you like it," Jane said, flushing with pleasure at Gracie's comments. "My sisters like the garden, but they sometimes think I spend too much time on it. Of course, they've mothered me all my life. They're twelve and fifteen years older than I am, so it's second nature for them to worry about me."

Gracie smiled sympathetically. "In our family, it's my son Arlen who's the mother hen. Since his father died five years ago, he's sure that I need watching so I won't get into trouble. He lives in New York with his wife and my wonderful grandson Elmo, so of course he has to monitor me by phone and e-mail. I start most days with a little note from Arlen."

"That's sweet," Jane said, "but my big sister Louise will think I'm a terrible hostess if I keep you standing out here in the sun. I haven't seen any of her piano students this morning, so she may be hard at work on the inn's finances. She keeps the books and pays the bills, thank heavens. It's my least favorite job. Do you mind going in through the side door? I always leave my shoes there when I've been in the garden."

"Not at all. I'm eager to see as much of the inn as you're willing to show me," Gracie said. "If the inside is as lovely as the outside, I'm blessed indeed to be staying here."

Inside, Louise Howard Smith, tall, blue-eyed and silver haired, looked at her watch for the third time in five minutes. She didn't mean to be impatient, but she had been expecting their latest guest sometime before noon. Just to be sure, she checked the reservation made in Gracie Parks's name. It was for today, Monday, June 12, through Sunday, June 18, just as she'd remembered.

Byrdie Hutchinson's friend wasn't overdue yet, but Louise had hoped to get her checked in and still have time to do some errands before her two o'clock music lesson. It was pleasant to have a light teaching schedule this summer, although she regretted that some of her pupils neglected their pianos during the school break.

Perhaps she was worrying more than necessary. Her better students tended to keep up their practice in spite of summer camps, family vacations, visits to relatives and all the other distractions of the season.

She was a little concerned that Jane spent every possible minute in the garden. Her youngest sister, she believed, had enough responsibility being in charge of meals, especially the lovely breakfasts they served their guests, without trying to compete in the demanding competition sponsored by the botanical society. Louise was willing to ease Jane's workload by helping out wherever she could. She didn't mind taking care of registration and making guests feel at home, but she couldn't cook nearly as well as Jane. Alice, too, was more than willing to help wherever she was needed, but she was busier than usual at the hospital substituting for nurses who were on vacation. Alice worked part-time, not ready to retire completely from nursing. At age sixty-two, she still had more energy than many younger nurses, and her superior at Potterston Hospital greatly appreciated Alice for the hours she was willing to work.

Louise heard a sound coming from the rear of the house and sighed deeply. No doubt it was her aunt coming to remind her of her promise to go to the bank with her today. Ethel Buckley, their father's half sister, lived in the carriage house on the property and could be something of a trial even though the sisters loved her. A widow with three grown children living elsewhere, she was a bit flighty and self-centered, characteristics that had nothing to do with her age, believed to be around seventy-five, although she was secretive about that issue.

Ethel's checkbook didn't balance, and rather than have Louise check her figures, she wanted to go to the bank where someone "high up" could straighten out her account. Louise didn't know how a farm wife managed to get to her age without learning to drive, but perhaps Acorn Hill was a safer place without Ethel behind the wheel.

"Oh dear, I am being grumpy today," Louise said under her breath.

She knew it wasn't Jane's garden, Ethel's sloppy checkbook, a tardy guest or her students' summer practicing habits that really had her in an uncharacteristic dither. It was the music ministry at Grace Chapel that distressed her. She loved music and saw it as a vital part of worship, but things were not going well with the choir, and she didn't know how to solve its problems.

"Louise, our guest is here," Jane called out, coming into sight a moment later still wearing her gardening overalls and swinging a big straw hat at her side. "We came in the back so I could leave my gardening shoes there."

"I'm Gracie Parks," the woman with Jane said. "I'm so excited to meet all of you. Byrdie has told me so much about you and your bed-and-breakfast. What a wonderful idea to turn your family home into a place where guests can enjoy welcoming hospitality. I'm sorry for Byrdie's distress over her house but absolutely delighted to stay here."

In spite of her preoccupation with her own problems, Louise smiled broadly at Gracie. Their new guest's good spirits were contagious, and Louise welcomed her as warmly as possible.

"We're so happy to have you," Louise said. "I understand that you're involved in your church choir, one of my personal interests."

"Yes, I sing in the Eternal Hope Community Church in Willow Bend and sometimes take over as director, but I'm not a professional musician like you."

Gracie beamed, and Louise returned the smile of the flame-haired woman toting a hefty cat in one arm.

"From what we've heard, you're also something of a Miss Marple," Louise said, remembering Agatha Christie's famous sleuth, although her own reading ran more to religious books and C. S. Lewis.

"I've been able to help solve a few puzzles, but perhaps it was more luck than detective work," Gracie said.

"Not according to Byrdie," Jane chimed in. "She thinks you make Sherlock Holmes look like an amateur."

Gracie's cheeks reddened. "I couldn't find my own shoelaces without the gifts God has given me. Sometimes if you listen to that still voice in your head, it turns out to be God letting you know what to do. But, of course, you grew up with Daniel Howard as your father. Byrdie thought the world of him. I'm preaching to the choir."

"Being a preacher's child is a great blessing," Louise said, "but we've all had to find our own separate paths to faith."

Gooseberry jerked in Gracie's grasp, and all three women immediately saw the reason. Wendell had strolled into the reception area looking completely in charge. He was a gray tabby with coal-black stripes. His four white paws and the black fur on the tip of his tail gave him a regal demeanor, and he was used to having unchallenged dominion over the inn. Louise held her breath when he sauntered up to Gracie and her somewhat tubby orange tabby.

Gracie stooped to give the two cats a chance to eyeball and sniff each other while still keeping them apart.

Nothing happened. Wendell seemed indifferent to the visitor, strolling away as casually as only a cat can.

"They don't seem to hate each other," Jane said hopefully.

"You can put Gooseberry down, and I'll put tidbits out for both of them. That way Wendell will associate your cat with unscheduled treats."

She went into the kitchen to arrange a party for the cats, and Louise smiled at Gracie.

"Wendell thinks he's in charge here. Sometimes he acts like the lord of the manor."

"Gooseberry is likely to act like a dog, especially when he follows me on my morning walks," Gracie said. "If they do mix it up, I can leave him with Byrdie."

"He's more than welcome," Louise said, meaning it. "And so are you. Perhaps I should check you in and show you your room."

"Splendid," Gracie agreed. "I am eager to see Byrdie."

Gracie felt the warm glow that always came to her when she made new friends. Jane shared her love of flowers, and Gracie looked forward to conversations with Louise about their mutual interest in music.

Louise settled her in a front room on the second floor, the one she called the Sunset Room. Gracie thought it was whimsical and sweet that each of the four guest rooms had a name, and she was also pleased to have one of the two rooms with a private bath. Because she would be there for at least a week, she was happy that her stay at the inn had begun so pleasantly.

She loved the terra-cotta wall treatment and the creamy antiqued furniture in her temporary home. The room was tastefully decorated with prints of impressionist paintings, including one of her favorites, *The Church at Auvers* by Vincent van Gogh. She always marveled that such a spiritually troubled man had created beautiful art. It was a reminder to her that there was potential for good in everyone, even those who were rejected by society. She prayed for the gift to see God's grace in everyone, even those who annoyed or harmed her.

She was tempted to slip out of her shoes and catnap for a short time. Road trips made her realize she was sixty-two, not exactly a kid anymore, and she had gotten up especially early to be on her way. But she wasn't here for a rest. Her friend had sounded so distressed on the phone that Gracie was praying the situation wasn't as bad as Byrdie had painted it.

She wouldn't be able to sleep anyway, not when her curiosity was fired up. Her new friends called her a sleuth, but she only used the gifts God had given her to help friends with their problems.

Since she hadn't taken time for her usual walk this morning, she changed into thick cotton socks and sturdy walking shoes. Acorn Hill was small enough that Byrdie's house wouldn't be too long a trip from the inn. Walking there and back would compensate for her missed morning exercise.

While she was at it, she would let Gooseberry follow along if he was so inclined. At seven years, the cat was comfortably middle-aged and, like his mistress, had a tendency to put on a bit of weight if he didn't get some exercise.

She'd just decided to leave her cell phone at the inn when it rang.

"Hello, this is Gracie," she said.

"Gracie, where are you?"

"Byrdie, is that you?" Her friend's voice had a hint of panic that made it hard to identify.

"Of course it is! When are you coming?"

"I'm about to leave Grace Chapel Inn and walk to your house."

"Oh, you're walking." Byrdie made it sound like a preposterous way to get from one place to another.

Gracie smiled to herself in spite of the stress in Byrdie's voice. Gracie knew Byrdie well enough to know that she thrived on crises and tended to exaggerate their seriousness. This time, though, Byrdie seemed uncommonly upset, perhaps with good reason.

The two of them went back a long way. Their husbands had been boyhood friends, and several times the four of them had taken vacations together. Byrdie's husband, Jake, died of a heart attack several years before Gracie's dear El, who was killed in a car crash five years ago. They'd been supportive of each other during these sorrowful times, and they still visited, although Byrdie didn't like highway driving and preferred that Gracie come to her house.

Gracie feared that some people thought Byrdie was dour, but beneath her somber exterior she was a warm person. She'd struggled with her faith after her husband's unexpected death, but Gracie prayed for Byrdie regularly and believed her friend was growing closer to the congregation at Grace Chapel.

"It won't take me long to get to your house," Gracie assured Byrdie. "I'll get directions from one of the Howard sisters. Can't wait to see you."

"I'm so glad you're here," Byrdie said, sounding relieved. "You always seem to know what to do."

Gracie didn't have a clue what she could do about a botched renovation job, but she could at least help Byrdie put it into perspective. Gracie was a great believer in perspective. Negative feelings made every bad situation worse. Convincing Byrdie of that might be a whole lot harder than her amateur sleuthing, though.

She hurried down to the main floor and then stopped in surprise. Jane was sitting cross-legged in front of the registration desk, tossing a ball of yarn for Gooseberry and Wendell to chase.

"They like each other," Jane said with a pleased grin. "I think it's going to be good for Wendell to have a friend."

"It's always good to have a friend," Gracie agreed. "I

thought I'd walk to Byrdie's and let Gooseberry follow along. He's like a dog that way, happy for an outing with me."

Jane sprang up with an agility that belied her fifty years. "I think Wendell is tuckered out anyway. He's not used to an active social life."

Gracie went out with Gooseberry and wished she had her walking hat, still tucked away in her luggage in her ten-year-old, dark-blue Cadillac. It was hotter than she'd expected under the noonday sun, but Acorn Hill's streets had lots of shady patches thanks to the abundance of stately trees.

Today Gracie hardly noticed the charm of the rural Pennsylvania town, and not many people seemed to be out and about to distract her. Maybe she should have driven to keep Byrdie from waiting long. As it was, Gracie's face was going to be beet-red by the time she got to the house. Friends always said she had good "color," enough that she rarely used much makeup, but hurrying in the heat of the day was making her face hot, and the resulting color might not be flattering.

She paused several times to make sure Gooseberry wasn't getting into mischief, but he seemed unusually sedate after his play session with Wendell. In fact, he was lagging, and she was almost ready, albeit reluctantly, to carry him when she saw Byrdie's house a half block ahead.

Her friend's house was a two-story late Victorian with a steep roof over the attic. Byrdie took pride in keeping it up to the standards her husband had maintained, and Gracie saw that it had been repainted recently. Byrdie had chosen a pale lavender shade with dark-blue trim around the windows. The somber tones were relieved by white decorative trim along the roofline and white rails on the long front porch. The house was a lot for her friend to keep up, but Byrdie made it her mission to keep it as attractive as it had been when she and her husband first restored it.

Byrdie was waiting for her on the front porch, not sitting in one of the three comfortable wicker chairs but pacing as though her movement could hurry Gracie along.

Gracie scooped up Gooseberry, who would be welcome as long as he stayed on the sun porch at the rear of the house, and waved to her friend with her free hand.

"I'm so happy to see you!" The usually reserved Byrdie hurried down the front steps and surprised Gracie with an especially strong hug.

"And it's good to see—"

"Come inside," Byrdie urged. "Do I have things to show you!"

Chapter ♫ Two

Byrdie played hostess to the best of her ability, serving bowls of canned vegetable soup, crackers, a pot of orange pekoe tea and store-bought gingersnaps, but Gracie could tell her friend's mind was on her problem, not the lunch. Not that Byrdie was ever one to put much effort into her meals. Lean herself, she liked to say that she believed in eating to live, not living to eat, and those who had eaten at her table learned that she acted on her beliefs.

"I like the way you're doing your hair," Gracie said to lighten the mood. "Soft waves are very becoming on you."

"The woman at the beauty parlor wanted to color it, but Jake always liked it salt and pepper. Said it suited my personality. Of course, it's a lot saltier than when he last saw it."

Gracie saw the sorrow wash over her friend's face and knew exactly how she felt. It was something they had in common.

"It's quite nice the way it is," Gracie said, although she certainly wasn't ready to let her own gray threads show through, not while she was still able to trot off to the beauty salon for a touch-up. Her El had loved her hair. If he looked down on her from heaven, he would still see the vibrant red he'd loved when they were young.

Byrdie cleared their soup bowls and pushed the plate of gingersnaps closer to Gracie.

"No, thank you," Gracie said, not feeling it was much of a sacrifice to pass up the dry little cookies.

She understood that Byrdie wasn't fond of the kitchen, but Gracie loved food preparation so much that she ran a part-time catering business to have an outlet for her creativity. She was looking forward to fabulous breakfasts at Grace Chapel Inn, part of the attraction of the bed-and-breakfast.

Byrdie was edgy, eager to tell her story, but she had shown good manners by serving lunch before she launched into her woes. Gracie appreciated her friend's restraint and was now more than ready to hear why her friend was so upset.

"Maybe I'd better show you what I'm so riled about," Byrdie said. "That is, if you don't mind climbing up to the attic. I brush the cobwebs away from time to time and set out glue traps to keep it free of mice and insects, but it's still not the most pleasant place."

"Let's see the scene of the crime," Gracie quipped, standing up from the scrubbed oak table that went so well in Byrdie's ultra-neat blue-and-white kitchen.

She was the only woman Gracie knew who didn't keep a single appliance on the countertop, although her blue-tiled workspace was abundant.

Byrdie led the way up gracefully curving stairs to the second floor, then to a small door to what Gracie had always assumed was a storage closet. The smell of fresh paint and a painter's tarp rolled into a corner reminded her of Byrdie's efforts to spruce up her home.

"It's pretty narrow," Byrdie warned. "Be sure you hang onto the rail. The steps are steep."

She snapped on a light that glowed weakly at the top of a staircase. The passage to the attic was so narrow that Gracie turned sideways to edge her way upward. Byrdie, whose hips were considerably leaner than Gracie's, made a frontal attack on steps that were inches steeper than average.

"The problem started with these steps," Byrdie explained. "There was a broken one third from the top. It just cracked and started to fall in. Jake always meant to fix it, but he never did get around to it. Not that he wasn't an absolute marvel about keeping the house shipshape. But there are always a lot of things that need doing in a house that's more than a hundred years old. He did his best, but the step was never a priority for him."

"I can see why it wouldn't be," Gracie said. "You probably don't have much reason to come up here."

"It's mainly a storage place," her friend agreed, "but once in a while I need something like the Christmas trim. It was hard stepping over the broken step, especially when I needed to carry something down. So I thought I'd hire a handyman to fix it instead of relying on my brother-in-law, Luther. He's been so good about helping me, but I didn't want to impose on him."

"Well, I see that you found someone." Even in the dim light Gracie could see the new board in the third step from the top.

"It's more like he found me, someone fool enough to believe what he said," Byrdie said bitterly. "I know not to let a stranger come to the door and sell me anything, but Eustace Sims advertised in the newspaper, our own *Acorn Nutshell*. I noticed his ad for a couple of weeks before I took a chance on calling him."

Gracie gratefully put both feet on the aged board floor of the attic, thinking that her morning walks hadn't conditioned her to be a mountain climber. She took a deep breath and looked around the large, open space of the attic.

It was spooky, no two ways about it. She gave Byrdie credit for having enough nerve to come up here alone. The single bulb, probably no more than a forty watt, dangled from a cord overhead, and a little light filtered into the space from a vent at the far end. Neither was enough to dispel the gloom.

"The problem is the insulation?" Gracie asked as she surveyed the jumbled contents that literally filled the attic.

Byrdie's house was extraordinarily neat on the first two floors, but she seemed to have saved every discard she'd ever owned and brought it up the narrow stairwell to store. There were boxes, large plastic bins and an antique trunk. A set of hard-sided luggage blocked the way to the back of the space, where an assortment of small furnishings was visible in outline. A rocking chair listed to one side, several small tables were loaded with more boxes, and an old metal headboard leaned against what appeared to be a large barrel.

"It's a terrible jumble, I know," Byrdie said as though reading her friend's mind. "I have to get up here and sort things out. I've been putting it off, so many memories, you know. Anyway, this is the new insulation." She made a sweeping gesture at the blanket of paper-covered pink padding between the attic joists.

"I'm afraid I don't know much about insulation," Gracie said, a little mystified about what she was supposed to see.

"The awful thing is, I can't see much difference between the old insulation and what he put here. Eustace Sims swore up and down that my old insulation was dangerous, but he put in the same kind as far as I can tell."

Gracie frowned and asked, "Did he say that the old stuff was made of asbestos?"

"Oh no, he was very clever. He implied it without using the word. He showed me places where it was coming loose, but now I think he ripped it loose himself when he was supposed to be fixing the step. I couldn't sleep nights for fretting about it. He kept calling, telling me he was worried about me living in a house with defective insulation. He had me convinced he could take care of it for a rock-bottom price. I'm furious at myself for not getting another estimate, but he scared me into thinking it had to be done right away."

"Do you have any bits of the old insulation? If it isn't dangerous, it would be evidence against him."

"No, he took every scrap with him. Said he was hauling it away for my benefit. It gets worse, Gracie. I had to sign a contract. I'll never do that again without showing it to a lawyer. The fine print said I had to pay extra for any related problems."

"I imagine there were some," Gracie said grimly, beginning to understand how badly her friend had been conned.

"I ended up paying nearly double!" Byrdie sounded close to tears. "Jake provided for me, but the house needs constant upkeep. I don't have that kind of money to waste."

"I would like to talk to that man," Gracie said, although she didn't have an inkling of what she would say. "What did you say his name is?"

"Eustace Sims, but he's disappeared. His ad isn't in the newspaper anymore, and I haven't found anyone who's ever heard of him. The police wouldn't do anything but take down my complaint."

"People don't just disappear in this day and age," Gracie said, trying to sound hopeful. "What other problems did he find?"

"Woodworms."

"Woodworms?"

"He said the attic was riddled with them and had to be treated before he could install the insulation."

"Did you see any worms?"

"No, they burrow deep into the wood. You can hardly see the holes they make, at least that's what Eustace Sims said."

"What did he do about them?"

"He sprayed some stuff, but he said it was too dangerous for me to be around it. I had to stay away from the attic for three days. I did get a few whiffs in my bedroom. It smelled dreadful."

"It would," Gracie said under her breath, more and more convinced that her friend had been the victim of a heartless scam.

"I know that if anyone can help me, you can," Byrdie said with touching certitude.

Gracie wasn't at all sure that anyone could get any of her friend's money back, but the more she heard, the angrier she got. If this Sims had cheated Byrdie, he had probably taken advantage of others, maybe some who could afford it even less than her friend. Someone had to stop him.

"Do you still have the contract?" Gracie asked.

"Oh yes, let's go downstairs, and I'll look it up. I think I filed it in my paid-bills folder."

"You go ahead. I want a better look at his work. Do you have a flashlight?"

"I keep one up here in case there's a power failure. I wouldn't want to be stuck up here in the dark."

Gracie heartily agreed with that. Taking the device her friend had indicated, she played a beam of light over a section of new insulation as Byrdie descended the steps.

The insulation at the front of the attic appeared to be the same as in her attic at home, but Gracie would be the first to admit she didn't know much about the product. She gingerly worked her way toward the rear and narrowly missed stepping on one of the glue traps Byrdie had set, this one riddled with small dark bugs, then bumped her shin painfully on the seat of a broken Windsor chair. She wanted to get to a spot where she could see the bare wood of the joists.

"Woodworms!" she scoffed.

She might believe the attic had termites or carpenter ants, but invisible woodworms sounded much too fanciful. So did Eustace Sims's smelly treatment. She sniffed, trying to pick up the scent of insecticide, but all she got was a very faint whiff of kerosene. El used to say she had the nose of a bloodhound, and it served her well in Byrdie's attic. She cautiously sniffed her way up and down the cluttered expanse, finally deciding there'd been a spill of nasty-smelling coal oil very close to the stairwell. That would explain the odor seeping down to the second story. He'd probably left an open can there and accidentally slopped a little.

Gracie decided not to tell Byrdie what she'd discovered, not yet anyway. It would only upset her friend more.

She cautiously made her way down the steep stairs, not remembering to leave the flashlight behind until she was at the bottom. She looked up the uninviting stairs and decided against another trip to the top. Instead, she placed the light on the bottom step, where Byrdie was sure to see it.

For the next hour she visited with Byrdie and watched her cut up carrots and celery for a stew she was preparing for their dinner. The Crock-Pot meal seemed more appropriate for a cold winter day, but Gracie was appreciative of any effort her friend made.

"I think I'll go back to the inn and freshen up before dinner," Gracie said, resisting the temptation to suggest ways to season the stew.

"I'll be happy to drive you back," Byrdie said as she added a tiny shake of salt to the Crock-Pot and replaced the glass cover. "It's pretty hot out."

"Thank you, dear, but Gooseberry and I need the exercise."

She found the big orange cat dozing on the sun porch. He'd made himself at home on a tropical-patterned cushion on Byrdie's wicker love seat, the only piece of furniture in her house where she tolerated him. Gracie knew that as soon as she left, Byrdie would vacuum for cat hairs. Her friend wasn't allergic to cats in particular, but she was hypersensitive to dust in any form. It was another reason why Gracie had suggested that she stay at a bed-and-breakfast. Whenever she visited Byrdie, she felt as though she was causing her friend an immense amount of work.

Byrdie was certainly right about the heat outside, but Gracie decided to set an easy pace and not tax herself or Gooseberry. She needed to be alone to get things straight in her mind. That meant some quiet time to talk to God. She was going to need His guidance to find a way to help Byrdie. Maybe she could give her friend the satisfaction of seeing justice done. A criminal shouldn't be allowed to go on hurting innocent victims.

Dear Lord, You know my weaknesses. I take too much pride in being able to solve problems. Give me guidance in pursuing the person who's wronged Byrdie, and help me to do it for the right reasons. If there's any way that I can help others, please show me the way. I know I can't do it alone.

She felt the crackle of Byrdie's contract in her canvas shoulder bag, and she couldn't get the nasty coal-oil smell out of her nostrils in spite of the sun-warmed scent of trees and flowers. What if Eustace Sims had moved on to another county or even another state? Was she giving Byrdie false hope by agreeing to look into the affair? Was there really anything she could do?

She walked slowly, scarcely noticing when Gooseberry investigated some bushes in front of a Cape Cod home with a brick path leading to the front steps.

The best thing to do was let her mind go blank. If God wanted her to go forward, she would know in her heart what to do next.

Louise was a little alarmed when she saw their new guest come through the front door of the inn. Her face was cherry-red, and her flaming curls stuck to her damp forehead.

"You didn't need to walk back from Byrdie's," Louise

said in her big-sister voice. "I would have been glad to go for you in my car."

"Oh, Byrdie offered to drive me, thank you," Gracie said cheerfully, "but I just ignored how hot it is today. I must look a sight. I turn beet-red when I'm hot, always have."

"I know what you need," Louise said. "Jane made a big pitcher of iced tea this morning after breakfast. It should be deliciously cold by now."

"Oh, I don't want to trouble you." Gracie blotted her face with a tissue from her shoulder bag.

"It's no trouble. I insist."

Louise smiled and realized that she would enjoy chatting with their new guest over a glass of tea. There was something about Gracie that invited friendship. She led the way to the kitchen at the back of the house.

"What a lovely, roomy kitchen you have," Gracie said. "I got a glimpse when Jane brought me in through the storage room, but it's even nicer than I thought. It's every cook's dream to have this much space."

Louise looked at the kitchen through her guest's eyes and nodded with approval. The black-and-white checkerboard tiles on the floor were shiny clean in spite of Jane's recent gardening activity. The rust-red paint on the cabinets wasn't a color she would have chosen, but it did give the room a warm glow. More importantly, the whole room was wonderfully efficient with a stainless-steel stove and dishwasher blending in well with the butcher-block countertop and the soapstone sink. Cooking wasn't Louise's contribution to the running of the inn, but even she could easily find what she needed on the rare occasions when she was called upon to prepare food.

"Did you have a pleasant afternoon?" Louise asked after she'd poured tall glasses of Jane's wonderful mint tea and added ice cubes.

Gracie hesitated a moment as she took a soothing swallow of tea.

"I'm not sure it was exactly pleasant. It was nice to see Byrdie. Our husbands were lifelong friends, and we've shared a lot of experiences. But she does have a problem. You don't know a workman named Eustace Sims, do you?"

"No, I'm pretty sure I don't. Is he the man who did something shady in her attic? There's been talk around town that she was swindled, but ordinarily I don't pay much attention to gossip."

"Unfortunately, it's not just gossip," Gracie said. "I think she paid for work that didn't even need to be done, but Eustace Sims has disappeared."

"Oh, that sounds bad." Louise sipped her tea, relieved that Gracie's color seemed to be subsiding. "I've heard of swindlers who go from town to town keeping a step ahead of the law."

"It may be something like that," Gracie agreed, frowning at the thought.

"Maybe someone else in town answered his ad. I could ask around a bit."

"That could be very helpful." Gracie's smile lit up her face.

"I don't hold out much hope, though. Maybe he only ran the ad here until he found a victim," Louise said.

She refilled Gracie's glass without being asked, sure that her new friend needed to be hydrated. Odd, she'd automatically thought of Gracie as a friend. The inn's guests didn't necessarily affect her that way, not that they hadn't had some lovely people stay here.

Maybe it was Gracie's connection to a longtime town resident that made it easy to relate to her, even though Louise had never been especially close with Byrdie Hutchinson. Naturally she'd helped with the funeral luncheon when Byrdie's husband passed away. She'd also invited Byrdie to join the choir, but the woman claimed to have no musical ability at all.

Louise was glad Gracie had come to visit Byrdie. She chided herself for being so wrapped up in music and the inn that she didn't connect with others more, but Alice would say she was too hard on herself. One person could do only so much.

It was advice Alice ignored herself. She'd always had a gift for taking people under her wing. It was a trait Louise admired but often couldn't emulate, at least not to the same degree. Her life was so full that Louise sometimes felt overwhelmed.

Gracie seemed to have the same gift as Alice, that of gathering others to her and making their sorrows hers. She set a fine Christian example.

"I don't know when I've tasted anything as refreshing as your iced tea," Gracie said with a smile.

"I can't take credit," Louise said. "Jane is a magician in the kitchen. Would you like to try a piece of her zucchini bread? She must know forty different ways to use zucchini. Most people grow it, then don't know what to do with all of it. We're forever finding a bag of it on our doorstep."

Louise was chattering, which was unlike her. Gracie had a demeanor that automatically put Louise at ease.

"I would love a slice," Gracie said.

Louise covered the bread and warmed it in the microwave to bring out the fresh-from-the-oven taste, then served it on one of her late mother's blue-and-white Wedgwood plates, usually reserved for special occasions.

"What a lovely plate," Gracie said before biting into the dark, succulent bread. "Oh, this is delicious, better than mine. Do you think Jane would share the recipe?"

"She'd probably be delighted," Louise said, feeling as pleased as though she'd baked it herself.

"Afternoon tea. What could be nicer?" Alice said coming into the kitchen through the front hallway.

"Especially with company," Louise said. "Gracie, this is Alice. Gracie is our new guest. She's here to visit Byrdie Hutchinson, but we're lucky to have her at the inn."

"Byrdie is having some renovation problems," Gracie said as though to dispel any doubt about her friend's hospitality. "It's nice to meet you, Alice. I'm going to love my stay at Grace Chapel Inn. Your sisters have been so gracious. I do believe Louise has saved my life with this wonderful tea. I was so hot walking back from Byrdie's that I wasn't sure I would make it."

"Alice is a nurse at Potterston Hospital. She's the one who loves mystery novels," Louise said. "Now you're getting to meet a real sleuth, Alice. Gracie is going to help Byrdie nab a swindler who cheated her."

"I'm going to try," Gracie said modestly. "It's doubtful whether I can do anything."

"Gracie is active in her church's choir too," Louise said. "We're going to have a lot to talk about."

"That's wonderful. I'm really pleased to meet you," Alice said, pushing her bobbed, reddish-brown hair back from her forehead. "I'll let you two get on with your tea party. I'm wilted. I can't wait to get out of this uniform and have a shower."

"Can I get you another piece of zucchini bread, Gracie?" Louise asked, not watching her sister as she left to change.

"Oh dear, no, I don't dare. I'd better save room for Byrdie's dinner. She was making a stew as I left."

"Stew in summer. That's an unusual choice. You must have dinner with us some night while you're here. And Byrdie too if she would like to come. Jane is a wonderful cook."

"'A magician in the kitchen,' isn't that what you called her? I would love to sample some of her magic," Gracie said, grinning broadly.

Louise found herself grinning too.

Chapter ♪ Three

A lice awoke before her alarm went off. By the time she remembered that there was no reason to get up early, she was wide-awake.

She wasn't scheduled to work at the hospital today, and Vera Humbert, her walking partner and longtime friend, was busy teaching a quilting class this morning. Alice had the whole day to herself, not that there wasn't always something to do around the inn.

In a leisurely mood, she took her time showering and dressing in a light-blue, crinkle-cotton dress and comfortable sandals. Her dress bore resemblance to a tent, but the outfit was amazingly cool on a hot summer day.

She made her bed, smoothing the yellow, green and violet patchwork quilt that went so well with the buttery yellow paint on her walls. Then, as she did every day of her life, she took time to thank God for having so richly blessed her life.

She was indeed blessed in having her sisters, her friends and a job that fulfilled her need to be useful. She also loved working with her ANGELs, the middle-school girls in the youth group she'd founded. Her life was full, and she treasured each new day.

Still, in spite of the promise of a fruitful, sunny day, she felt an unexpected sadness. She alone of the three Howard sisters had lived with their father until he died at the age of ninety-two. He had been a gentle, kind father who raised his three daughters alone after their mother died giving birth to Jane. He retired from his ministry ten years before his death but still continued to reach out to people through his sermons and counseling.

Alice celebrated his long life, his love for his daughters, and his many years of faithful service to the Lord, but she still had moments when she missed him terribly. For some reason, her feeling of loss was acute this morning.

She went quietly down from her third-story bedroom to the foyer on the first floor that served as a reception area for the inn's guests. She intended to ask Jane if she needed help with breakfast, but the door of her father's study beckoned to her. It was closed, and she traced the letters on the sign they'd put on the door: The Daniel Howard Library.

It was the room where she still felt closest to her father. She went in, closed the door behind her and remembered the many times she'd sat here with her father. They'd shared the problems and small triumphs of everyday life, and sometimes they would read in companionable silence. She hadn't known how much their times together had meant to her until he was gone.

The room was papered in mossy-green. Mahogany bookshelves held a large collection of religious and philosophical books and her father's set of Shakespeare, his favorite recreational reading. She sat in one of the two russet-colored chairs and let happy memories wash over her.

Dear Lord, she prayed, *I know my beloved father is with You, and I still have a ways to go and things to do. Give me faith and strength to do Your will.*

Her melancholy mood lessened, and she went to the kitchen to see whether she could help her younger sister.

"Good morning. Is there anything I can do?" Alice asked as she walked into the kitchen.

"Are you home all day today?" Jane asked.

"Yes, unless I'm called in for an emergency. Do you want me to set the table?"

"That would be wonderful, thanks. Since Gracie is our only guest, I thought we should eat in the dining room with her instead of in the kitchen."

"Fine. Shall I use the everyday china?" Alice asked.

"Yes, I'm sure Gracie would rather have company and a relaxed atmosphere than a fancy table all to herself. She fell in love with my garden, especially the roses. I'm hoping she'll be able to spend some time in it today. She may have some suggestions that will help me get ready for the competition."

That partly explained Jane's enthusiasm for their guest. When Jane took on a project, she went into it wholeheartedly, expecting others to share her excitement. Perhaps Alice and Louise had been too critical of all the time Jane was putting into the garden. Neither of them intended to be negative, but old habits died hard. They worried that she was overdoing it, overworking herself. They were accustomed to mothering Jane, but perhaps she needed support more than advice.

"Good morning," Louise said, walking into the kitchen. "Has Gracie come down yet? What are you making for breakfast?"

Alice noticed that there was a tantalizing aroma of bacon in the air along with the welcome scent of freshly brewed coffee. She inhaled the breakfast fragrance and wrinkled her nose with the pleasure of it.

"I have a special breakfast casserole in the oven," Jane said. "It has to be mixed up the night before so the egg-milk mixture can soak into the dry bread overnight. I put in chopped bacon, shredded cheddar cheese and mushrooms, then added my butter-and-cornflakes crumb topping this morning. I hope Gracie will like it as much as I do."

"Our guests always love your breakfasts," Alice said as she folded paper napkins to place by the plates.

"It's nice to have such a congenial guest," Louise remarked. "We had a very pleasant conversation yesterday. I shouldn't have let her walk to Byrdie's though. It was really too hot yesterday."

Alice knew it wasn't like Louise to fret over what strangers did, nor did she usually show so much enthusiasm for a guest. Apparently Gracie had made friends with both her sisters. Well, a person couldn't have too many friends, but Gracie was here to see Byrdie, who, unfortunately, needed more friends than she had. Alice wondered if she'd been remiss in not making more of an effort to befriend Byrdie in the time after her husband's death.

"Good morning!" Gracie's cheerful voice called out as she walked into the dining room. "Hope I haven't slept through breakfast. I rested like a baby all night, well, not like my baby did. My son Arlen was more a howler than a sleeper when he was tiny."

"I know what that's like," Louise said. "My husband used to joke that my Cynthia was born with a soprano's lungs and an owl's sleeping habits."

"Alice, there are fresh berry cups in the fridge, if you wouldn't mind bringing them in. The casserole and biscuits are nearly ready," Jane said, then turned and beamed at Gracie. "If you have a few minutes to spare this morning, the garden is at its best early in the day. The morning glories were closed when you came yesterday."

"I would love to see it," Gracie said.

Louise sat down at the dining-room table, looking forward to a delicious breakfast and enjoyable company. She asked a blessing on their meal and on Gracie's visit. Then Jane put the steaming casserole on a hot pad in the middle of the table.

"This is marvelous," Gracie said after her first bite. "I've made egg casseroles, but never one this good."

"I vary the ingredients," Jane said. "Sausage or ham

makes a good substitute for the bacon, and I often experiment with different spices. I'd be glad to give you the recipe."

"I'd love to have it if you don't mind sharing. Oh, these biscuits are outstanding."

Louise didn't blame anyone for admiring Jane's cooking. It was a big reason why guests came back for second and even more visits, but she was eager to finish the meal and talk to Gracie about the Grace Chapel choir. Maybe Gracie's choir experience in Willow Bend would give her some insight on how to help here. Louise had been concerned for days, especially since the most troublesome problem was Florence Simpson. No one had ever found a way to curb Florence's bombastic ways. Now that the choir was having difficulties with matters like attendance and music selection, she seemed to think that her role was even more important.

After receiving compliments on her excellent breakfast, Jane spirited Gracie out to the garden, and Louise busied herself clearing the dining room table and putting away leftovers. She hoped that Gracie wasn't in a hurry to go to Byrdie's house. An outsider's opinion might be just what she needed to get a fresh perspective on the choir. Rev. Kenneth Thompson, Grace Chapel's pastor, had asked her to take charge temporarily, and Louise didn't want to let him or the church down.

Florence, however, was determined to run the choir herself. She seemed to fancy herself a major talent, the most gifted member. The truth was that she had an adequate but certainly not outstanding voice. At this moment Florence might be home picking music and planning solos for herself.

Louise shook her head, knowing that her idea of a choir differed greatly from Florence's. Louise loved music and saw it as one of the ways to worship God. That meant an effort that involved all the members contributing to the best of their abilities in a spirit of faith and love. Choir politics distressed her, but she wasn't sure how to discourage Florence from trying to dominate the group. Her problem was compounded by the fact that Florence was really good at heart, and Louise didn't want to hurt her feelings.

Gracie came back to the kitchen alone and announced that Jane had a few things to do outside while it was still cool.

"I'm really impressed," Gracie said. "Jane's roses are so lovely."

"Yes, they are," Louise agreed, inviting Gracie to sit and have another cup of tea.

When they were settled over their teacups, Louise had a qualm of conscience. Was it fair to discuss the choir's problems with an outsider? After a moment Louise decided to plunge ahead.

"You've had a lot of choir experience," Louise said, referring to their earlier conversation. "Maybe you have some ideas I can use. I'm more used to accompanying the choir than directing it, but when our minister asked me to take the job temporarily, I didn't want to let him down. Our choir director moved, and the church board hasn't found a permanent replacement yet."

"Is it a very large choir?" Gracie asked, sounding genuinely interested.

"No, especially not since some members resigned. They say their schedules are too busy, but I suspect it's really because of internal problems," Louise said sadly.

"That sounds distressing." Gracie rested her arms on the table to listen sympathetically.

"I've been lying awake nights trying to think of ways to bring harmony to the group," Louise confessed, "and I don't mean musical harmony."

Gracie nodded to show she understood.

"I don't want to sound malicious." Louise sighed, torn between wanting to tell Gracie everything and not wanting to seem harsh about Florence.

"I'm sure you won't," Gracie encouraged, "but I can't help if I don't know the problem."

"You're right." Louise smiled, relieved by Gracie's understanding. "The major problem is one of our members, Florence Simpson. She's trying to exert a strong influence on the choir, and in the process she's creating chaos. People have left because she's been so aggressive in promoting her ideas. She really believes that she's the backbone of the choir, the lead soprano."

"I'm guessing she's not," Gracie said.

"If all the choir members had to audition today, she might be among the last picked," Louise conceded. "That doesn't mean she can't sing, only that she isn't better than all the other members. The choir hasn't sung at any of the services since the director left, and Rev. Thompson would really like to have them back."

"It does seem a shame to go all summer without a choir, although our church does allow some time off when many of the members are on vacation."

"Most of our members seem to be in town," Louise said. "It's just that we're not up to snuff right now. I've scheduled special practices on Tuesday and Thursday evenings, but last Thursday was something of a disaster. Florence wasted a great deal of time arguing against one of the selections and insisting on a choice of her own. I dread going to the practice tonight for fear that people just won't come. We have a faithful few who are reliable, but they're distressed at the way the choir has gone downhill. It's my responsibility, but I'm at my wits' end."

"A choir is no place for a prima donna," Gracie agreed. "Have you talked to Florence in private?"

"Yes," Louise said, trying not to sound as discouraged as she felt. "It's like having a conversation with the radio. She talks but doesn't listen."

"I've known a few people like that," Gracie said. "Other people's ideas bounce off them like ping-pong balls off a wall. They think they're having a conversation, but all they're doing is reaffirming their own opinions."

"Yes, that's it exactly." Louise felt relieved just talking to a person who understood her problem with Florence. "We did have such a lovely choir. It breaks my heart that it's not up to its usual standards, but I don't seem to be making much headway as a choir director."

"I doubt that's the problem." Gracie frowned as though weighing all aspects of the situation. "I did plan to stay here for a week, but I can stay longer if I can be helpful. It may take longer to help Byrdie with her situation. Maybe I'll be able to make some suggestions if I come to a choir practice with you."

"That would be wonderful!" Louise said. "Would you mind if I introduce you as my temporary assistant? That way, you'll be more than a visitor. Florence might pay more attention."

"Perfect!" Gracie said. "Maybe I'll get some ideas to take back to the Eternal Hope choir."

"I can't tell you how grateful I am," Louise said, feeling some of the burden lift just from having shared her distress. "I can't thank you enough."

"I haven't done anything yet," Gracie protested. "Your Florence sounds like something of a challenge."

Gracie finished her tea and had a refill, pleased that Louise seemed more relaxed. She didn't have a clue what she could do about Grace Chapel's choir problems, particularly because one person seemed determined to dominate the group. Louise didn't seem like a person who could be easily intimidated, which made Gracie curious to meet Florence.

She somewhat reluctantly took leave of Louise, thanking her for the tea and confirming the time of the choir rehearsal.

"We can walk to the chapel together," Louise said. "I like to go over around six-thirty, and the choir members get there at seven. And thank you again."

Gracie didn't bother to look for Gooseberry before she went back to her room. She knew that he had adapted well to the hospitable atmosphere of the inn, where he'd been given his own water and food bowls.

She was happy for the time she'd spent with Jane and Louise but still troubled by Byrdie's problem. She took the folded contract out of her shoulder bag and skimmed through it again. There was a lot of fine print, and it would appear that the contractor had every right to charge more than the initial estimate if he found any problems. But had he found them or faked them? Gracie was skeptical about everything he'd done.

The first thing to do was find out if the contract was valid. Fortunately her adored niece, Carter Stephens, was a lawyer working with the Cook County District Attorney's Office in Chicago. Gracie was pretty sure her niece would be at work by now. The delicious breakfast, Jane's tour of her garden and the talk with Louise had taken longer than Gracie had expected.

Gracie used her cell phone to reach Carter's extension, then gave her name to a secretary. Carter came on line almost immediately.

"Aunt Gracie, what a nice surprise to hear from you. Are you coming to visit?"

"No, I'm visiting a friend in Pennsylvania, but it's wonderful to hear your voice, dear. I'm hoping you'll spend some of your vacation with me this summer."

"I can't think of anything nicer, but I'm tied up here for now."

"I understand," Gracie said. "I'm afraid this is a business call."

"Uh-oh." Carter knew Gracie's sleuthing ways and sounded a bit wary. "You're not involved in something dangerous, are you?"

"No, not at all," Gracie assured her, honestly believing a

confrontation with Florence might be more hazardous than trying to find a swindling contractor.

"Then how can I help you?"

"My friend here in Acorn Hill, Byrdie Hutchinson, paid to have the insulation replaced in her attic. I'm not at all sure it was necessary, but the man who did it scared her into having it done along with some other work."

"Did he say it was asbestos?" Carter asked.

"No, he was too cunning for that. Worse, he used the fine print in the contract to charge her more than the agreed-upon price. I wonder if you would mind taking a look at it."

"Of course, Aunt Gracie. Can you fax it to me here at the office? I can't get to it immediately, but I'll read it as soon as possible."

"Thank you so much, dear. I don't know what can be done about it. The man seems to have disappeared. But I would like to know if the contract is unusual in any way."

Gracie said good-bye, not wanting to bother Carter more than necessary at her office. She didn't have a plan to foil Eustace Sims, but at least she'd taken the first step. Now she had to locate a fax machine. At the risk of being a nuisance, she went to the kitchen and found Louise making a shopping list.

"You can use the inn's," the oldest Howard sister said cordially. "It's in the foyer behind the registration desk. Do you need help?"

"No, I'll manage nicely," Gracie assured her. "Thank you very much."

Moments later she stood beside the fax machine trying to remove the staple that held the three pages of the contract together. It seemed like a long document for a simple insulation job. She managed to separate the pages without breaking a fingernail, but she was so absorbed in the task of getting the pages ready that she didn't notice someone coming toward her until she spoke.

"Is there something I can help you with?" an older woman with short red hair said in a challenging voice.

"Louise said it would be okay to use the fax machine," Gracie explained. "I'm staying here."

"Well, if my niece said so, I guess it's all right. I'm Ethel Buckley, the Howard sisters' aunt, but I couldn't love them more if they were my own children."

"I'm Gracie Parks," she said, trying to be patient and sociable although she very much wanted to get the contract sent to Carter.

"You must be Byrdie Hutchinson's friend. Jane told me all about you. No, maybe it was Louise. I'm in and out a lot because I live in the carriage house next to the inn. I try to help the girls in any way I can."

"That's nice," Gracie said, looking into the pale-blue eyes of a slightly plump woman who was probably in her seventies. "Your nieces have made me feel very much at home at Grace Chapel Inn. I'm sure I'll enjoy my stay here."

"Now how does that machine work?" Ethel said, maneuvering between Gracie and the fax. "I recall watching Louise send something once. Let's see if I can remember how the page goes."

"It's nice of you," Gracie said, "but I think I can do it."

"I feel responsible for things at the inn, although my nieces don't expect me to do any of the work. Not that I'm not willing, but my plate is full. I'm on the church board, and I help out at the chapel wherever I can. That doesn't mean I'm not concerned about everything that goes on here. How is Byrdie holding up, do you think? I'm a widow myself, so I know how lonely a person can feel, not that I'm lonely here in Acorn Hill. People here look out for one another."

"If you'll excuse me . . ." Gracie managed to get within reach of the fax.

"That's an official-looking paper," Ethel said. "Not that it's any of my business. I wouldn't dream of meddling in a guest's private business."

Gracie wasn't secretive as a rule, but she didn't feel comfortable talking about Byrdie's problem. She had a hunch Ethel was digging her for information. On the other hand, she probably knew all there was to know about Acorn Hill. Gracie decided to do some digging of her own.

"I'm sure you wouldn't," Gracie said, "but it's nice of you to take an interest in the people around you. You probably know a lot about what goes on in the town."

"I've gotten to know a lot of people since I moved here ten years ago. Even the mayor is a friend of mine. My late husband was a farmer, and it got lonely on the farm after our three children grew up and moved away. It was wonderful of Daniel to invite me to live here after my Bob passed on."

"Do you know a man named Eustace Sims?" Gracie asked.

"Eustace, that's a name I haven't heard before, but I did know a Sims family when I was young. Theodore and Ebenezer. Seems like people with short last names like to give their kids long first names. No, maybe it wasn't Sims. It could have been Crims. Something like that anyway."

"Oh, you've met Aunt Ethel," Louise said, coming into the foyer. "Are you having any trouble with the fax machine?"

"No, I'm just about to send," Gracie said. "I really appreciate using it."

"Our home is your home while you're here," Louise said with a smile.

She linked arms with her aunt and gently steered her away from Gracie and the fax machine.

"Now, do you still want me to drive you to the bank this afternoon?" Louise asked.

Gracie turned her attention to the contract. She hoped against hope that Carter would find something irregular about it, but there was still the problem of finding Eustace Sims. If he made his living bilking older women, he must still advertise somewhere. That notion gave her some ideas about how to track him down.

Chapter ♪ Four

Jane added a couple of items to the grocery list that Louise had been preparing. She felt a bit guilty because it really wasn't Louise's responsibility to shop for groceries or check the cupboards, freezer and refrigerator to see what they needed.

"I really appreciate this," Jane said, handing her sister the revised list. "It gives me the opportunity to walk around town and check out my competition."

"You do more than your share around here," Louise said, tucking the list into her purse. "It won't hurt me to make a trip to the grocery store."

Alice came into the kitchen. "Is one of you going to the store?" she asked. "I noticed we're low on cat treats."

"My fault," Jane said. "I probably gave Wendell and Gooseberry more than they needed, but I wanted to encourage them to like each other."

"You seem to have succeeded," Alice said. "They've been acting like old friends."

"I'm going to do the shopping today," Louise said. "I'll put cat treats on my list."

"Louise is doing me a tremendous favor," Jane said. "I

really want to walk around town and see what other people have done with their gardens. Maybe I'll see some ways to improve mine."

"Do you know who will be entering the botanical society contest?" Alice asked.

"Not everyone, but I understand that they always get a lot of entries. People in Acorn Hill must love their gardens. If I'm going to win—and I have high hopes—I need to compare mine to others'."

"Jane, this is the first year you've entered. I hope you don't get your hopes up too high," Louise said.

"When does our Jane ever do things halfway?" Alice teased. "No weed would dare raise its head in the Howard garden when she's on duty."

"True," Louise agreed, "but there are some wonderful gardens in town. The Bentleys' garden is pretty spectacular. They've won several times in the past."

"The judges were dazzled by their statuary," Alice said. "At least that's what I've heard. I'm not sure stone creatures are a substitute for good gardening, but it might be something you want to check out, Jane."

"I've heard there are some nice ones on Village Road behind the Methodist church," Jane said.

"Yes, but it's pretty hot for a long walk. Maybe you should drive instead," Louise cautioned.

"No, I would feel too conspicuous stopping the car every time I wanted a closer look," Jane said.

"Ah, we have a spy in the family," Alice teased. "Maybe you should disguise yourself. Would you like to borrow my oversized sunglasses?"

"And my big floppy straw hat?" Louise added.

"You two are terrible!" Jane said, laughing. "Next you'll want me to buy some garden gnomes."

"That's not a bad idea," Alice said with mock enthusiasm. "You could use your painting talent to give them striped hats and plaid coats. That would impress the judges."

"More likely it would distract them. I'm counting on my roses to give me first place. And don't either of you try to dissuade me."

"We wouldn't dream of it," Alice said more seriously. "We just don't want you to be disappointed. There really is a lot of competition for such a small town."

"Also you shouldn't work yourself to a frazzle in this heat. We have guests booked for the weekend, and that will make more work for you," Louise warned.

"I love to cook for a group. It's not that much more work than making breakfast for the three of us," Jane assured her. "Anyway, most of the hard work in the garden is done. I just have to maintain it. Some rain would be nice, but meanwhile, I'll be out there with my trusty hose."

"If you're determined to go on a garden tour of your own," Alice said, "be sure to look at the Holzmanns'. Their color is usually spectacular."

"Do you think so?" Louise asked. "Their flower beds always look crowded to me. I'd rather see more planning and spacing."

"I like the spontaneous look," Alice said. "The Bentley garden always seems a little too contrived, too formal."

"You two!" Jane said. "If the judges disagree as much as you do on what makes a good garden, maybe mine—ours— will be a compromise winner."

"No, you were right the first time," Alice assured her. "It is your garden. It was a disaster when you took charge of it. You deserve full credit for bringing it back. You know we're both pulling for you."

"I know, and I appreciate your support. By the way, Louie, be sure we have enough buttermilk," Jane teased, knowing that it was a favorite of her older sister.

"While I'm out, maybe I'll look for a pink plastic flamingo to put in the rose garden," Louise threatened in a good-natured response to the use of Jane's pet name for her.

Jane left smiling. Her big sister was in an unusually playful mood. Maybe it was because Gracie Parks was going to help with the choir.

The sun was hot, but Jane had taken her gardening hat on the way out. Not many people would be out working in their gardens this close to noon, which was fine with her. She felt the way she imagined a spy would feel, and it was fun. Was this how Gracie felt when she was sleuthing?

Jane's excitement made her want to hurry as if to see every garden in Acorn Hill. But she restrained herself and tried to stroll in a nonchalant way, deciding she could only cover a few homes today. Those along Acorn Avenue and Village Road seemed particularly promising, so she took a shortcut on the path that led from Grace Chapel to the rectory, now occupied by Associate Pastor Henry Ley and his wife Patsy. They were working at a youth camp for the summer, and they wouldn't mind Jane's cutting through their yard even if they were at home.

She wouldn't see the Bentleys' statuary garden on this walk, but the Holzmanns' house wasn't far. Flowers grew in a thick blanket all around their house, a profusion of colors in no particular pattern or order. She walked to the back garden and found the same riotous display of mixed flowers. She had to agree with Louise about liking more order in a garden. The Holzmanns certainly had green thumbs, but they seemed to have scattered seeds indiscriminately and let nature take its course.

Jane mentally scratched off the Holzmanns as serious competition and wandered through their neighborhood, looking at other gardens. The people in this area seemed to like growing vegetables as well as flowers, and she saw some wonderful plants that would soon be heavy with ripening tomatoes. Leaf lettuce and cabbages sprouted in neat rows along with the intricate lacy tops of carrots. As a chef, she could do creative things with fresh produce, but today she was only interested in flowers and shrubs for their beauty.

She spotted one splendid little garden behind a neat brick bungalow with curtained windows. She was somewhat uncomfortable walking on the private property of people she didn't know, but she couldn't resist going to the back of the house for a closer look. The garden had a functioning water-wheel and neat crushed-stone paths, but the owner had had bad luck in one section. Several dying shrubs marred the perfection of the plantings. Jane didn't see any serious competition here either, and a sudden outburst of angry barking inside the house made her realize that the family dog saw her as an intruder. Only a sliding-glass door separated her from an agitated and menacing Doberman.

She hurried out of the yard, feeling as though she'd been caught doing something underhanded. Maybe she should knock on doors and ask permission before going into back-yards. Of course, she would have to explain why she was so interested. It would be too duplicitous to pretend that she'd just been attracted by a glimpse from the street.

Did Gracie suffer pangs of guilt when she was investigat-ing? Or were her motives so laudable that her conscience was at ease when she made inroads into other people's space? Jane's respect for Gracie grew when she considered how hard it was to reconcile the need to know with the right to privacy. It was such a knotty problem that Jane walked past several homes without checking them for gardens.

Maybe it would be better to look early in the morning or in the evening, when serious gardeners were likely to be out watering. That way she wouldn't feel so sneaky, and she would also have a chance to ask people if they were entering the contest. Besides, the next dog that objected to her nosi-ness might not be confined.

Yes, that was the answer. She wasn't cut out to be a spy. As much as she wanted to win, she didn't like trespassing. She continued her walk for the pleasure of getting some exercise, but she didn't go into any more gardens.

Back at the inn Alice had left to run some errands of her own before Louise ran hers, and Louise felt vaguely dissatisfied with her day's schedule. She had more choir matters she felt drawn to discuss with Gracie, but their guest would probably spend most of the day with Byrdie. As much as Louise wanted to fill Gracie in on the problems, maybe it was better to let her meet the choir members and form her own opinions.

Louise was too honest with herself not to wonder whether her own inexperience caused her to exaggerate Florence's disruptive influence. After all, Louise was only a substitute director. She much preferred accompanying the group to trying to direct it, so maybe Florence was worried about not having a permanent leader.

For all Florence's bombastic ways, she did manage to get things done. Underneath her aggressive exterior, she had a good heart and didn't wish the choir any harm. Under a strong director, she usually contributed to the choir without disrupting it.

If worse came to worst, Louise could ask Rev. Thompson to speak with Florence. She was more apt to defer to him than to anyone else at Grace Chapel. Louise wondered if it was because their minister came from an affluent Boston family, then chided herself for being uncharitable. The whole congregation was enthusiastic about their minister. He truly cared about other people and he put the Lord's work first. Louise hoped she wouldn't have to bring Rev. Thompson into the situation. She didn't want to put him in the position of having to side with one chapel member against another.

Louise closed her eyes and prayed fervently that she and

Florence could resolve their differences as good Christians should.

Please, Lord, give me the patience and wisdom to do Your work even when it's difficult.

Something brushed against her ankle, startling her for a second. She looked down and saw Gracie's big orange cat.

"Gooseberry, I haven't seen you all morning," she said, bending to stroke the cat's luxurious fur.

It was a relief that Wendell had taken to the visiting feline rather than ignoring or challenging Gooseberry with his usual haughty demeanor. Wendell was king of the Grace Chapel Inn and could be terribly territorial if he felt threatened.

"If touchy male cats can become friends, then certainly I can find a way to get along with Florence," she said aloud.

"Did someone mention my name?"

Louise looked up, horrified that Florence might have heard what she'd said.

"I let myself in the front door. Since this is an inn, and strangers walk in and out, I didn't think a dear friend's letting herself in was like invading a private home." Florence smiled as she provided her explanation.

"I was just talking to our visiting cat," Louise said to change the subject. "His name is Gooseberry."

Either Florence hadn't heard clearly or she was willing to ignore Louise's remark. She launched into the reason for her visit without bothering with small talk.

"I think we should do something about the choir robes," Florence announced.

Louise was too flabbergasted to respond. She stared into Florence's eyes, slate gray below brows that had been plucked and penciled into thin, stark lines. As usual, Florence's brown hair was pulled back into a neat twist, and she was dressed in a stylish, if somewhat flashy, yellow chiffon dress with a pattern of huge orange and white flowers that did nothing for her plump shape.

"Every choir in the country has the same kind of robes, all one color with no way of distinguishing individual members," Florence said.

"Ours are very nice," Louise said defensively. "The navy looks nice on men and women, and the touch of gold at the collar makes them quite elegant."

"Of course, we would need to have a fund raiser or the like to buy new ones," Florence went on as though Louise hadn't spoken.

"There's no reason to replace them," Louise said firmly. "They have quite a bit of use left in them, and there are better reasons to raise money. The food pantry—"

"What I have in mind," Florence interrupted, "are multicolored robes."

"Choir robes like Joseph's coat of many colors?" Louise would have laughed if the other woman hadn't looked so earnest and determined.

"No, of course not. I was thinking of different colors for different members." Florence fiddled with one of the large gemstone rings on her left hand. "What I meant is that no rule says every member of the choir has to wear exactly the same kind of robe."

"It's a fine tradition," Louise said stiffly. "We're praising God with one voice. The robes underscore that."

"Well, God must like a lot of colors or He wouldn't have made so many."

Louise knew it could be a mistake to argue with Florence, but this was no time for that stubborn woman to campaign for new choir robes that weren't even needed.

"I'm sure the chapel has greater needs right now," Louise insisted. "Our different outreach committees are always in need of funding, and you know how much the upkeep is on our wonderful building."

"Yes, yes," Florence said impatiently. "My idea is to assign different colors according to the choir member's expertise and years of experience. For example, a soloist with twenty years in the choir would wear a gold robe. A newcomer would start with pale blue and work his or her way up through other shades, say royal into navy blue. I'm flexible on the colors, of course. They don't have to be blue and gold. The important thing is that one color should distinguish the more talented senior members."

"Who would assign the colors?" Louise didn't try to keep the dismay out of her voice. Florence was going too far with this latest brainstorm of hers.

"We would have a committee, of course. I'd be happy to chair it."

Louise groaned inwardly and remembered her prayer for patience.

Florence wanted to enhance her status in the choir by having a special robe that set her apart. It would never occur to her that others were more talented or more deserving of special recognition. Her idea had the potential to create disharmony among the choir members. Feelings would be hurt, and no good could come of it. Ill will could spread to the whole congregation and make color-coded robes a major issue.

"Florence, I don't think we should make any major changes until we've hired a new choir director."

"On the contrary, doing this now will help us hire a creative, imaginative director if the applicants see that we're not locked into the same old traditional robes. We don't want someone stodgy."

Louise seriously doubted that the color of the robes would have any bearing on the selection of a new director, but she also knew how futile it was to argue. She needed time to organize her thoughts and find an objection that Florence would accept.

"For now, we have some serious work ahead of us to get the choir running smoothly again," Louise said dejectedly.

"I'm willing to help any way I can," Florence said, "but I think I should at least present my idea at choir practice tonight."

"Please don't, not tonight. We need to focus on our singing," Louise said.

Louise didn't know any way to put it plainer. The last thing they needed at the practice tonight was the turmoil of discussing one of Florence's self-serving ideas.

"Well, you are the *acting* director," Florence said unhappily.

"We have a great deal to do tonight."

"I may just toss around the idea a bit during our break. I know the others look up to me, and a little informal brainstorming can't hurt."

"There won't be time. We're having a guest," Louise said as a desperate last resort.

"Someone who wants to join?"

"No, a visitor from out of town, someone with a lot of choir experience. She may be able to give us a few pointers."

Louise had said more than she'd intended. It had seemed wiser to spring Gracie without warning, but she needed to discourage Florence from bringing up the subject of new robes.

"Ah, imagine if she could meet the choir in their new attire. Imagine how impressive it would be for an outsider to visit Grace Chapel and see them robed in multicolored splendor." Florence closed her eyes as if to envision it.

"I don't think anyone in the choir has the time or energy for a big fund-raising project right now."

"You don't have to worry about that," Florence said with a sly smile. "Not only am I willing to head up the effort, I've talked with my husband, and Ronald has agreed to donate a generous amount, so we only need to raise part of the cost of new robes."

"Indeed!" Louise said briskly, at a loss how to dampen

Florence's enthusiasm and not at all impressed by her self-serving generosity. "That doesn't change the fact that we don't need them."

Florence and Ronald Simpson were one of the wealthiest couples in Acorn Hill. They didn't have children, and they could probably afford to contribute handsomely for new robes. The point was that even if the choir needed new robes, Florence's idea of using a variety of colors to denote status was dreadful.

"I couldn't wait to share my idea with you," Florence said, ignoring Louise's negative reaction. "Now I have to get going. You have no idea how much I have to do today. I want to keep my husband happy by taking his favorite suit to the cleaners, and I haven't had a manicure for ages. I owe it to the choir to look my best, don't you think?"

Louise could only respond with a patient nod. The problem with the choir had just gotten worse, and she was still at a loss about how to handle Florence.

The church board wouldn't begin the process of hiring a new choir director until fall, relying on Louise to keep the choir going until they found someone. She was determined not to let Grace Chapel down, but Florence was creating problems faster than Louise could solve them. Louise would pray for peace and harmony among the choir members, but in her heart she knew that God had given her the responsibility for making it happen.

Florence's pointy heels made clacking sounds as she went through the foyer to the front door, and Alice, just returning, stepped aside to let her pass.

"Hello, Florence," Alice said.

"Sorry, no time to visit," Florence said, sounding a bit breathless. "You've no idea how much I have to do today."

"I'm sure you'll be busy," Alice said mildly, watching as Florence went out.

She turned around to see Louise coming toward her.

"Florence was certainly in a hurry," Alice said, immediately reading the distress on her sister's face.

"She can be impossible!" Louise said, agitated.

"What did she do to upset you?"

"I can't talk about it now," Louise said. "I might lose my temper. I haven't done the grocery shopping yet, and tonight is choir practice. Jane needs some of the things on the list for our dinner, so I have to get going."

"Would you like me to do your shopping for you?" Alice asked.

"It's sweet of you to offer, but I can manage," Louise said. "I'll just run upstairs and get my purse. If you see Jane, tell her I should be back in less than two hours."

"All right." Alice watched her sister hurry up the stairs, wondering if she would race that fast all the way to the third floor, where the sisters had their bedrooms.

It wasn't like Louise to be so rushed. Whatever Florence had said, it certainly did not sit well with her sister. Alice's instinct ordinarily would have been to follow Louise and try to help, but her sister had made it clear that she didn't want to talk right now.

Alice wandered back to the kitchen with a vague idea of having some iced tea. Instead, she sat at the table and did something unusual: She did nothing. She was rarely without places to go and things to accomplish, but on this warm summer afternoon there was absolutely nothing that needed her attention. It gave her an unpleasant, empty feeling.

Elbows on the table, she propped her chin in her hands and wondered why her sister was so upset. Louise wasn't one to suffer in silence, but it wasn't hard to figure out that it had something to do with the choir.

Alice knew there was little she could do to help with Louise's choir problems, but that didn't stop her from wishing she had some answers.

At least Louise had Gracie. Maybe an outside opinion would help her with the choir.

"Anybody home?" Jane called out from the storage-room entrance to the house.

She emerged with a flushed face and dark strands of hair escaping from her usually neat ponytail.

"Just me," Alice said. "You look exhausted."

"No, just hot. I think I'll jump into the shower before I have to start dinner."

"Louise just left. She said to tell you she'll be back in a couple of hours. Florence was leaving when I got back. I don't think things went well between them."

Jane filled a glass with water from the faucet and drank deeply before speaking.

"When you're really thirsty, there's nothing like water." She emptied the glass and set it on the counter. "Louise can handle Florence. And she has Gracie to help."

"Yes, I'm sure Gracie will be a big help," Alice agreed. "How did your tour of gardens go?"

"Fine—except for a big dog that barked at me. Fortunately he was behind a sliding glass door."

"Are you still confident that your garden measures up?"

"At dinner I'll give you and Louise a rundown on those I saw. Right now I'm so sweaty I can hardly stand myself."

"Run along and have your shower," Alice said. "If you want help with dinner, I'll be in Father's study."

Chapter ♪ Five

Gooseberry was contentedly napping in the sunroom at Grace Chapel Inn when Gracie was ready to leave Tuesday morning. Because he was getting along so well with Wendell, she decided to leave him there.

She made sure to stow her cell phone in her big shoulder bag, then decided it would be best to go by car. Much as she enjoyed a morning walk, she might need it to track down Eustace Sims.

First, though, she wanted to hear from Carter. Her niece would know if there were any loopholes in the contract. Even if everything about it was perfectly legal, Gracie was highly suspicious of Sims's activities. She knew kerosene when she smelled it, and there wasn't one good reason to have such a flammable substance in an old attic.

When she got to Byrdie's house, her friend was brewing a pot of tea. She served it in the kitchen along with a plate of the same gingersnaps that had been a part of yesterday's lunch. Gracie could honestly say that Jane's breakfast at the inn had been too filling for her to have a midmorning snack.

They settled down for tea using Byrdie's cherished china cups with delicate painted violets and gold trim. Gracie appreciated her friend's gesture of hospitality but wished the tea didn't taste so much like wet cardboard. However, there was more to friendship than food and drink. Byrdie never claimed to be a good cook, and Gracie had to admit that her own standards were pretty high. How delightful for her that she could look forward to Jane's wonderful breakfasts during her visit.

She and Byrdie were having a pleasant time reminiscing about happy events when a ringing sound came from her shoulder bag.

"My cell phone," Gracie explained, hurriedly unzipping the bag and locating it. "Hello."

"Aunt Gracie, it's Carter."

"Oh, it's so nice of you to call so soon. I'm really concerned about the work that was supposedly done here."

"I'm afraid my news isn't good," Carter said. "The contract is legal. I don't see any way that your friend can challenge it in court unless the work didn't need to be done. Then it's a case of fraud, but it could be hard to prove that."

Especially if we can't find the man who swindled Byrdie, Gracie thought.

"I was afraid of that," she said.

"I did take it a step further," Carter said. "There's an intern working in our office who's a whiz on computers. She tried to locate Eustace Sims every way she could. No phone for him is in service, his address is bogus, and the Better Business Bureau in your area has no record of him. As far as we can tell, he's not licensed to do any kind of contracting. In fact, he doesn't seem to exist, at least not under that name."

"Oh dear." Gracie didn't want to say anything that would alarm Byrdie, who was listening attentively, but it confirmed her worst suspicions. Eustace Sims was probably a career criminal.

"Sorry I couldn't give you better news, Aunt Gracie," Carter said. "I'm afraid there's nothing you can do. Maybe this is one time when it would be better not to investigate. He doesn't sound like the kind of person you should confront even if you can find him."

"You're probably right," Gracie reluctantly agreed. "Thank you so much for all your help, dear. I can't tell you how much I appreciate it."

"It's my pleasure to help you, especially if it prevents you from doing anything rash," Carter said with a soft laugh. "Much as I'd like to talk more, I have some work that has to be done."

"Thank you again," Gracie said before she broke the connection.

"It's bad news, isn't it?" Byrdie asked in a woeful voice.

"Pretty much so," Gracie was forced to admit. "The contract you signed is legal, and my niece had an assistant in her office search for Eustace Sims on the computer. There's no trace of him."

"He has a telephone. Won't his number show up somewhere?" Byrdie asked hopefully.

"It's either out of service or listed under another name. I'm so sorry, but Eustace Sims doesn't seem to exist under that name."

"Oh dear." Byrdie took a deep breath and seemed on the verge of tears. "I didn't have much hope of getting any of my money back, but I hate seeing such a bad man get away with cheating people. I feel so dumb for having anything to do with him."

"Don't feel that way." Gracie went over to her friend and put her arm around her shoulders. "It's not your fault."

"Since Jake died, everything has been so hard." Byrdie produced a tissue from the pocket of her green-and-white checkered housedress and blotted her eyes. "I'm not good at making decisions."

"You're a dear friend, Byrdie, and you're doing a wonderful job of keeping up the house," Gracie assured her.

She was thinking fast, wondering if there was anything else she could do. It was tempting to forget all about Sims. Byrdie wasn't destitute. No doubt she would recover from the financial loss. But the swindler had robbed Byrdie of her confidence, and that was irreplaceable.

"Jake would be so disappointed in me," Byrdie insisted. "He warned me so many times never to trust workmen we don't know."

"Jake was able to do most of his own home repairs," Gracie said, deciding it was time to be practical. "You aren't. You have to depend on help. You did the right thing picking someone who advertised in the local paper. It was bad luck, not bad judgment."

"Do you really think so?" Byrdie asked, brightening a little.

"I'm sure of it, and I'm not through looking for Mr. Eustace Sims." Gracie spoke impulsively, knowing even as she said the words that she might come to regret them.

"Do you really think there's a chance of finding him?"

"I certainly hope so. He has to buy supplies somewhere. He has to live somewhere. Just because a man disappears from computer scrutiny doesn't mean he's not still around somewhere."

Dear Lord, what am I getting myself into now? If there's any way I can stop this man from hurting others, please help me. I know I can't do it without You. Gracie prayed in silence.

"Of course," Byrdie said more cheerfully. "Why didn't I think of that? He put in new insulation. He must have bought it somewhere."

"We can check the phone book for places that might sell insulation." Gracie was glad to have something concrete to do. "There can't be very many in a town this size. Of course, he didn't necessarily buy locally or use his own name. Is there anything distinctive about his looks?"

"Not really." Byrdie pursed her lips in thought. "He was

pretty ordinary looking. Not tall or short, not skinny or heavy."

"What color were his eyes?"

"I'm sure they were brown, kind of flat brown, not warm brown like my Jake's."

"And his hair?" Gracie prompted.

"I never saw much of it. He always wore a baseball cap on backward. Odd though, it wasn't a Phillies or a Pittsburgh Pirates cap. That's mostly what you see around here. His was dark blue. Let me think what team it was." Byrdie frowned in concentration.

"What color was the logo?" Gracie asked, trying to be helpful.

"Just a minute. Yes, I see it. It was a Detroit Tigers cap."

"Well, there can't be too many of those around here."

"And he has a beard," Byrdie said triumphantly. "Quite a full beard. It was sort of mixed black and gray. Not very attractive. I remember thinking he would look better if he shaved it off. My Jake never wore a beard, thank heavens. They always seem to collect food spills. Nasty, really."

Gracie didn't agree with her friend on that point. She thought a beard could be quite handsome when it was neatly trimmed, but she wondered if Eustace Sims wore one to disguise his looks.

"Can you think of anything else about him?"

"His ears sort of stood out. I remember wondering if kids had teased him about them when he was a child."

"That's a good distinguishing feature. It's good you remembered it," Gracie praised her friend. "How about his clothing? Did he dress in any particular way?"

"Just what you'd expect a workman to wear—jeans and usually a grubby long-sleeved shirt. One day he came to work with a denim jacket. It was whitened in spots from being washed a lot. And he had heavy workman's boots. You know the kind. They come up over the ankles and have thick laces.

I did ask him to wipe them on the doormat before he came in. He seemed a little surly about that, but I thought it was a reasonable request. Anyway, he did it every time after that."

"Did he talk much?"

In Gracie's experience, people who talked a lot inevitably gave away information about themselves.

"Only about my attic problems. He was quite a talker, I can tell you that, but not about himself. I asked him once if he had a family, and he said, 'Don't like to talk about 'em.' That's odd, don't you think?"

"It could mean he's divorced. Did he ever mention how far he had to drive to get home?"

"No, he was closemouthed about things like that. Of course, I didn't want to pry."

"What did he drive?"

"A pickup truck. It was a dirty old thing. Once I got a look inside. It was cluttered with fast-food garbage and news-papers and I don't know what all. I was worried he would leave a mess in the attic, but he was neat in his work."

"Do you know what make the truck was?"

"No, I don't pay much attention to things like that."

"Do you remember seeing a license plate?"

Byrdie started to pour more tea, but Gracie quickly gestured that she didn't want seconds. "It was a Pennsylvania license. I'm pretty sure of that."

She scrunched her face in concentration, and Gracie let her think without interruption.

"I remember not being able to read the number because it was caked with mud. I thought it was odd because we hadn't had rain for quite a few days, but I took it to mean he hadn't washed the truck in a long time. Now I wonder if he smeared it on purpose so he couldn't be traced through his license plate. I'm afraid that's all I can tell you about Eustace Sims. Now that I think about it, he didn't want me to know much. He never mentioned where he lived or where he grew up. Most folks tell you something about themselves, but he was pretty careful not to reveal much that was personal. That should have warned me."

"He was fixing your house. You didn't need to know anything about his personal life," Gracie said, not wanting her friend to feel guilty.

"I suppose," Byrdie said.

"I have to admit that Eustace Sims is getting to me," Gracie said thoughtfully. "The man is slick. That's for sure. If it had been my attic, I probably wouldn't have done anything differently. It's not your fault that he took advantage of you. He's probably done it to plenty of people before you, and he'll do it again and again if we don't find a way to stop him."

"That's what I'm afraid of," Byrdie said. "But what can we possibly do?"

"I don't know yet," Gracie admitted. "There's nothing to do until we can find him. Let's take a look at the phone book and see how many building-supply places are near here."

With Byrdie looking over her shoulder, Gracie flipped through the yellow pages until she found the section on building materials. There was only one listing in Acorn Hill.

"Miller's Building Supply on Keystone Road. Is that far from here?" Gracie asked.

"I'll drive you there. Appearing in person would probably be more effective than just phoning." Byrdie made the offer with enthusiasm. "I could kick myself for not thinking of it sooner. He had to buy the insulation somewhere."

Gracie wasn't optimistic. A man who was involved in shady dealings wasn't likely to waltz into the nearest business where they might remember a stranger. Still, she wanted to be thorough.

"I have my car here," she said.

"No, it's only fair that I drive. You drove all the way from Willow Bend to help me."

Gracie followed her friend out to the garage in back of

the house, where Byrdie ceremoniously opened the door with a little black control box. There was room in the unusually clean and neat garage for two cars, but just one car, a large, dark-green Plymouth station wagon was parked there like a museum display. In fact, it had been a long time since Gracie had seen a model like it.

"It's a terrible gas burner," Byrdie admitted as they got in, "but it was the last car Jake bought for me. I can't bring myself to part with it. Fortunately, I can walk most places, so I only take it out for an occasional excursion. It would be a shame to trade in a vehicle with less than forty thousand miles."

"It looks almost new," Gracie said, admiring the highly polished surface. Even the tires looked newly scrubbed.

"I try to keep things nice." Byrdie sniffed a little, probably remembering how her efforts in the house had led to trouble.

Gracie was sure this was the cleanest car that she'd seen outside of a dealer's showroom. The upholstery looked new, and there wasn't a scrap of paper or even a bit of lint anywhere in sight. She realized that Byrdie was giving her special treatment by letting her ride in it.

The trip to the supply place wasn't long, but it did prove to be hair-raising. Byrdie didn't seem to be able to drive safely and talk at the same time, and she was in an unusually chatty mood.

"The stop sign!" Gracie cried.

It was too late. They sailed through it as Byrdie chatted on about Jake's favorite auto garage, one she patronized faithfully on the occasions when the car needed servicing.

Thank You, God, Gracie thought when she realized that no cars had been coming on the cross street.

As soon as she left the business district behind, Byrdie accelerated, shattering the stereotype of mature women as careful drivers. She drove like a teenage boy, whipping down town roads with one hand on the steering wheel and one gesturing as she talked a mile a minute.

"You're so smart to think of the place where he bought the insulation," Byrdie said for the fourth or fifth time. "I don't know how I can thank you."

"I haven't done anything yet," Gracie said, bracing her feet against the flooring and watching with consternation as Byrdie took her other hand off the wheel to pat her hair.

The car swerved over the centerline, but God was certainly watching over them. A moment after Byrdie returned to the general vicinity of the right lane, a huge farm truck came over a rise directly in front of them on the opposite side of the road. Gracie pulled her seat belt tighter against her and prayed harder, not knowing if it would help to ask Byrdie to slow down. It might make her nervous and even more dangerous.

Much to her relief, a sign ahead on the left indicated that they'd reached Miller's Building Supply.

"There it is," Gracie said, expecting Byrdie to slow down and make the left turn.

Instead her friend swerved across the road without bothering to signal or look for oncoming vehicles. She scattered gravel and came to a bumpy stop a few feet from the entrance.

"There," Byrdie said, apparently satisfied that they'd made it in one piece. "You'd better do the talking. You're so much better at getting information."

Gracie didn't know about that, but she got out of the big Plymouth and set her shaky legs on terra firma. Now that she thought about it, this was the first time she'd ridden with Byrdie behind the wheel. One of their husbands had always done the driving when the couples traveled together.

"We'll see what they have to say," she said weakly.

Inside the barnlike metal building, a lean, weather-beaten man with rolled-up sleeves and baggy overalls somewhat grudgingly asked how he could help them.

"A man who did some insulation work for my friend may have bought his supplies here. He left some things at her house, but we don't know where to contact him."

Gracie mentally crossed her fingers. She didn't like coming close to a fib, but she didn't want to embarrass Byrdie, and it was certainly true that Eustace Sims had left suspicion and bad feelings behind him, not to mention his outrageous contract.

"You better talk to the boss," the man said.

He disappeared somewhere in the rear of the building, apparently to summon his employer. As he did, Gracie wandered toward the back between stacks of freshly milled lumber while Byrdie timidly hovered near the front counter. The smell of new wood was pleasant, but the building was poorly lit and crowded enough to make Gracie a little claustrophobic.

"Hello?" she called out, hoping the surly man had actually told someone they were there.

She heard a heavy door close, and a portly man in gray work pants and a plaid summer shirt ambled toward her.

"Is there a problem, ma'am?" he asked when he was a few yards from her.

"No, we just had a question." She glanced back at Byrdie, who was too far away to be part of the "we."

"How can I help?"

"A man who did work at my friend's house may have bought insulation from you. We need to contact him." That sounded more truthful to her. "Is it possible that you know Eustace Sims?"

"Never heard of him," the man said a trifle impatiently.

"He may not have given his name. He's medium height and weight with a bushy, salt-and-pepper beard. He usually wears a Detroit Tigers baseball cap."

"Doesn't ring a bell." The man hitched up his trousers by the belt and looked ready to leave.

"Could you possibly check your records to see if you made a sale around the time he bought supplies?"

"It wouldn't do any good if he paid cash. Do you know if he used a credit card?"

It seemed unlikely that a criminal would leave that kind of trail, but Gracie waited while her reluctant informant checked somewhere in the back. After what seemed like ages, he came back to the counter shaking his head.

"If he bought anything here, it must have been a cash sale. Anyway, I think I would remember a Detroit Tigers cap. We don't see those around here."

Gracie thanked him, satisfied that Sims probably hadn't bought the insulation in Acorn Hill.

"Well, that didn't help," Byrdie said glumly when they were back in the car.

She tried starting it, but the engine only gave an anemic cough.

"We've eliminated one possible source of the insulation," Gracie assured her. "The man seemed pretty sure about not seeing a Detroit Tigers cap."

Byrdie tried starting the aging Plymouth a second time, and it sputtered to life.

Gracie had mixed feelings about the car's recovery. She took a deep breath, wondering if she could caution Byrdie about her driving without hurting her feelings.

"I haven't seen this part of Acorn Hill," she said as the car pulled onto the road. "Perhaps you could give me a relaxing tour. It's such a pretty town. I love all the old trees, and people take such good care of their yards."

"Yes, they do," Byrdie said, brightening a little. "I'll turn down Acorn Avenue when we get to it. There's a pretty stone cottage you should see."

Much to Gracie's relief, Byrdie drove sensibly, then

turned and proceeded slowly down the residential street, pointing out the houses of people she knew.

"Would it be too much trouble to stop at Grace Chapel Inn?" Gracie asked. "I'd like to pick up my camera. It might not be a bad idea to take a few pictures of the work in your attic."

"No trouble at all," Byrdie said, "but you are having supper at my house, aren't you? I'm planning macaroni and cheese."

"Yes, I'll just be a minute at the inn."

Gracie knew the evening menu. She'd seen the box on the counter, and Byrdie didn't leave things out unless she intended to use them right away.

Byrdie stopped the car on the road in front of the inn.

"I'll wait here and keep the motor running," she said. "Sometimes when I stop and try to start again right away, it stalls on me."

"I can walk back to your place," Gracie offered, remembering that she'd missed her morning walk.

"Oh no, I'm happy to wait. I can't tell you how much I appreciate your help."

"All right then."

Gracie hurried into the inn and up the stairs to her room. There she rummaged in her suitcase to find her little camera. She was on her way out again when she saw Jane and Alice talking beside the registration desk.

"Hi, Gracie," Jane called out as Alice smiled pleasantly. "Are you enjoying our town?"

"It's lovely, but I've been at work trying to learn where Byrdie's contractor, Eustace Sims, bought his materials."

"Have you tried Miller's out on Keystone Road?" Jane asked.

"Yes, they're pretty sure he didn't buy from them."

"The best person to ask is Fred Humbert at Fred's

Hardware," Alice said. "I don't think he sells insulation, but he knows where to go for supplies in the county. His store is just down the road from us. I would be happy to go there with you and introduce you. His wife Vera is my walking partner and an old friend."

"That's a good idea," Jane said, "but why don't I save you a trip, Alice? I'll go there with Gracie. I've been meaning to ask Fred if he has a hose nozzle that will deliver a finer spray for my roses."

"Very well," Alice said. She seemed disappointed.

"That's awfully nice of you, Jane. And thank you for the idea, Alice. Byrdie is waiting outside in her station wagon. She's afraid if she turns off the engine, the car won't start again. I'll tell her to go on home, and I'll walk there after we go to the hardware store. I've been wanting to stretch my legs."

Byrdie protested mildly when Gracie told her the plan but seemed relieved to take the aging Plymouth back to her garage while it was still functioning.

As Jane and Gracie walked the short distance to the hardware store, Jane talked about the gardens she'd seen on her morning excursion. "I was enjoying myself until a noisy dog made me realize I was trespassing," she said with an embarrassed chuckle.

"I'm sure people who plant gardens want others to enjoy them," Gracie reassured her.

Fred's Hardware was old-fashioned in the nicest possible way. It was a jumble of the expected merchandise with sections for gardening supplies and for small appliances. There was also a toy shelf with miniature tractors and cars, puzzles, small dolls and games. Gracie noticed some wax lips, something she hadn't seen since her own childhood, and a barrel of packaged caramel corn.

A sandy-haired middle-aged man smiled at them when

they entered and greeted Jane cordially by name. He was alone in the store except for a gray-haired man in blue striped overalls who was examining drill bits.

"Gracie, this is Fred Humbert. Gracie is visiting Byrdie Hutchinson but staying with us at the inn because Byrdie's house is undergoing renovations."

Fred reached across the wooden counter that separated them and offered Gracie his hand. "A pleasure to meet you, Gracie."

Gracie couldn't help returning his smile and pleasantries. He seemed like a man who would help her if he could.

"It's a little more than a social visit, I'm afraid," she explained. "Byrdie had some insulation work done in her attic, and it appears she was cheated. Worse, the contractor told her she had woodworms and charged her plenty to get rid of them. I suspect he just opened some kerosene to make it smell like he'd done something to get rid of the critters."

"She had woodworms in her furniture?" Fred asked with a puzzled expression.

"No, in the attic."

"First I've heard of something like that. You maybe should talk to an exterminator."

"Have you ever met a workman named Eustace Sims?" Gracie asked.

"No, I'm pretty sure he's not local."

"That's what Byrdie thinks. He's disappeared, and my niece couldn't trace him on the Internet. We thought that if we can learn where he bought his supplies, we might get a lead."

"Gracie is something of a sleuth," Jane said. "She's solved some real crimes in her hometown."

"The police do that," Gracie was quick to explain. "I just like to work my way through puzzling things."

"Sounds interesting. Say, have you checked with Miller's out on Keystone Road?" Fred asked.

"Yes, and the man there was pretty sure he'd never seen our contractor. Sims always seems to wear a Detroit Tigers baseball cap."

"That's one we don't see around here as a rule," Fred said. "He could buy supplies in any one of a number of places in the county. Afraid I can't suggest one in particular."

"Well, thank you for listening," Gracie said, trying to conceal her disappointment.

"Wait a minute. Why don't I drop by Byrdie's place and see just what this fellow did. It might give me some ideas about where he bought the insulation. Have to admit, I'm curious about this woodworm story."

"That would be wonderful!" Gracie said. "I'm sure Byrdie would be grateful."

"I'll give her a call when I can get away from the store," Fred said.

"Now, Fred," Jane said, getting down to her business, "do you have a hose nozzle that will mist my roses? One that's really gentle but delivers a wide spray?"

Gracie said her good-byes and left Jane to learn about the merits of different nozzles.

Chapter ♪ Six

Despite the fact that it was ordinarily a favorite meal for Louise, she ate little of the grilled catfish served with hush puppies and spinach salad that Jane had prepared for dinner. She saved most of her portion as a treat for Wendell and Gooseberry, then excused herself to get ready for choir practice.

This evening she felt more apprehensive than enthusiastic about working on the hymns for Sunday. Florence's idea for new choir robes was the last thing a floundering choir needed to consider.

Part of her was a little embarrassed to be taking Gracie as a guest when there was sure to be turmoil at the practice. As a musician she liked to present the choir in the best possible light, but she needed help badly. Maybe an outsider's viewpoint would help her see ways of dealing with Florence without hurting her feelings or generating conflict within the choir.

Louise prayed for peace for the choir and a chance to carry out the music ministry at Grace Chapel without strife. She knew in her heart that Florence's plan to elevate some members, especially herself, by assigning different colored robes was a bad one. It could only lead to trouble, but when Florence got a brainstorm, she was almost impossible to dissuade.

After she freshened up, Louise went down to the foyer to wait for Gracie, only to find that she was already there.

"What a pretty dress," Gracie said. "Blue is certainly your color."

"Thank you."

"Maybe I should change," Gracie said.

"No, there's no need. Our choir members are very casual at rehearsals. Your slacks and tunic are fine. We can start walking over to the chapel."

On the short walk Louise told her about some of the members but was careful not to say more about Florence. It seemed better to let Gracie form her own opinion of the situation.

"Only one person called to be excused from practice," Louise said. "One of our tenors took his family to visit relatives in Maryland. I'm pretty sure he doesn't intend to quit the choir. I just hope all the others will be there. We can't afford to lose more voices."

"It's a lovely church," Gracie said as they approached the white clapboard building built in the late nineteenth-century. "You can tell just by looking that a lot of loving care has been lavished on it over the years. I do love a belfry. It reminds me of a finger pointing toward heaven."

"Grace Chapel has been blessed with many good stewards," Louise said. "And we're fortunate to have a pastor who cares a great deal about our place of worship. He even refinished some of the pews himself by hand."

She held open one of the double doors in front to let Gracie enter.

"We have a pipe organ in good repair that I usually play to accompany the choir, but tonight I have someone to play the piano for the practice."

She led the way between wooden pews that glowed with a rich patina. The interior walls were creamy white, and they surrounded stained-glass windows that glowed with deep colors. By a trick of light, the red carpeting gave a pinkish tinge to the walls that was especially pronounced at this time of evening.

"It's quite inspiring," Gracie said.

"I'm glad you feel that way. I wanted you to see the chapel at its most peaceful. I'm concerned that the mood might be shattered when the choir arrives."

"Perhaps they'll surprise you." Gracie smiled. "People sometimes do."

"I am being pessimistic," Louise admitted. "Maybe it's because I'm out of my element acting as director."

She hoped that she was worrying for nothing. The members had had time to rethink their personal goals for the choir. They might come tonight with renewed dedication.

Florence was the first to arrive.

"Gracie, this is Florence Simpson, one of our sopranos," she said. "Florence, Gracie Parks is the friend who's generously offered to give us some help with the choir. She's very active in her church choir."

"Nice to meet you," Florence said with offhand courtesy. "I've called several members about the new choir robes, Louise. No one has objected to bringing up the subject tonight."

Louise was at a loss for words. She'd emphatically asked Florence not to bring up her idea until the choir was reorganized and on track.

"I'd love to see your old robes," Gracie said as if sensing Louise's consternation. "I always feel so elevated when I wear a robe, as if I've consecrated my efforts to the Lord in a special way."

"Yes, that's exactly how I feel," Florence said, a trifle breathlessly. "Putting on a robe creates an excitement that's hard to express to those who don't sing."

"I think we have time for a quick look before rehearsal starts, don't we?" Gracie asked Louise.

"Certainly," Louise agreed. "I'm sure Florence will be glad to show you."

The robes were in a closet on the lower level near the Assembly Room, the large room set aside for a variety of church activities. Louise wasn't sure why Gracie had asked to see them, but it gave her breathing space to greet the other choir members.

They arrived singly and in pairs, giving Louise a chance to express her gratitude for the time they were giving to the choir.

"I know two practices a week take a lot of effort on your part, but it's the only way we'll be ready to perform again any time soon," she said to Loueda Ullman, a quiet older woman who had been in the choir for just about a year.

"I'm happy to come as often as you feel necessary," Loueda said.

By seven o'clock, when the rehearsal was scheduled to begin, most of the members were assembled. Louise breathed a sigh of relief. By her count, all the remaining regulars were there except Rhonda Rockwell. Unfortunately, Rhonda and Florence had exchanged some harsh words after the last rehearsal. Louise would have to call Rhonda and try to soothe her hurt feelings. Still, the attendance was better than she'd worried about.

She'd intended to introduce Gracie right after their opening prayer, but Florence and their guest hadn't returned from seeing the gowns.

"We'll begin with 'Amazing Grace' the way we practiced it last week," Louise said. "I know it feels strange at first to sing familiar words with new music, but it will be lovely when we've mastered it."

She was a bit relieved to begin rehearsal without any delays. Florence had held up the last rehearsal by passing out copies of a hymn she'd found when she went through her grandmother's sheet-music collection. Louise had wasted valuable time trying to explain that she needed to see music ahead of time to be able to direct it.

"I didn't know you would start without me," Florence said, loudly returning in the middle of the first hymn.

The choir's pianist continued to play, but the choir let their voices fade away at Florence's interruption, and soon the music stopped altogether.

"I wondered what was keeping you," Louise said pointedly, unhappy with herself for letting Florence cause another disruption. "But now I can introduce our visitor. Gracie Parks has kindly consented to help us while she's visiting in Acorn Hill. She's active in the choir at Eternal Hope Community Church in Willow Bend, Indiana. I'm sure none of you will object that I've made her honorary assistant choir director."

The choir erupted with warm welcomes, and several people asked Gracie questions about her background. Louise couldn't follow the conversations because Florence drew her aside.

"Gracie thinks it would be better to talk about new robes when we've hired a real choir director," Florence said. "I'm not sure I agree. It can't hurt to toss around a few ideas—"

"Your ideas," Louise interrupted, ignoring the implication that she wasn't qualified to lead the choir. "Since we have a guest, I think we should table any discussion of robes. Now, if you'll take your place, we can get down to business."

"We have to leave at eight," Toni Glendenning said. "Our babysitter has to go to another job."

Toni and her husband Eric were the newest members of the choir. Louise especially hoped to attract some younger singers and didn't want to discourage them by wasting time.

"Before you leave, you'll want to hear about my idea for new choir robes," Florence said.

"If they're paying a sitter, they want to sing, not sit around jawing," Jack O'Hara said.

Jack was an animal-control officer who worked in

Potterston but lived in Acorn Hill. He could be outspoken, especially when Florence was trying to push her ideas on the group. An ex-marine with bright-red hair and a distinctive handlebar mustache, he was an excellent baritone and a staunch supporter of the choir. He and Florence had gotten into a few heated disagreements in the past.

"We'll try once again with 'Amazing Grace,'" Louise said firmly.

"Oh dear, you're determined to use the new music," Florence said. "The regular music is so dear to all of us. I don't know why you decided to change."

"The choir should be a learning experience," Louise said, looking directly at Florence.

The practice proceeded. Florence muttered under her breath whenever there was a pause, Jack once cautioned her to hush up, and the Glendennings left fifteen minutes before eight. Louise thanked them for coming and invited them to come to the Thursday rehearsal.

"We'll have to see if my mother can watch the children," Toni said in a doubtful tone.

Louise fervently hoped they wouldn't be the next members to drop out.

By the time the last choir member left, shortly after nine o'clock, she was exhausted. This was harder work than six piano lessons without a break. Of course, when she gave lessons to children, she enjoyed more control than she felt she had had tonight.

Gracie smiled sympathetically. "It didn't go too badly," she said.

"I'd give three sopranos for one good tenor," Louise said. "I had high hopes for Eric, but now I'm not sure whether he or his wife will come again."

"It's hard for couples with young children," Gracie said, "but you don't know that they'll quit. It could strengthen their marriage to share a dedication to the choir."

"You and I know that," Louise said wearily, "but do they?"

"Maybe you could find someone in the church who would volunteer to babysit for them during practices."

"That's a wonderful idea!" Louise said, perking up. "Alice works with the girls in the congregation. She moderates a group called the ANGELs. I'm almost sure she could find some volunteers. Maybe other parents would be interested in singing with the choir if free babysitting was available."

"It's not really my idea," Gracie said modestly. "Our choir has tried it with some success."

"It was wonderful for you to suggest it. Maybe the choir will grow instead of shrink. I know we'll hire a regular director in the fall, but I feel responsible for maintaining things in the meantime."

Louise turned out the lights and locked the church for the night, then walked back to the inn with Gracie.

"I am curious," Louise said. "Did you make any progress convincing Florence that our choir robes don't need replacing?"

Gracie chuckled softly. "She is a determined woman."

"At least she let the subject drop so we could actually practice tonight."

"I think she's regrouping for a new assault," Gracie said. "Oh dear, that sounds so militant."

"When Florence gets an idea, she's practically unstoppable. Believe me—I've seen her in action. But despite her disruptions, I really don't think she realizes the negative effect that she's having."

"Perhaps the hardest thing our Lord told us to do is turn the other cheek."

"Sometimes it's hard to do without letting someone like Florence take advantage. I don't want to hurt her or lose her participation, but people have avoided the choir because she can be so bossy."

"I think there's only one thing we can do now," Gracie said seriously. "If we both pray for guidance, I'm sure God won't let us down."

"It means a lot that you'll add your prayers to mine," Louise said. "Sometimes I worry that I'm too much like Florence, insisting that things be done my way."

"Your goals are different. Florence wants vindication for her ideas. You want the best possible choir to carry on the music ministry at Grace Chapel."

"Thank you, Gracie."

"I haven't done anything."

"You've made me see things more positively."

"That's what friends do, Louise."

And in His wisdom, Louise thought, *God knows when someone needs a friend.*

Jane woke up even earlier than usual Wednesday morning. She wanted to take a walk to see more gardens, with luck while their owners were out watering.

Breakfast was ready for Gracie and her sisters. Jane had prepared a blueberry blintze soufflé and a Canadian-bacon-and-cheese quiche, so her guest and sisters were well served.

Gracie was still their only guest, although that would change today. They were booked solid through the weekend thanks to a family reunion and a wedding at the Methodist church. This morning offered Jane her best chance to explore. After setting out the meal on a heated serving tray to keep food warm, she was eager to go.

Somewhat to her surprise, she met Gracie coming down the stairs.

"Good morning, Gracie. You're an early bird today."

"I woke up and couldn't get back to sleep. I have to confess that Byrdie's situation is on my mind. There's a criminal out there taking advantage of defenseless people."

"Will she be able to take him to court?"

"My niece doesn't think Byrdie has a good case unless we can prove fraud. Right now we can't prove anything. We can't even find Eustace Sims. Most likely that's not his real name."

"That is a problem," Jane said sympathetically. "What can you do in a situation like this?"

"I did have one thought. When people choose a false name, they sometimes use the letters in their real name. That's partly why I couldn't get back to sleep. I was trying to make a new name out of *Eustace Sims*."

"Like a party game," Jane said. "I used to like word games at showers and such. I've even won a few times."

"You're just the one I need," Gracie said enthusiastically. "I've written his name and made a start, but not a very good one."

She showed Jane the paper.

"Sam, that's good. Sam Tice, unusual but possible," Jane said. "Tim works, but I've never known anyone whose last name is Seat. Ace would be a nickname for a gambler. This is tough. There are too many vowels."

"I may be way off course," Gracie admitted. "His name may be something common like John Smith."

"Why don't you take your paper to breakfast and explain the challenge to my sisters. The three of you can think it over, and I'll have a try when I get home."

"Oh, I'm sorry if I've held you up."

"Not at all," Jane assured her. "And I hope you enjoy your meal."

"I'm certain that I will," Gracie said cheerfully.

Jane hurried out of the inn before her sisters came downstairs. She enjoyed their quiet breakfasts together when the inn had few or no guests, but she was eager to get out and see what other gardeners were doing. Time was growing short with the competition scheduled for the end of next week, but there was still time to make small improvements if she saw something to inspire her.

She wasn't planning to copy what other gardeners had done. She'd worked hard on her plan before changing the original layout, but it was always possible to improve. Maybe what she hoped to gain from seeing other gardens was confidence. Was she getting her hopes up too high, as Louise had tactfully suggested? Was she wasting a great deal of effort with little chance of winning?

Jane went in a different direction this morning, taking Chapel Road to Berry Lane, which ran east and west through town. The homes tended to be older than those on Village Road, but that meant the gardens might reflect years of care and dedication. She expected her toughest competition to come from that area.

She did see some lovely gardens, including the Bentleys' spacious, prize-winning garden with its wildlife statuary. Somewhat to her surprise, there was someone out watering at the Bentleys', but it wasn't the doctor or his wife Kathy. A slender, somewhat stoop-shouldered man with weather-beaten skin and sparse, graying hair was hard at work misting their flowers.

Jane didn't know the man, but she had seen him doing yard work around town. Apparently the Bentleys were using a professional gardener. As far as Jane knew, it wasn't against the botanical society's rules, but it took some of the luster from their floral displays. She liked to think of a garden as a creative expression of the person who planted and cared for it.

As much as she was enjoying her walk on the quiet early morning streets of Acorn Hill, Jane couldn't help being distracted by Gracie's search for Eustace Sims. Was it possible his name was locked inside the letters of his false identity? She found herself rearranging letters in her head without much success. The name could be a clue to where he lived or who his parents were. Or maybe he'd found the name in a book or heard it on a television show. Jane didn't hold out much hope of finding the man through his name, but it was intriguing to consider the possibilities.

Just as she'd imagined, several gardeners were out watering

in the cool of the morning. She stopped to admire George Henry's garden. He was a retired man who loved to chat, so it took several minutes to determine that he wasn't entering the botanical society's competition.

"I entered one year," he said, "and they told me my climbing roses needed pruning. I happen to like them just the way they are. I don't need a plaque to tell me my garden is nice."

"It's beautiful," Jane agreed, edging her way back toward the street. "I'm glad I saw it, but I have to keep walking. There's a lot of work waiting for me at the inn."

Her excuse was true, but she also wanted to see a few more gardens before she hurried home.

She walked by a small brick cottage set way back on a large corner lot. It caught her eye and she noticed a name on the curbside mailbox: Harry Grayson. This had to be Elma Grayson's house, although she'd been a widow for many years. Jane had seen her at the chapel and had a nodding acquaintance with her. She usually went to church alone and left right after the service. As far as Jane knew, she wasn't involved in any social activities. Elma had to be at least eighty, a frail-looking woman with soft-spoken ways and an innate dignity.

Her garden was a surprise. In fact, it was hard to tell where the yard began and the garden ended. There were small patches of grass in random places, but for the most part, the whole of the large lot was filled with plants and flowers.

Jane walked by slowly, then turned and retraced her steps for a better look. There didn't seem to be any pattern to the plantings. A paving-block path meandered through the maze, stopping and starting for no apparent reason. The flowers weren't grouped together in any organized fashion. Marigolds were crowded in with peony bushes and bachelor's buttons, only to reappear yards away in a cluster of zinnias. Against one wall of the house, a rather spectacular lily was tied to a stake to support its long stalk next to a big pot of begonias.

Jane was fascinated. The whole yard was a crazy quilt of varieties and colors almost as though a giant hand had scattered seeds and bulbs in a random toss. Yet, in spite of the disorderly array of flowers, every one seemed to be flourishing.

She walked past it again, no longer concerned about being conspicuous. A small patch of horseradishes was tucked into one of the beds and marked with a small hand-lettered sign to identify the plantings. Jane smiled at this unusual mixing of plants.

Her sisters had teased her about gnomes, but Elma had one of those too. A mischievous little face peered out under a bright red cap, looking very much the master of a clump of periwinkle.

"Well, it looks as if you're the keeper of the garden," Jane said.

She smiled at her own silliness for talking to a garden gnome, but it was a garden that inspired a fanciful comment.

Everywhere Jane looked, she saw a surprise. A wooden squirrel made his home under a pink climbing rose, and a plastic flamingo lorded over a patch of snapdragons. This was nothing like the Bentley garden, where a majestic granite column held center stage. It was more like a child's playroom badly in need of straightening but charming in spite of the clutter.

Jane had work to do and her own garden to tend, but she tore herself away from this hodgepodge of growing things with some reluctance. Hurrying back to the inn, she was still bemused by Elma Grayson's garden. Of course, it would never win a prize. Jane could imagine what the judges would say about the helter-skelter layout and random planting of things like horseradishes. She hoped Elma wasn't entering the competition. It would be a shame if her feelings were hurt by critical comments from garden experts.

There was nothing random about the Grace Chapel Inn garden. Jane had followed the basic scheme begun by her mother, adding to it based on gardening books she'd studied. She went over it plant by plant in her mind as she walked. After seeing a few other gardens, she was satisfied that hers would stand up to rigorous judging.

Don't get overconfident, she warned herself.

Louise and Alice had been right about the quality of the gardens in Acorn Hill. She was facing stiff competition.

Jane knew herself well enough to know that it wasn't besting other gardeners that drove her to excel. She put her all into projects and was her own harshest critic. When she started something, she wanted it to be perfect, or as close to perfect as she could get.

Before going into the house, she took time to mist her flowers using the new nozzle Fred had recommended. She loved the way her roses looked with tiny droplets clinging to their cool, smooth petals. After making sure every plant had just the right amount of water, she went inside, feeling that her morning jaunt had been a success.

Chapter ♪ Seven

Gracie intended to check in with Byrdie, then go to the library. Louise had confirmed that there was a collection of recent phone books there. Gracie needed the names of building-supply companies that might have done business with Eustace Sims. It would be like looking for a needle in a haystack, but at the moment she didn't have any better ideas.

Only one problem kept her from leaving the inn. Gooseberry was nowhere to be found. Louise had mentioned that other guests were expected today, and Gracie didn't want him to be underfoot. There was no way of knowing whether new arrivals would be partial to cats, and Gracie didn't want to take advantage of the sisters' hospitality by leaving him there all day.

A cat could go a lot of places where a good guest shouldn't snoop. Gracie searched the main floor and the yard without success, then returned to the kitchen on the theory that Gooseberry was never too far from the source of food. There she met Jane, who had just returned from her garden touring. She also encountered an untouched dish of cat food that had been set out for her pet.

"Did you have a nice walk?" Gracie asked.

"Very nice. I feel more confident that my garden measures up."

"Oh, I'm sure it must. It's lovely. You didn't happen to see Gooseberry while you were out, did you?"

"No, now that you mention it, I haven't seen Wendell yet this morning either. Of course, he'll probably show up when it's time for his ten o'clock treat. Maybe he took Gooseberry to the woods to chase butterflies or whatever it is that he does there."

"I want him to walk along with me to Byrdie's house," Gracie explained. "I can't ask you to keep him here when you're expecting more guests."

"I'm afraid it's out of our hands," Jane said, laughing softly. "Wendell thinks Gooseberry is his guest. By all means, feel free to leave him here. Gooseberry hasn't been the least bit of trouble."

"If you're sure—"

"Absolutely."

"Then I will get started," Gracie said. "I'm so glad this is a cat-friendly inn."

"It's our pleasure to have him here. Oh, Louise and I wondered if you and Byrdie would like to have dinner with us one evening, maybe tomorrow if you're going to choir practice again. I could drive Byrdie home when you and Louise leave for the chapel."

"That sounds wonderful," Gracie agreed. "I'll look forward to it, and I'm sure Byrdie will too."

Gracie took her leave and walked at a brisk pace toward her friend's house. She still had a little nagging guilt about making Jane responsible for Gooseberry, but it was pleasurable to move along without keeping track of her big, sometimes lazy, orange cat.

Byrdie was waiting for her on the shady front porch, eager to hear how choir practice had gone the evening before.

"I did hear a rumor that some in the choir don't like the music Louise picks," Byrdie said when they were settled into her kitchen with a cup of ginseng tea, which Byrdie swore was good for arthritis.

"Louise is using untraditional music for 'Amazing Grace,'" Gracie explained. "I'm sure the choir will love it once they get the hang of it, but there's always some resistance to learning new music for a familiar hymn. I don't think it's fair for anyone to be critical of Louise. The choir is fortunate to have her fill in until the church can hire a permanent director."

"Yes, I guess you're right," Byrdie said. "Some people just enjoy complaining."

Gracie thought Byrdie's version of ginseng tea was only a tad tastier than warm tap water, but she reminded herself not to judge her friend. She noticed a can of okra and a boxed mix for scalloped potatoes on the countertop and remembered Jane's kind invitation.

"We're invited to have dinner at the inn tomorrow," she said. "I told Jane I was pretty sure you would accept."

"How lovely!" Byrdie said with genuine pleasure. "Can I bring something? Maybe my Mexican peppers and corn."

"I suspect Jane likes to plan the entire meal herself since she's a professional chef. Maybe you can put together a bouquet from your garden for the table. Jane has entered the botanical competition and probably isn't cutting any flowers from her own garden."

"Yes, I could do that. I can put together a nice bouquet using irises. They were spectacular when Jake was taking care of them and they're still very attractive."

"That sounds lovely. Now, would you like to come to the library with me? I'm going to look for building suppliers in the area phone books."

"Of course, if you need me."

"Only if you have the time," Gracie said. "It will probably be a bit tedious."

"I need to go to the post office for stamps. It's right across from the library, so I'll walk there with you, then pop over to the bakery to get some of their fresh-baked whole-wheat bread for lunch. Then I'll come back to the library. We can walk home together."

The Lord was watching over her, Gracie decided. Byrdie hadn't suggested driving her car. Gracie felt considerably safer on her own two feet, but she wouldn't hurt her friend's feelings for anything.

Gracie found the Acorn Hill Library to be a handsome, compact brick building. Inside, a generous portion of the floor space was devoted to a children's section, with plastic tables and open shelves in bright primary colors. A friendly young librarian with a winning smile directed her to the adult reading area at the south end of the building.

Gracie found a shelf of phone directories, not all current but recent enough for her purposes. She set about jotting down the names and phone numbers of building-supply companies.

When the librarian passed by the table, she whispered, "If you have a lot to copy, you might want to use the library's copy machine."

"Why didn't I think of making copies?" Gracie said, laughing at herself.

"We do have to charge by the page," the young woman apologized. "The library has a pretty tight budget."

"It's more than worth it. Thank you so much for suggesting it."

Gracie realized that she was so wrapped up in her hunt for Eustace Sims that she wasn't thinking things through the way she should. Her friends might call her a sleuth, but she knew how often she struggled with simple tasks. She had to settle down and seek guidance from the Lord. Otherwise she would be useless to Byrdie and all the other innocent people who might be cheated by the unscrupulous contractor.

As she went through the mechanics of copying pages, Gracie tried to organize her thoughts and plan her course of action. She felt at odds with this task, out of her element in trying to deal with a dishonest contractor. She didn't know the people and businesses in and around Acorn Hill the way she knew those in her hometown, but she couldn't succumb to discouragement. Jesus had showed the importance of taking a stand against evil in a Bible passage she'd taught many times in Sunday school. She went over the familiar words in her head:

Jesus entered the temple area and drove out all who were buying and selling there. He overturned the tables of the money changers and the benches of those selling doves. "It is written," he said to them, "'My house will be called a house of prayer,' but you are making it a 'den of robbers'" (Matthew 21:12–13).

Gracie knew that her task was very small compared with challenging corrupt practices in the temple, but it was one that had been given to her. Who knew what suffering and hardship she could prevent by exposing Eustace Sims?

She gathered together the copies and replaced the phone directories on the shelf. Perhaps she might not be able to find Sims this way, but she would put her trust in the Lord and pray for further guidance. Meanwhile, she would use her cell phone to contact out-of-town businesses that might remember the contractor's name or his Detroit baseball cap.

Finding him was only half the problem. What would she do when she caught up with him?

She folded the pages, put them into her shoulder bag and hurried out of the library to wait for Byrdie. Her friend was walking toward her along Acorn Avenue with a white bakery bag in one hand and her straw summer handbag in the other.

"Have you had any luck?" she called out when she got near.

"I have a lot of numbers to call," Gracie said, walking up to her.

"I'll help you after we have some lunch," Byrdie promised. "I'm resigned to never getting back any of my money, but it will make me feel better if we can stop that man from bilking other people."

Gracie walked back to Byrdie's house, absentmindedly responding to her friend's conversation. A man couldn't disappear into thin air. If he was working in the area, he had to buy materials somewhere. With Byrdie's help, they could cover all the businesses on her list this afternoon.

At the inn, Louise was glad to have the distraction of a new pupil. Mandy was one of the blond, blue-eyed Gardner twins. Her mother had wisely decided to allow the five-year-old girls to pursue different activities, and Mandy seemed to have an interest in music. When working with children her age, Louise tried hard to make lessons enjoyable. At the first session, her main goal was to establish rapport and learn more about her pupil.

The early afternoon lesson went quickly, and Mandy seemed eager to learn. Louise was far less optimistic about the choir's willingness to try anything new. This morning she'd received two phone calls questioning her choice of music for "Amazing Grace." One was from Florence, of course. At least she hadn't brought up the issue of new gowns again. Louise was grateful for that small favor, although she knew Florence too well to believe she would drop the subject.

The other call was from a person who said she wasn't in the choir. The woman had called anonymously, purporting to be a friend who didn't want to see the choir go downhill. She claimed to be doing Louise a favor by warning her about opposition to her leadership. The only specific thing she mentioned was the music for "Amazing Grace."

Louise didn't for one moment believe that the caller was acting out of kindness. There was something furtive and off-putting about a person who called to complain without giving her name. Louise could only compare it to a poison-pen letter whose purpose was to inflict pain.

She hadn't had a chance to mention it to either of her sisters and she didn't think she would. They would be upset for her sake. Louise wasn't at all sure she wanted to know who the anonymous caller was. She'd found a wonderful home in Acorn Hill after losing her husband. Most of the people were warm and friendly, and the return to her childhood town had been healing. She wasn't going to let this sly troublemaker change her feelings toward her neighbors.

There was bookkeeping to do and preparations to be made before new guests arrived late this afternoon. Louise went to work determined to put the unidentified caller out of her mind, but she knew it wouldn't be easy.

Was she wrong to try new music? The choir had talented and dedicated members. They wouldn't find the alternate arrangement too challenging. People often resisted change at first, but Louise had confidence in the choir. They would do a splendid job.

Nevertheless, she felt it prudent at least to consider whether to abandon the new music. It would be easier on her to choose only familiar pieces, but was it fair to the choir in the long run? There was an excitement about trying new things that could energize them and help them to bond.

Since she was only a temporary director, it was tempting to take the easy way, but she couldn't bring herself to do it. It would mean giving in to Florence. Also, it would be giving in to a person who didn't even have the decency to identify herself. Louise was sure Florence wouldn't stoop to asking someone to make an anonymous call. She wasn't shy about speaking her mind, but she'd never been shifty or underhanded.

Louise steeled herself to stand firm but wished she could talk to her sisters without distressing them. More than ever she realized what a blessing it was to have Gracie staying at the inn. Gracie had attended a choir practice and would understand Louise's doubts and anxiety.

Gracie went back to Byrdie's house with her friend and tackled the chore of phoning building-supply businesses close to Acorn Hill. Byrdie was eager to help and made several calls on her own, but it was soon obvious that she wasn't asking the right questions.

"I'm looking for a man named Eustace Sims," Byrdie said. "He might be using some other name, but he has a beard and wears a Detroit Tigers cap."

A few seconds later she hung up and sadly reported her lack of success.

Gracie didn't want to lecture her friend on ways to extract information, so she punched in another number on her cell phone and gestured for Byrdie to wait a minute.

"This is Gracie Parks," she said when a weary-sounding woman answered the phone. "My friend had some insulation work done, and I believe the man who installed it may have purchased it from you."

"Is something wrong with it?" the woman asked suspiciously.

"No, not at all. I would like to speak to him about some work that needs doing, but I can't find his number in the book. His name is Eustace Sims. Do you remember selling the insulation to him? He has a salt-and-pepper beard and usually wears a Detroit Tigers baseball cap. Since I'm on my own now, I really do have to rely on qualified workmen."

"I don't remember selling insulation to anyone like that, but if he shows up, I'll give him your number," the woman offered.

Gracie gave her cell phone number and thanked the woman.

"You do it so much better than I do," Byrdie said. "No

wonder everyone calls you a sleuth. I never can think of what to say on the telephone."

"You're probably too honest," Gracie assured her, not proud of the need to approach fibbing in order to find Sims.

She hoped God would forgive her for the white lies. She was angling for information that was really none of her business, at least in the opinion of people at the supply companies. She had to give them some reason for her interest in Sims. So far, though, her technique had been a total failure.

Byrdie gave up on calling and went to prepare lunch. Gracie was grateful for the break when she joined Byrdie at the kitchen table for tuna-salad sandwiches and fat-free soy chips. Byrdie's tuna salad was a bit dry and lacked special touches like chopped onions and celery, but the delicious fresh brown bread made up for it.

"I can see why you went to the bakery this morning," Gracie said. "This sandwich is delicious."

Byrdie, unaccustomed to praise for her meal preparation, beamed, reminding Gracie how important it was to tell people when they did something well.

The afternoon didn't bring success. Gracie's ear ached from pressing the phone to it, and she was afraid she would run out of minutes on her cell-phone plan before she could cover all the businesses on her lists.

Byrdie hovered but didn't make more calls or offer any suggestions. Gracie's frustration grew as the afternoon passed without a single new clue concerning the contractor's whereabouts.

At last she had to give up. She couldn't call every building supplier in Pennsylvania, and for all she knew, Eustace might be hundreds or thousands of miles away by now. The apparent attempt to conceal the license plate on his truck with mud, the cancelled phone service and his unwillingness to talk about himself were all bad signs. It appeared that he was going to great pains to keep his identity a secret.

Late in the afternoon, Byrdie made iced tea from a powdered mix, and Gracie was glad to join her on the front porch. They sipped the beverage, which bore a distant resemblance to the tea Gracie had enjoyed at the inn, and avoided talking about her phone efforts. When Byrdie wanted to go inside and start the packaged scalloped potatoes, Gracie insisted on treating her to dinner in a restaurant.

The usual ANGELs meeting had been called off on Wednesday evening. Alice, having worked a couple of hours beyond her scheduled shift, was still in her nurse's uniform when she registered two new guests, Karla Kennedy and Minna Newton. They were staying in Acorn Hill because they were bridesmaids in the wedding at the Methodist church on Saturday.

"You won't see much of us," Karla said. "We'll mostly be at our friend's house."

"Yes, I understand you're here for a wedding," Alice said, smiling at the tall, dark-haired girl. "We serve breakfast from seven—"

"Oh, you don't need to fix breakfast for us," Minna said. "We're not morning people."

"If you like, we can leave the fixings for a cold breakfast in the dining room." Alice wasn't sure how to handle guests who weren't eager to partake of Jane's breakfasts.

"No, really, we're just grateful for a bed. Our friend Christy—she's the bride—offered to let us stay at her house. We want to see her as much as possible before the wedding. She's so much fun to be around, but she has three aunts and two uncles staying there already."

"I've known Christy since she was little," Alice said. "I always loved her curly blond hair and her sense of humor."

"She still loves to play tricks on people," Karla said, "but she's never mean."

"Staying here is so much nicer than driving back and forth to Potterston for a place to stay," Minna said. "I'm excited to see our room. This is a lovely house."

Alice smiled at their enthusiasm and gave them two keys to the front bedroom next to the one Gracie was using. The girls would need the private bath to get ready for the wedding events. The people who had reserved the other two rooms for the Johnson family reunion would share a bath at the rear. They weren't expected until Thursday evening, so Jane wouldn't need to prepare a large breakfast on Thursday.

Alice went looking for Jane to tell her about the guests who didn't eat breakfast and found her in the garden.

"It's looking lovely," Alice said. "I can't imagine any way to improve it."

"Do you think so?" Jane bent and removed a bit of clover. "Maybe I should have planted some petunias around the bird bath. Louise did that one year."

"I'm surprised you remember them. You couldn't have been more than ten when she made that brief venture into gardening. Anyway, the garden looks complete just the way it is."

"Maybe you're right. Fullness isn't necessarily good."

"Our new guests checked in," Alice said. "The two bridesmaids. They don't want breakfast tomorrow."

"If they want to sleep late, I could set out some cereal and sweet rolls," Jane said.

"I offered, but they seem more interested in going to the bride's house."

"Thank you for calling about having to miss dinner. How was your meal at the hospital?" Jane asked.

"Not like the ones I enjoy at home, but we were so busy that I had little choice."

"You know I can always whip up a quick supper. That's why I freeze leftovers."

"I know," Alice agreed. "I just didn't want to be a bother."

"Oh no, I see some crab grass over there. Look, just beside the path. I was sure that I had taken care of it."

"Your eyes are better than mine," Alice said, laughing. "I would need a magnifying glass to keep things as perfect as you do."

Jane was already attacking the invading crab grass, so Alice wandered back inside.

Louise was standing beside the registration book.

"Alice, how was your day? I see that two of our new guests arrived."

"Yes, they seem like nice girls, but I doubt we'll see much of them. They'll be at the bride's house most of the time. They specifically don't want breakfast."

"Well, Jane will have a good group Friday and Saturday when the reunion guests are here. You worked a long shift. You're still in your uniform."

"I had dinner in the cafeteria. Jane would have insisted on cooking for me, and you know how involved she is with her garden these days. I didn't want to make extra work for her."

There was the sound of the front door opening and closing, and Alice looked over her shoulder to see who it was.

"Oh, Gracie, just the person I want to see," Louise said.

Alice saw their guest coming toward them. Her red curls looked limp, and her cheeks were bright pink as though she'd been hurrying.

"Just let me catch my breath," Gracie said. "I saw that rascal Gooseberry darting between bushes along the side of the house. Apparently he didn't want to stop playing. He wouldn't let me catch him."

"He didn't miss his supper," Louise assured her. "Of course, Wendell never does either."

"Louise, I had such a frustrating day," Gracie said. "Alice, how are you?"

"Fine."

"I called here and I called there, but no one seemed to know Eustace Sims or a man matching his description. At least none of the people at the building-supply places would admit to it," Gracie said.

"You must be exhausted," Louise said. "We have an assortment of herbal teas, just the thing to relax after a hard day. Will you join me for a cup?"

"Speaking of hard days," Alice said, feeling somewhat left out of the conversation. "It's been a trying one for me. I think I'll go to my room for a soak in the tub and some reading before I turn in."

Louise and Gracie both wished her a relaxing time, but neither suggested that she join them for tea. Alice couldn't begrudge her sister a new friendship, because she treasured her own friendship with Vera. She went up to her third-floor bedroom feeling more tired than usual.

Louise had thought often that day about the anonymous phone call. It was something new to her, and she fervently wished the caller had been open enough to give her name. It was one thing to work out her differences with Florence. It was quite another to have a secret critic.

"You look disturbed," Gracie said as they settled down at the kitchen table for their tea.

"I'm afraid I am. In your sleuthing, have you ever had a situation with an anonymous caller?"

Gracie shook her head. "Do you mean a threatening call?"

"More a complaining call. A woman phoned me this morning and said the choir didn't like the new music for 'Amazing Grace.'"

"Someone in the choir?"

"She said she wasn't. And it certainly wasn't Florence. However, she also called with the same complaint."

"Would Florence get somebody to make an anonymous call just to reinforce her own opinion?" Gracie asked.

"I don't think so. Florence has always been open. She doesn't hesitate to express her opinions, but I doubt she would ever stoop to that."

"If the caller isn't in the choir and isn't acting on Florence's behalf, why did she bother to phone you?"

"That is what's disturbing me."

"I hate to see you upset," Gracie said, "but we've both lived long enough to know that some people like making trouble. It could be someone who doesn't have the talent to be in the choir. Or possibly it isn't even a member of Grace Chapel. Some people are malicious for little or no reason."

"It had to be someone who knew about the rehearsal."

"True, but she may just have a talent for turning an innocent remark into gossip. Anyway, you can't let an anonymous caller interfere with what you're trying to do with the choir. I'm sure even those who prefer the familiar music of 'Amazing Grace' will come to love the new rendition."

"I hope you're right," Louise said, "Please, don't say anything about it to my sisters. We're not a family that keeps secrets, but I know this would really disturb them. I don't want to distress them when there's nothing any of us can do about it."

"Of course, I won't say anything to anybody."

Chapter ♪ Eight

Gracie walked to Byrdie's house right after breakfast Thursday morning. She hadn't decided what to do next about finding Eustace Sims, and Byrdie's only suggestion was to put their heads together over a cup of ginseng tea.

"You probably think ginseng comes from China," Byrdie said, "but it's grown right here in this country. The climate in Wisconsin is just right for the roots. I read about all the things it's good for, but I forget what they are."

"That's nice," Gracie said, in no way intending her comment to apply to the taste of the tea, which she found mediocre at best.

The doorbell rang, and Byrdie hurried to see who was calling on her. Gracie stayed in the kitchen, taking the opportunity to pour the contents of her cup down the sink drain. Her need to dispose of the brew outweighed her feelings of guilt.

"Gracie, come see who's here," Byrdie called from the front entryway.

Gracie quickly returned her empty teacup to the saucer and hurried to meet the visitor.

"You remember Fred Humbert from the hardware store," Byrdie said.

"Yes, of course. Nice to see you, Fred."

"And you too. I can take a look at the attic if you still want me to," the genial, sandy-haired man said.

"That would really be nice of you," Gracie said. "Anything you can tell us would be helpful. So far we haven't been able to locate Eustace Sims. We're not even sure that's his real name."

Byrdie led the way to the second story, then opened the narrow door to the attic. Gracie handed him the flashlight she'd left on the bottom step, and both women followed Fred up the stairs.

"The light isn't too good," Byrdie said.

Gracie followed Fred as he explored the far reaches of the attic, using the flashlight to examine the wooden joists and the insulation packed along the walls. He stooped down near the back and clucked with disapproval.

"The insulation is all new, but your man fudged on putting in as much as he should have. Look here. Back in the corner where it's dark, he didn't install nearly enough. Your hunch is right if you think he did an inferior job, Gracie, but there's no way I can tell whether the old needed to be replaced."

"What about the woodworms?" Byrdie asked in an unhappy voice.

"Your wood looks sound to me. I don't see any sign of the little holes woodworms would leave." Fred tapped an overhead beam with the end of the flashlight. "I'm not an exterminator, but I haven't seen any sign of insect damage. I would say this is an exceptionally sound attic. I'm sorry, Byrdie, but I suspect that this Sims character cheated you. Jake took good care of the house, and it shows."

"Yes, he did," Byrdie said smiling at Fred's praise of her husband. "I want to keep it up as well as he did, but it's hard to know what needs doing."

"Looks to me like you're doing a fine job," Fred said. "It

was just your bad luck to run into a crooked contractor. It could happen to anyone."

"That's what we're afraid of," Gracie said. "If he cheated Byrdie, he's almost sure to be doing it to other people. Unfortunately we haven't been able to learn where he bought the insulation. I was hoping to trace him that way."

"It's a pretty standard type," Fred said, stooping to keep from bumping his head on the ceiling.

"If you're done looking, would you like to have a cup of tea with us?" Byrdie asked.

"Afraid I'm not much of a tea drinker." Fred turned off the flashlight and started down the narrow stairway.

"I'd be happy to fix a pot of coffee. Jake was always partial to coffee too."

"Now that does sound inviting," Fred said.

Gracie decided that Fred was one of those people who inspire trust. A person couldn't help but like him right away. If he said the work was poorly done and possibly unnecessary, she was absolutely convinced of it. Byrdie threw herself into making coffee for Fred. She took a coffee maker with a glass pot from a lower cupboard and took great care in grinding some beans and measuring the coffee.

"I hope you'll enjoy this brew," she said. "I keep some fresh beans on hand in case someone comes over and wants a cup."

"Awfully nice of you to go to all this trouble," Fred said. Then he added apologetically, "Say, I didn't give you the good news. I have one bit of information you might be able to use. I heard through the grapevine, so to speak, that a lady named Matilda Singleton over in Potterston was madder than a wet hen over some work she arranged to have done on her house. She wanted to have the contractor arrested. Claims he ripped everything apart in her kitchen, then refused to do the work until she paid him all the money up front."

"Did she pay?" Gracie asked.

"She'd already paid half. When she wouldn't pay the whole amount ahead of time, he disappeared. She had to hire someone else to do the work."

"He kept her money and left things a mess?" Byrdie asked.

"That's about the size of it. He tore the kitchen apart thinking that then she would have to come up with more money. A lady who's been married as many times as Matilda Singleton doesn't put up with any nonsense from a man, I can tell you that," he said with a smile.

"I wonder if she would talk to us," Gracie said.

"I have a hunch Ms. Singleton will talk to anyone who will listen, but I don't know if Eustace Sims is the fellow who cheated her," Fred said. "Mention my name if you like. Alice Howard knew her in college. Matilda moved to Potterston not long ago with her last husband, but he passed away shortly after the move."

"What do you think?" Gracie asked when Fred had finished his coffee and left. "Should we talk to Matilda Singleton and see if it was Sims who swindled her too?"

"It's worth a try," Byrdie said, confirming what Gracie thought.

"We should call first, then I'll check at the inn to see what Gooseberry has been doing. I'll come back for you in my car."

"That's a call I can make." Byrdie sounded happy to have the opportunity.

For her part, Gracie was glad Byrdie hadn't insisted on driving. She hurried back to the inn, glad to have started the day with two good walks and a promising lead.

It wasn't long before Gracie and Byrdie were headed toward Potterston in Gracie's aging, dark-blue Cadillac. Byrdie was familiar with the town and had directions from Matilda Singleton to find her house. They located the Cape

Cod house with dormer windows on the second floor without any trouble. It was in a neighborhood of gracefully aging homes shaded by stately maples and clumps of birch.

Matilda Singleton opened the door before they had a chance to press the buzzer.

"One of you is the lady who called, right? Why don't you both come on in? I tell you, I'd like to see that swindler behind bars."

"I'm Byrdie Hutchinson. I made the call. This is Gracie Parks, my friend from Indiana. She's had some experience dealing with crooked folks, so she's helping me run down Eustace Sims."

"You're a private detective?" Matilda asked, holding the door open and motioning them to enter.

"No, nothing like that, Ms. Singleton." Gracie said with a self-deprecating laugh. "I just like to solve puzzles."

"For goodness' sake, call me Mattie. I haven't figured out whether to call myself Mrs. since I'm a widow or Ms. because I'm single again. Guess the easiest thing is to get married again."

She hooted with laughter, a deep throaty bellow that went with her statuesque figure and broad, good-natured face. Mattie had to be around sixty, because she'd gone to college with Alice, but her only concession to age was a pair of eyeglasses pushed up into her bushy, pale-blond hair. When she talked, the top half of her face didn't move. Gracie had seen enough cosmetic surgery to recognize it in the tightly stretched skin of Mattie's forehead.

"Come on in and have a seat," Mattie said, ushering them into the front room.

It was a remarkable room with Wedgwood-blue walls, a white velvet couch and matching side chairs, antique-gold carpeting and several landscapes in ornate gesso frames hanging on the walls. In contrast, there were piles of magazines and newspapers, the remnants of a couple of microwave meals, an overturned knitting bag with balls of yarn spilling out and a collection of general clutter that completely covered the coffee table.

"Don't mind my mess," Mattie said offhandedly. "Without a man around, it doesn't seem worth the bother to clean up."

Mattie didn't seem to notice Byrdie's frown of disapproval, and Gracie plunged into their reason for coming.

"We understand that you had bad luck with a contractor," Gracie said.

"Everybody in the county knows that," Mattie said emphatically. "I made enough of a stink to smoke out a grizzly, but the louse has disappeared, clean as a whistle."

"What was his name?" Byrdie asked still standing.

"He told me it was Tim Houston."

"The man who swindled me called himself Eustace Sims," Byrdie said excitedly.

"We were playing with the letters in his name to see if they could be made into another name, possibly his real name," Gracie explained. "We didn't have any luck, but Tim and Sim rhyme. Houston and Eustace both have the *u*, *s* and *t* in sequence."

"Maybe his home town is Houston," Byrdie suggested.

"He didn't sound like a Texas boy to me," Mattie said. "More like he came from hill country in Pennsylvania or West Virginia. My second husband grew up in a little coalmining town, so I can usually latch onto the accent."

"*Must, crust, dust*—there are a lot of words with *u*, *s*, *t*," Gracie said thoughtfully.

"Let me show you the kitchen now that someone else finished it," Mattie said, leading the way toward the back of the house. "It took a big chunk of my late husband's insurance money to renovate it, thanks to Tim Houston ripping everything out and making off with half the payment."

"It's very nice," Byrdie said politely, unconsciously turning

up her nose at the clutter covering the new granite counter-
tops and the round breakfast table.

"A dolphin faucet. What an interesting touch," Gracie
commented.

"Thanks. I had to argue with the new contractor to get
him to install it."

Turning the conversation back to Mattie's first contractor, Gracie asked, "What did this Tim Houston fellow look
like?"

"I didn't notice much besides the beard. It was big and
bushy, black streaked with white. I like a man with facial hair,
but my floor mop is better lookin' than his beard."

"Was there anything distinctive about the way he
dressed?" Gracie asked.

"He wore the standard workman's jeans and T-shirt.
Some hostess I am," she said with a hoot of laughter. "What
can I get you ladies to drink?"

"Nothing, thank you," Byrdie quickly said.

Gracie's mind wasn't on refreshments.

"Did he wear a cap?" she asked.

"Now that you mention it, he always had a dusty-looking
baseball cap stuck on his head. Didn't have the manners to
take it off in the house."

"What color was it?"

"Oh, nothing distinctive. I would remember a Pittsburgh
cap. I'm an avid Pirates fan. Now that I think, it was probably dark blue."

"Did it have a logo?"

"A big *D*, I think. Of course! It was a Detroit Tiger's cap.
Why didn't I think of that sooner? Guess I was so darn mad
that I wasn't thinking clearly."

"What did he drive?" Gracie pressed.

"A beat-up truck. I didn't look at it close up."

"So you didn't see the license plate?"

"Afraid not. I tried describing him to the police, but the

best I could come up with was average. He's average height, average weight, and average looks. A lump of bread dough is more distinctive. I can't even say what color his eyes are because he kept his hat on and never looked me straight in the eye."

"Sounds like our man," Byrdie said. "Eustace Sims has a sly look—foxy, unsavory."

Gracie was afraid Byrdie was letting her imagination run away. Sims had seemed trustworthy enough to hire for the work, but there was nothing to be gained by challenging her description.

"He was a smooth talker, though," Mattie said. "I thought I knew a lot about men until he showed up."

"Did you sign a contract?" Gracie asked.

"You bet. I read it very carefully, and it specifically said the second half of the payment wasn't due until the work was done. Instead he demanded to have it as soon as he'd ripped the place apart."

"That's odd," Gracie mused. "He did the work for Byrdie before demanding the final payment. Maybe he works differently according to the situation."

"We did have some artistic differences. The fool wanted to use some tiles behind my sink that he picked up at a warehouse closeout. They were puce, if you can imagine that color in my kitchen," Mattie said, gesturing broadly at the bright yellow walls and shamrock-green floor tiles.

"He didn't want to do things your way?" Gracie asked mildly.

"That's the understatement of the year! I insisted he haul off the rubble right away. I mean, how does it look to have a kitchen sink in the front yard? He tried to tell me that I had to hire a trash man to take the old appliances and cupboards to the dump. You'd better believe I told him what I thought of that."

"So he gave you a hard time while he was working?"

"He was the most uncooperative, mule-headed man I've ever come across, and that includes my first husband, Bernie. Bernie thought it was woman's work to carry out the garbage."

"There's no way to be sure, but I think Tim Houston and Eustace Sims are the same person," Gracie said. "How did you get in touch with him?"

"He advertised in the newspaper. I had exorbitant estimates from two local contractors, and I thought it couldn't hurt to get a third. His was twenty percent lower. That's a lot when you're doing a whole kitchen, so I jumped at the chance to get the work done more reasonably."

"Have you tried to contact him since he walked out on the job?" Gracie asked.

"Have I! The pond scum has disappeared. I even hired a private detective to trace him, but all that did was cost me more money."

Gracie met Byrdie's eyes and knew that they'd learned all they could here.

"We really appreciate hearing your story, Mattie," she said. "If we learn anything, we'll let you know."

"He should be in jail," Mattie said. "If it weren't for the fine print in that contract, the law might do something."

"What fine print?" Byrdie asked.

"I don't know how I let it get past me, but if the work wasn't completed for any reason, he reserved the right to keep any monies paid as compensation for planning and other services rendered. I can't pursue criminal charges because I refused to pay the second half of the money. If he'd failed to do the work then, I would have had a case."

"Diabolical," Byrdie said softly.

"I wonder where he'll strike next," Gracie said sadly, then thanked Mattie for sharing her experience with them.

They left and drove back to Acorn Hill in a somber mood.

"It's worse than I thought," Gracie said thoughtfully. "I wonder how he learned to draw up such a tricky and misleading contract."

"He's a smooth one," Byrdie agreed unhappily. "I'm afraid we'll never find him, and even if we do, what then?"

"What then indeed?" Gracie asked pensively. "At least we have dinner at Grace Chapel Inn to look forward to. If Jane's dinner is as good as her breakfasts, I'll have to take a long, long walk tomorrow morning."

Jane finished setting the large mahogany table in the dining room, then put out a silver candy dish filled with her signature Swedish mints colored pale pink, green and white. They were still cold from the freezer where she kept a supply. They added a nice touch in a room with green walls and chair pads in a subtle shade of pale green and ivory damask.

She plugged in the warming tray on the buffet, preferring to serve her lasagna there instead of at the table. This way she could keep the remainder warm in the glass pan in case anyone wanted seconds.

The sisters seldom ate in the dining room, using it mostly to serve breakfast to their guests or to entertain company. Jane had decided to make the meal more festive by using china that Louise had received as a wedding gift. The plates were large with delicate blue flowers and a thin silver band. They weren't permitted in the dishwasher, of course, but it was worth hand washing them. She thought Louise would be pleased to see the set in use. Her older sister had seemed a little down recently, no doubt because the choir wasn't doing as well as she'd hoped.

"I was going to offer to help," Alice said, coming into the dining room, "but I see you're as efficient as always."

"Once I've prepared the lasagna, it's an easy meal," Jane said. "With any luck, the guests coming for the reunion won't be here until I've had time to clear the table and clean up the kitchen. It's been fun, planning a meal for invited guests. I'm certainly enjoying Gracie's company."

"Yes, we're lucky to have her here," Louise said as she came into the dining room. "I'm so grateful that she's willing to go to choir practice with me again tonight. Sometimes I feel that I'm in over my head trying to direct it."

"Of course you're not," Alice said emphatically. "If you weren't so busy with the inn and your private lessons, you'd be the ideal person to be the permanent director."

"I seriously doubt that," Louise said.

"The lasagna smells wonderful. We haven't had it in ages," said Alice.

"It's not exactly a warm-weather dish," Jane said, "but if Byrdie can serve stew . . . Actually, I was in the mood for Italian."

Gracie and Byrdie arrived exactly when expected, which Jane appreciated. Nothing ruined a meal quicker than guests who were late. Because Louise liked to leave for choir practice shortly after six-thirty, Jane had planned an earlier-than-usual meal.

Byrdie presented her with a lovely arrangement of flowers. Jane admired the deep-purple irises, thanked Byrdie for the arrangement and put it on the table as a centerpiece.

The women seated themselves, and Alice led them in a blessing, asking that they join hands and bow their heads. Jane found inspiration in her sister's deep faith and felt warmed by the fellowship around the table.

Then, with appreciative comments from everyone, Jane put an aromatic serving of lasagna on each plate and handed it over to the table. They passed around a bowl of greens with sliced Roma tomatoes topped by Jane's special Italian dressing, and a plate with thick slices of warm garlic bread.

"Almost everything Jane serves is homemade," Louise said, "even the bread."

"Your flowers are so lovely, Byrdie. If you like, after dinner I'll show you my garden," Jane said.

"Gracie mentioned that your garden is really lovely," Byrdie said. "I only had a glimpse as we came up the walk."

"Speaking of gardens—"

"It's Jane's favorite subject," Alice teased.

"I've already told Gracie and Louise, but I saw a really unusual garden while I was scoping out the competition. It's Elma Grayson's."

"Vera and I have walked past it," Alice said. "It's hard to tell where the yard ends and the garden begins."

"That's the one," Jane said. "Everything is all mixed up. She's even growing horseradish in a flowerbed. The whole thing is like a crazy quilt."

"I like her wooden squirrel," Alice said.

"Her little figures are curious additions, but they work for her. Of course, it's not the kind of garden that wins prizes, but it does have charm," Jane said.

"I'll have to see it before I leave Acorn Hill," Gracie said.

"How did your day go, Gracie?" Jane asked, noticing that Gracie looked a little downhearted.

"We went to Potterston," Byrdie said. "Turns out a woman named Mattie Singleton—someone I think you know, Alice—was cheated by a contractor. We're almost certain it was Eustace Sims, but he called himself Tim Houston."

"Of course I know Mattie," Alice said. "She was an acquaintance in college."

"She came out worse than I did," Byrdie said. "He tore apart her kitchen, then disappeared with money she'd paid in advance."

"We may not have been totally wrong about the letters in his name," Gracie said. "Tim rhymes with Sim, and he used u, s and t in both names. Unfortunately we're not any closer to learning his real name or finding him."

When their main course was finished, with many compliments from her guests and sisters, Jane brought out stemmed glasses filled with lemon sherbet accompanied by a plate of homemade macaroons. "What a lovely dinner," Byrdie said. "I really should do more cooking from scratch. Thank you for inviting me."

Alice offered to clean up, giving Jane a chance to show Byrdie her garden before driving her home. Louise was eager to get to the chapel before the choir members arrived, so immediately after dessert, she hurried up to her room to freshen up and get some things she needed for the rehearsal.

"It was a lovely dinner, Jane," Gracie said. "I like your lasagna recipe even better than mine."

"I'll be glad to share it," Jane offered. "I can print it out on the computer."

"Thank you," Gracie said. "There are so many benefits to staying at Grace Chapel Inn."

Chapter ♪♪Nine

Louise's spirits lifted a little as she walked to Thursday-night choir practice with Gracie. It had been heartening for Louise to hear that Fred had helped to provide useful information about Eustace Sims.

"When Byrdie and I talked with Mattie Singleton," Gracie said, "she didn't know how to find him either. He does seem to be playing games with his name, and we don't know his real one yet."

"At least you're making progress," Louise said. "I still have no idea who my anonymous caller is."

"You haven't gotten another call?" Gracie asked with concern.

"No, but I have decided to sign up for caller ID sometime in the near future. I'm sure Jane and Alice will see that it can be a convenience."

"You still haven't told them?"

"No, I know how upset they would be. Both of them have enough concerns of their own without fretting over mine. I am only a temporary choir director, so the selection of music won't be my problem after the church board hires a new director. Oh, by the way, would you like to direct a hymn or two this evening? You are the assistant director."

"I could try one that I've done before when I substituted for our director back home," Gracie said, "if you don't expect too much. In fact, it would be fun for me."

Louise held the door for Gracie when they reached the chapel, then followed her inside. She was surprised to see someone there ahead of them, then realized it was Rev. Thompson.

"Louise, I hope you don't mind if I sit in on choir practice awhile," he said.

"Not at all, Kenneth. It will be a pleasure to have you. This is Gracie Parks, a guest at the inn and a new friend. She's going to help me by directing a hymn or two tonight. Gracie, Rev. Kenneth Thompson is our minister, and we're very fortunate to have him."

"I'm pleased to meet you," Gracie said. "I've heard good things about you in the short time I've been here."

"Grace Chapel's congregation has been very kind, no one more so than the Howard sisters," he said.

Rev. Thompson was a tall, lean man with short, dark hair and arresting hazel eyes. Louise thoroughly approved of his conservative manner of dress. Even though it was a warm summer evening, he was wearing dress slacks, a white button-down shirt and a navy tie with narrow gray pinstripes.

He asked Gracie where she lived, and Louise slipped away to prepare herself for the choir. It seemed much harder to face them now that she'd received the anonymous phone call. She didn't want to be suspicious, but it would be hard to look at the members without wondering if one of them had made the call.

Choir members began arriving. Louise was happy to see Eric and Toni Glendenning. Alice had enlisted some of her ANGELs as volunteer babysitters, and the couple had been the first to make use of their services. Louise hoped it would encourage other young parents to join the choir.

Oddly enough, when they were ready to begin, Florence wasn't there. Louise asked Rev. Thompson to lead them in an opening prayer, then began with "Amazing Grace" using the new music. She was pleased that no one protested. It went much better than on Tuesday, perhaps because the choir put more heart and less protest into it.

She was ready to move onto the next hymn when Florence burst through the double doors at the rear of the church and hurried up the aisle. The tardy choir member was flushed and breathless when she took her place after dropping a large shopping bag on a nearby pew.

"I went to Potterston," she said, aware that she had everyone's attention. "I apologize for being late, but time slipped away from me. The mall there has a religious book-and-supply store, and I wanted to look at the robes they had in their catalog." Rev. Thompson, who knew nothing about Florence's obsession with choir robes, looked puzzled, but no one reacted to her latest pronouncement.

"I was just about to turn over the choir to Gracie," Louise said with all the patience she could muster.

"Oh."

Florence didn't protest, and Louise was grateful for that.

Gracie led the choir in "Blest Be the Tie That Binds," a hymn familiar to the members. Louise sat on a pew and enjoyed it. There were some lovely voices at Grace Chapel, and she fervently hoped there wouldn't be any turmoil to discourage the faithful from remaining part of the choir.

"Very nice," Rev. Thompson said after Gracie finished and set down the baton.

He stood and spoke enthusiastically. "It sounds to me as if the choir is ready to begin singing at services again," he said. "Do you feel up to doing at least one hymn this Sunday?"

Louise looked at the choir members, not sure how to answer. They certainly weren't ready to perform "Amazing

Grace," although this evening's practice had been an immense improvement. She was running hymns through her head, wondering how to respond, when Jack O'Hara spoke up.

"I thought we sounded pretty good on 'Blest Be,'" the animal-control officer said. "Any reason why we shouldn't go with that one?"

"None at all as far as I'm concerned," Rev. Thompson said. "What do you think, Louise?"

"Gracie directed it. Are you willing to lead us in church this Sunday, Gracie?"

Her friend looked more pink-cheeked than usual, perhaps a little flustered at being asked to direct the choir before the whole congregation, but she readily agreed.

"I'll be happy to if everyone is in agreement," Gracie said.

"Fine," Florence said, "but why do just one? We were working on 'I Love to Tell the Story' last spring. I had the solo part. I'm sure I could be ready to sing it by Sunday."

Rev. Thompson looked at Louise, his back to the choir and his brows slightly arched in a silent question.

"Since we won't have another practice before Sunday," Louise said, "why don't we plan on just one hymn this week. We can work on 'I Love to Tell the Story' for another Sunday."

"That sounds good," the minister said. "I'll put 'Blest Be the Tie That Binds' in the bulletin for Sunday. I'm sure the congregation will be happy to have the choir back. I know that I will."

They went over the hymn for Sunday several more times until Gracie complimented the choir on how well they'd done.

"Now we can work on 'I Love to Tell the Story,'" Florence said insistently.

When no one protested staying longer, Louise took over the directing again.

Her worst fear about the hymn was realized. The choir did well enough, but Florence's solo was light years away from being ready. She simply couldn't sing the high intervals. The solo required an outstanding voice. Florence's was adequate for choir singing, but she was reaching beyond her ability. Louise was afraid that no amount of practice would help. The problem, as Louise saw it, was to dissuade Florence without throwing the choir into chaos. She didn't know how much to assert her will. Should she allow Florence to solo and let the new director cope with her campaign for new robes? What was best for Grace Chapel? Louise was honest enough with herself to wonder if pride was part of what kept her from confiding in her sisters. She walked back to the inn with Gracie, hesitant at first to rehash the rehearsal with her. She didn't want her companion to think that she was a complainer, but Gracie seemed to sense her unease.

"Perhaps Florence will realize that the solo is too much for her," Gracie suggested.

"Maybe," Louise said doubtfully.

"No, I guess not." Gracie laughed softly at her improbable suggestion.

"I'll have to think of some way to discourage her," Louise said more to herself than Gracie. "Oh my, I haven't thanked you for agreeing to lead the choir on Sunday."

"You don't need to. It's my pleasure. You and the choir have made me feel right at home."

Jane was waiting for Louise by the registration desk when they got back to the inn. Gracie said good night and went up to her room.

"Our reunion guests are here," Jane reported. "They may want breakfast Saturday, but tomorrow they're going to a breakfast for their branch of the family."

"Has Alice gone to bed?"

"She went to a movie with Vera," Jane said. "Fred needed to stock shelves at the hardware store, so they drove to Potterston for a late show."

"Good. Alice was overdue for some recreation."

Louise sought out the quiet comfort of her father's study. There she decided to pray for God to give her guidance and to strengthen her trust that the choir problems would be resolved in a spirit of love.

Gracie awoke Friday morning and was surprised that she'd slept past eight o'clock. Gooseberry was stretching his legs at the door, making it clear that he wanted to get out. She cracked the door and watched as his thick tail disappeared from sight. Then she hurried to shower and dress for the day in white slacks, a bright yellow tank top and a yellow-and-white striped cotton shirt worn open like a jacket.

She'd deliberately picked a cheerful outfit. If there was anything she could do to brighten Louise's day, she wanted to do it. Louise had a problem with the choir, and Gracie didn't see an easy solution.

If Florence were being deliberately nasty and difficult, she wouldn't be so hard to thwart. As it was, the overly zealous choir member thought that she was helping. It probably never occurred to her that others might react negatively. Florence was a longtime choir member, and in some situations seniority meant a lot.

Gracie didn't know Florence well enough to guess what insecurity or feelings of inadequacy prompted her to be so pushy, but she sympathized with Louise, who balanced her striving for perfection with a natural kindness. Gracie admired her patience and diplomacy. By the time Gracie went down for breakfast, her thoughts had turned to the problem of finding Eustace Sims or Tim Houston or whoever the man really was. Both Byrdie and Mattie had gone to the police, but the law officers' hands seemed to be tied. There was no proof that Byrdie was a victim of fraud, and no clue to the identification of Mattie's crooked contractor.

"Good morning," she said when she entered the kitchen.

Jane and Louise were lingering over the remains of their breakfast. "Have your other guests had breakfast?" Gracie asked.

"No," Jane said. "The reunion people left for a family breakfast, and the bridesmaids prefer to sleep late. Alice is working at the hospital this morning. Her shift began at seven. So there are just the two of us."

"I can't think of better breakfast company, if you'll permit me to eat with you here," Gracie said. "But you've almost finished, and I'm not that hungry this morning. If I may, I'll just have one of those pecan rolls and be on my way."

"Of course you may. I'll fix a fresh pot of tea," Jane said, getting up and walking to fill the kettle. "I'd be happy to fix you an omelet."

"No thank you, really."

"What are your plans for the day?" Louise asked.

"I wish I knew," Gracie said wistfully. "In this day and age, people don't just disappear. Eustace Sims is probably out taking advantage of some poor soul even as we speak, and I'm fresh out of ideas on how to find him.

"Is there anything we can do?" Jane asked as she put a cup and saucer in front of Gracie.

"We would be happy to help any way we can," Louise said.

"I think that your prayers would help more than anything else at this point. I need the Lord to point me in the right direction. It's going to take more than my amateur sleuthing to run down Eustace Sims."

"We'll be happy to pray for God's guidance," Louise said.

Jane echoed her sister's thought and suggested that they pray together. They joined hands and each prayed aloud that Gracie would be able to protect other innocent people from wicked schemes.

Gracie felt her confidence renewed. "Maybe I'll phone Matilda Singleton to see if she can remember more that might help. It's too soon to be discouraged. You've both helped me more than you know."

Jane quickly cleared the breakfast table after Gracie and Louise had left the kitchen. She wanted to look at more gardens, especially Elma Grayson's remarkable blending of lawn, vegetable patch and flower garden. Something about it had impressed her so, although she wasn't sure what.

Armed with sunglasses and her big straw hat, Jane set out for Berry Lane. She felt a little like a schoolgirl playing hooky, but she really wanted to see Elma's garden again. Mostly she wanted to know why it had stuck in her mind when she hadn't regarded it to be the kind of garden that was likely to win awards.

She walked briskly because she'd promised to drive Ethel to the dentist in Potterston. They would have to leave by ten o'clock to be on time for her aunt's appointment. She was mentally making a list of things she needed at the big discount store near the dentist's office, but she lost her concentration when she got within sight of Elma's garden.

Slowing her steps, she enjoyed the profusion of colors and textures that surrounded Elma's little brick house. It reminded her of pictures she'd seen of old English gardens with rows of hollyhocks nodding in welcome.

It took her a minute to notice another straw hat near a bed of marigolds. Elma was kneeling on a rubber mat, engrossed in spading around a cluster of plants.

"Good morning," Jane said from a distance so she wouldn't startle the frail-looking, elderly woman.

"Oh," Elma said, slowing getting up to greet Jane. "You're one of the Howard girls, aren't you? I've seen you at Grace Chapel."

"Yes, I'm Jane. I've seen you at the chapel too. You have a lovely garden, Elma. This isn't the first time I've admired it."

"Thank you, Jane. It's been a lot of years in the making. Harry and I started it when we were first married. Now that he's been gone for nearly ten years, nothing gives me more pleasure than being out here with my plants and my memories."

"Do you take care of it all by yourself?" Jane asked.

"Oh my, no. My neighbor across the way brings his rototiller over in the spring and gets the beds for annuals ready to plant. He does my lawn in summer and scoops away the snow in winter. I don't know what I'd do without him."

"Then you do your own planting?"

Elma grinned and brushed a lock of gray-white hair out of her face. "I'm afraid I'm something of a Tom Sawyer these days. My niece brings her grandchildren for a stay, and I persuade them all that it would be a hoot to pitch in and help. The children seem to have such fun doing it. Lucy is in middle school. She's a hard worker. Cindy is nine and has a regular little green thumb."

"It sounds like a family project," Jane said, admiring a cluster of blue bachelor buttons.

"Oh, more than that. I have dear friends who help me look after it during the summer. It's getting a bit warm. Would you like to come inside for a glass of lemonade?" Elma invited.

"I would love to, but I've promised to drive my aunt to the dentist in Potterston."

"Come another day then," Elma said in a tone that showed she meant it. "I don't need any notice. You're welcome whenever you're in the neighborhood."

"That's very kind of you," Jane said. "I'm sorry I have to rush away today."

"Before you go, maybe you can give me an idea of where to put the newest resident of my garden."

She led the way closer to the house, where a painted

wooden skunk attached to a ground stake was lying on the small front porch.

"The boy down the street made it for me in woodworking class and painted it in his garage." She picked up the small skunk with gleaming black and white paint. "I believe I'll name him Elijah because God sent Elijah to a widow for bread and water."

"I remember the story," Jane said with pleasure. "Because of her kindness, Elijah told the widow that her jar of flour wouldn't be used up and her oil jar wouldn't go dry until the drought was over."

"It's my way of remembering that God is looking after me even though I'm not as strong as I once was," Elma said.

"Do all the creatures in your garden have names?" Jane asked, fascinated by the depth of thought that helped to shape Elma's garden.

"Oh my, yes. There's Moses," she said, pointing toward a wooden squirrel. "I call him that because he gathers nuts the way God's people gathered manna in the wilderness. It's an important name for such a little creature, but he reminds me that God cares for all of us."

"What an extraordinary garden," Jane said, taken aback by Elma's explanations.

"Everything here jogs my memory, which isn't what it once was. I grow horseradishes to remind me of the bitter herbs eaten with the Passover lamb. But here I am, rattling on when you need to be on your way. Do come see me when you have the time."

"I certainly will," Jane said, reluctantly saying good-bye to the extraordinary gardener.

Chapter ♪ Ten

The unmistakable fragrance of cinnamon wafted up to Gracie's room even before she was ready to go down for breakfast. It was Saturday morning, the big day for the inn guests who'd come for a wedding and a family reunion. So far she had only glimpsed the two bridesmaids when they were on their way out the day before. She'd met the reunion guests, but only briefly when their paths crossed in the foyer.

She knew Jane had prepared a big breakfast this morning. Based on earlier discussions, Gracie imagined that it would be a feast. Because she and Byrdie had plans for the day, she took her purse and cell phone with her to the dining room, where she found that she was the first to answer the silent summons of the cinnamon.

"Good morning, Gracie," Louise said cheerfully, carrying a tray of tableware and napkins to the dining room table. "You're the first one down for breakfast. Jane is almost ready to start serving."

"I can wait for the others," Gracie said. "I don't want to be a bother."

"You couldn't possibly be. We're enjoying your visit so much that we just might adopt you into the Howard family."

"That's so nice of you to say that," Gracie said, beaming. "Grace Chapel Inn is starting to feel like a second home. It was my good fortune that you had room for me. Byrdie feels bad that her guestroom is still torn up. Her second floor is barely usable what with renovations still in progress, but she has a nice bedroom for herself on the first floor."

"Eustace Sims wasn't supposed to finish the work in her spare bedroom, was he?" Louise asked with concern.

"Fortunately not. She has a workman lined up to finish it, but he's too busy doing outside jobs while the weather is nice. What she needs is a rainy streak so he has time for her job."

"It's certainly been a long process for her, hasn't it?"

"She started last fall. Her idea was to redo the house so that she could have everything she needs on the first floor."

"It sounds as if she's planned well for her later years," Louise said as she finished setting the table. "It's unfortunate that Sims treated her so poorly. Have you learned anything new since I saw you yesterday?"

"Byrdie and I drove to some of the building-supply places. We were hoping that face-to-face contacts would bring more results than phone calls, but so far, no luck."

"That is a shame," Louise said. "Oh, what's that?"

Gracie realized that her cell phone was sounding and quickly located it in her purse. She'd talked to Arlen, her son, last evening, so it was most likely Byrdie.

"Hello," she said as Louise left the room.

"Gracie, you're not going to believe what I just did," Byrdie said in a distressed voice.

"What's wrong?"

"I fell. I was taking some trash out to the container by the garage, and I twisted my ankle in a rut. I don't know how I could've done something so foolish, but my ankle has swollen up to the size of a melon."

"Oh, that's terrible. I'll come right over and drive you to the emergency room. Do you think it's broken?"

"It's probably just sprained," Byrdie said, "but there's no way I'll be able to do more investigations with you today."

"Don't be concerned about that," Gracie said. "The important thing is to stay off your ankle until a doctor checks it."

"Yes, I'm certainly doing that," Byrdie said with a half-hearted laugh. "I'm sitting on the couch with an ice pack on it."

"I'll be right over," Gracie assured her.

"Have you had your breakfast? You don't have to miss it on my account."

"No, but skipping a meal won't do my figure the slightest harm. Don't move until I get there."

She said good-bye, returned the cell phone to her purse and went into the kitchen to tell Jane and Louise that there would be one fewer for breakfast.

"That was bad news, I'm afraid," Gracie said. "Byrdie twisted her ankle when she took the trash out this morning. She says it's swollen like a melon, so I'm going to drive over right away. Chances are she should go to the emergency room and have it looked at."

"Oh, what a shame," Jane said as she took a pan of fried apples, the source of the wonderful cinnamon scent, off the stove. Wait just a minute, and I'll make up a plate for the two of you. You don't want to go to the emergency room without breakfast. It might be a long wait if they're busy."

"I don't want you to go to any trouble," Gracie said, although the aroma in the kitchen was making her mouth water.

"It's no trouble at all." Jane heaped food upon a large, white plate. "I made enough to feed an army, and odds are, the bridesmaids will only nibble if they even come down for breakfast. We're having Gournay cheese omelets and hash browns with the fried apples. I have a cover that will keep breakfast warm for you and Byrdie. But don't dawdle."

Gracie smiled. "I promise that I won't."

"If there's anything I can do to help, please feel free to ask," Louise said.

"That goes for me too," Jane said, "and I'm sure I can speak for Alice as well. She was called to work at the hospital today, but her shift ends at three."

"You're all so kind," Gracie said. "I'm sure Byrdie would appreciate your prayers for a quick, uncomplicated recovery. And thank you for breakfast. It smells wonderful."

Louise walked to the car with Gracie, making her promise to call if there was anything she could do to help.

Gracie wasted no time in driving to her friend's house, then carried Jane's gift of breakfast to Byrdie's front door and knocked softly.

"Come in. It's not locked," Byrdie called out.

Gracie found her with legs outstretched on the couch and a plastic bag of ice cubes propped on her ankle.

"I didn't want to go upstairs to look for my ice bag with everything in disarray, so I improvised," Byrdie said. "I'm afraid it's started to leak."

"I'll get you fresh ice and double-bag it inside a towel," Gracie said. "Oh dear, you weren't exaggerating. Your ankle has really ballooned up. As soon as we have some of the lovely breakfast Jane sent, I'll drive you to the emergency room."

"A trip like that is too much trouble," Byrdie said. "I'm sure my ankle will be fine if I stay off my feet awhile."

"It's not trouble. It's the only sensible thing to do," Gracie said in a determined voice.

"I can't go to the hospital in Potterston wearing this dreadful housedress. I only put it on in the morning before I do my chores."

Gracie had to agree that the black sack-dress with chartreuse flowers wasn't the height of fashion, but she wouldn't take no for an answer about having the ankle examined by a doctor.

"Have a bit of breakfast," she said. "Then you can tell me what you want to wear, and I'll find it in your closet. You can change while I bring my car around to the back. That way you won't have to hobble down those steep front steps. You don't have any crutches, do you?"

"Yes, now that you mention it, I do. I had some surgery on my knee a few years back, but I don't remember where they're stored. Maybe in the cellar, but I can't ask you to go down there. It's really not a nice place."

"I've seen lots of basements. Yours can't be all that bad, but first we'll savor Jane's breakfast."

Gracie placed a small table beside the couch, hurried to find plates, flatware and napkins in Byrdie's methodically organized kitchen, arranged those items on a tray along with coffee that Byrdie had prepared, and rejoined her friend for breakfast.

Delicious as the meal was, Gracie's delight in Jane's cooking was tempered by concern that her friend might have broken her ankle, not that a sprain wasn't unpleasant enough. Byrdie ate with gusto, though, enjoying the breakfast in spite of her pain. Gracie left her to finish her meal while she went to the cellar to hunt for crutches.

A door beside the walk-in pantry led to the cellar. Gracie went down the wooden stairs very cautiously, but they seemed sturdy enough in spite of the narrow boards. The floor was hard-packed dirt, perhaps not unusual in a house as old as Byrdie's but a surprise to Gracie. A square of shabby linoleum was laid at the bottom of the steps, and she could make out odds and ends of discarded carpeting scattered around the open space like stepping-stones.

The light wasn't strong, coming as it did from a single bulb suspended from the unfinished ceiling at the bottom of the stairs. She made her way to a long workbench on the right, where another bulb hung in a metal shade. She found a string and pulled it to illuminate the cellar further.

Byrdie had warned her. The old gray stone foundation and the low ceiling made it a dismal place, and Gracie could see that she might have trouble finding the crutches. The basement was a warren of rooms with separate doors leading off from the main space. Some doors were shut, and others were open, but everything about the dimly lit basement was uninviting.

She surveyed the open space without spotting any place that could conceal a pair of crutches, so there was no choice. She had to explore behind all the doors since Byrdie's ankle was much too swollen for walking.

The first door she tried was stuck. She couldn't push it open with her hand, so she pushed against it with her shoulder and hip, finally budging it enough to squeeze inside. She shrieked aloud when something brushed against her face, then laughed at herself. It was only the cord to another light, and she gladly pulled it. The metal bulk of the furnace and the white enameled tank of a water heater filled most of the space, but she checked all the corners and shadows anyway. There were no crutches in this room, so she pulled off the light and tried another cubbyhole.

She explored a fruit cellar that contained dusty Mason jars of brownish peaches and other preserves. There were cardboard boxes on some of the shelves but none big enough to contain crutches.

A third little room was even less inviting. She had to find an old broom and brush away the cobwebs in the open doorway, and the overhead bulb was as dim as a light could be without burning out completely. Two walls were lined with shelves, most of them filled with corrugated cardboard boxes marked with black crayon or felt pen. A third wall held the switch box for the house's electrical system. Gracie had just decided that the crutches weren't there when something caught her eye.

Jake had been as neat as Byrdie when it came to hanging

tools, labeling boxes and generally keeping things orderly. Nothing was lying on the basement floor except the long aluminum flashlight under the switch box. It wasn't surprising that a homeowner would keep a light handy in case of power failure. It was unusual that Byrdie would just leave it on the floor against the wall.

Gracie picked it up carefully using a tissue she'd stuffed in the pocket of her pale-blue summer slacks. She expected it to be dusty from a long sojourn on the dirt floor, but instead it looked shiny and clean. Was it possible a workman had left it there recently? She studied the shiny metal cylinder and decided to ask Byrdie about it.

Fortunately, she found the crutches on a shelf in the next spooky little niche. They were wrapped in transparent plastic that was clouded by age and dust. Sighing with relief, she extinguished the lights and trudged up to the main floor carrying crutches and the flashlight.

She unwrapped the crutches outside the kitchen door and discarded the plastic in a container by the garage, being careful not to trip in the same depression that had brought Byrdie to harm. The crutches were old wooden ones with the red foam rubber on top crumbling with age, but they would be a big help in getting Byrdie into the car.

Byrdie had left the couch and hobbled into her room to change clothes by the time Gracie got back to her. She was sitting on the edge of her bed wearing a navy linen skirt and a white knit top.

"I'm afraid I'll have to wear sandals without pantyhose," she said unhappily.

"It won't matter in the least," Gracie said. "I found the crutches nicely wrapped on a shelf."

"I'm grateful that you did," Byrdie said. "I'm afraid there are still preserves in the fruit cellar that have been there for years. Cleaning down there is my next project after the remodeling is done. Some days I think I've bitten off more than I can chew. I don't know where I'll find a handyman to haul things out of the cellar."

"You'll work something out," Gracie assured her. "I did want to ask you about this."

She held up the flashlight, and Byrdie gave her a blank look.

"I found it by the switch box. I thought it was odd that this was the only thing in the basement left lying on the floor."

"It's not mine," Byrdie said. "Jake always insisted that I keep our flashlight for the basement in the kitchen drawer where it's easy to find. I've never seen this one before."

"I had a hunch it wasn't yours," Gracie said. "Do you know whose it is?"

"Oh dear, I've had several workmen in the house."

"Did any of them go down to the switchbox?" Gracie asked.

"Yes, now that I think of it, Eustace Sims overloaded the circuit with some tool or other. He had to go to the basement to pull a switch. I suppose that could be his flashlight. He was careless about leaving tools about. I was always reminding him to take something or other with him."

"If it is his, then he probably left fingerprints on it. I was careful to pick it up with a tissue. This may be a way of finding his true identity."

Gracie laughed because she sounded like a dime-novel detective, the kind in stories that she'd found on her grandmother's shelf many long years ago. Still, it was encouraging to think that they might have real evidence to take to the police, even though she knew that she was playing a long shot: Local authorities would probably be disinclined to investigate fingerprints in this kind of situation.

"He may not have been the only workman who went into the cellar," Byrdie said somewhat skeptically.

"Well, all that matters now is that we get you to the emergency room."

Gracie drove to Potterston. She was so familiar with the route now that she didn't need any directions from Byrdie. Hospital signs were prominently displayed along the side of the road, so she was able to drive there without further delay.

Byrdie insisted on hobbling into the emergency waiting room on her crutches instead of riding in a wheelchair, but once inside she gratefully settled onto a chair while her friend took her insurance card to the registration desk. Gracie counted six other groups and individuals waiting for attention and hoped Byrdie would get her turn without a terribly long wait.

Her optimism faded as an hour passed with only one patient called. At this rate, they might spend most of the day at the hospital. She had hoped to stop at the police station with the flashlight she'd found in Byrdie's basement.

Another half hour passed, and several people were summoned. Byrdie was entertaining herself with copies of magazines scattered on the table beside her, but Gracie was too restless to read. The flashlight was the first hard evidence that could lead them to Eustace Sims, and she couldn't wait to present it to the Potterston police.

At last Byrdie got her turn and was taken to one of the curtained examining stations while Gracie remained in the waiting room. She emerged forty-five minutes later pushed in a wheelchair by a familiar nurse.

"Alice, I didn't know that you work in the emergency room," Gracie said, rising from her chair.

"I don't usually, but I'm filling in for a nurse who's on vacation. I didn't know that you were out here until Byrdie was called in. She has a severe sprain, but there's no fracture. If she keeps it elevated and iced, it should be better in a few days. She has a prescription for pain."

"I'm glad it's not broken," Gracie said with relief.

Gracie could usually talk to anyone at any time, but she felt reserved with Alice. She was getting to know Louise and

Jane quite well, so it bothered her a bit that she didn't feel a stronger connection to Alice. The sisters were three different personalities, each likeable in her own way. Perhaps before she left Acorn Hill, she would find some common interests with Alice.

"I'm glad you were here to look after Byrdie," Gracie said.

"I'm happy it isn't more serious. Is your car close? It might be easier to use the wheelchair instead of crutches, Byrdie."

"I'll bring the car to the entrance. Thank you so much, Alice." Gracie smiled, glad to have something to do at last.

When Byrdie was comfortably settled in Gracie's big Cadillac, she expressed her willingness to wait in the car while Gracie went into the police station.

"There's nothing more that I can tell them about the flashlight," she said. "It definitely isn't mine, and it is possible Eustace Sims left it there. He isn't a very tidy man."

The Potterston police station was housed in a modern brick building that was more functional than attractive. The lobby had brown floor tiles, and the walls were painted a dull beige. Directly ahead, behind glass windows that ran the length of the room, was a long desk staffed by a uniformed officer. Gracie opened the door and went in with some trepidation, self-consciously carrying the flashlight in a transparent plastic food bag. Now that she was actually here, she worried that her evidence wouldn't interest them.

"What can I do for you?" the burly officer behind the counter asked without looking up from a ledger in front of him.

"I'd like to have the fingerprints on this flashlight checked. There's reason to believe that it belongs to a contractor who has been working scams in the area."

He looked up and raised his eyebrows.

"Have you filed a complaint?"

"No, but you have one on file from Mrs. Matilda Singleton of this town. The other person who was swindled is Mrs. Byrdie Hutchinson of Acorn Hill."

"That's out of our jurisdiction. You have to talk to the police in Acorn Hill about that."

"Yes, she already has, but we think the man who cheated her is the same man who swindled Mrs. Singleton, only he called himself Tim Houston instead of Eustace Sims."

"He left the flashlight at Mrs. Singleton's house?"

"No, at Mrs. Hutchinson's. I found it in the cellar on the floor by the switch box. We're pretty sure Eustace Sims left it there."

"He was the only one who had access to . . . what's her name's house?"

Gracie took a deep breath, exasperated because the man was still paying more attention to the book in front of him than he was to her.

"Is there a detective I could speak with?" she asked sternly.

"Yes, ma'am. Lieutenant Fraser is here. Just a moment. I'll see if he's available."

Gracie stood by the counter, resisting the urge to tap her foot. She reminded herself that amateur sleuths in books always had a hard time getting the police to take them seriously.

"I'm Lieutenant Fraser." A tall, thin man with short hair and a long, pinched-looking face walked up to the counter. "What's the problem?"

"I have potential evidence that might help track down the contractor who swindled Mrs. Matilda Singleton," Gracie said, grateful that the man was at least giving her his full attention. "This flashlight probably has his fingerprints on it."

"You found it at Mrs. Singleton's house?" he asked, pushing up one sleeve of his blue shirt.

"No, at Mrs. Byrdie Hutchinson's in Acorn Hill. We

strongly suspect that the man who cheated her on insulation work is the same one who victimized Mrs. Singleton of Potterston. Their names have a similar ring to them: Tim Houston, Eustace Sims."

"Ma'am, we don't have jurisdiction in Acorn Hill. We can't investigate a crime there. She'll have to go to the authorities in Acorn Hill."

"She has," Gracie said making an effort to be patient. "She was told hers is a civil case, but Mrs. Singleton's is a criminal one. If the same man is involved in both—"

"I'm sorry," he said. "You didn't find the flashlight in our jurisdiction. We can't process evidence in a civil case in Acorn Hill."

Gracie went back to Byrdie in the car, knowing she'd hit a solid wall of resistance. Even though instinct told her the same man had defrauded both women, she wasn't going to get any help from the Potterston police. The flashlight fiasco made that clear, and now Gracie knew that she and her friends were on their own in tracking down Eustace Sims.

"They can't process evidence found in Acorn Hill," Gracie said dejectedly as she started the car.

"Oh dear, I've caused you so much trouble. I guess the only thing to do is forget about Eustace Sims once and for all."

"No," Gracie said emphatically. "He's out there some-where, and he'll swindle more innocent people if we don't stop him. I've made up my mind. I'm not going to give up."

She drove Byrdie home, went to fill her prescription, then returned and fixed a light lunch of grilled-cheese sand-wiches and tomato soup, the best Byrdie's kitchen had to offer. By midafternoon her friend was happy to nap on the couch while Gracie returned to the inn.

Jane was standing in her garden when Gracie got back.

"I keep thinking something is missing," she said when Gracie got within earshot.

"I can't imagine what," Gracie said. "It's absolutely lovely."

"Oh well, maybe I just have precompetition nerves," Jane said with a light laugh. "How is Byrdie doing?"

"She'll have to keep off her ankle for a few days. I thought I might stay a bit longer if my room isn't booked for next week."

"As luck would have it, it's free. We had reservations for all four rooms, but one of our guests canceled. I'll be sure to tell Louise not to book it. It's sweet of you to stay to take care of Byrdie. How can we help?"

"I'm sure she would like some company later on," Gracie said. "Meanwhile, I left her napping on the couch. They gave her pain medication that made her sleepy. Oh, I saw Alice. She was working in the emergency room."

"She's been filling in wherever she's needed this summer. I hope she won't have to work so many hours next week." Jane stooped to pull a weed so tiny that a hawk might not have noticed it. "Her job is supposed to be part-time, but they always seem to need her. Oh well, it makes her happy to be useful."

Gracie smiled, recalling how Alice had helped when Byrdie was at the hospital. She hoped that Alice was aware of how much they appreciated her help and her thoughtfulness.

Gracie had come to Acorn Hill to visit Byrdie for a week and to help her to deal with a crooked contractor. So far she'd run out of time while also running into more predicaments than she'd ever expected in the sleepy little town. She still didn't know how to handle Florence in the choir or how to find Eustace Sims, not to mention what to do if they found him.

Gracie definitely needed to stay another week.

Chapter ♫ Eleven

Gracie dressed carefully Sunday morning, regretting that she hadn't brought her best summer dress to Acorn Hill. Her dove-gray cotton slacks and lacy white tunic would have to do. Even though a choir robe would cover most of her clothing, she would feel more suitably attired wearing her pale lime sheath with the little jacket.

When she'd done all she could to tame her flaming curls and brush the dust from her best leather sandals, she turned to the most important preparation of all. She took out the paperback Bible that she carried when she traveled and turned to a favorite psalm.

She read with thoughtful concentration until she came to a verse that spoke to her: "I will sing to the LORD all my life/ I will sing praise to my God as long as I live" (Psalm 104:33). She didn't know why she'd been called to lead the Grace Chapel choir this morning, but some of her nervousness vanished as she prayed for peace.

The dining room was empty when Gracie came down for breakfast, and the dishes from the guests who had eaten earlier had been cleared away. She was about to inspect the homemade muffins on the sideboard when Jane came through the swinging door from the kitchen carrying a plate of hot food.

"Good morning, Gracie. When I heard you moving about upstairs, I took the liberty of fixing your breakfast so that you wouldn't have to wait. This is called Topsy-Turvy French Toast a l'Orange, a specialty of the inn. I hope you enjoy eating it as much as I like announcing its name." She laughed gaily and went back to the kitchen for Gracie's tea.

"This looks awesome, as today's youngsters might say," Gracie called after her hostess. She broke off a piece of the crisp bacon that accompanied her toast and closed her eyes in delight as she savored it.

"And here's your tea," Jane said upon her return. "I hope that you can eat in peace. Things get a little hectic on Sunday morning with all of us trying to get ready for church."

"It doesn't matter," Gracie said. "I'll do justice to this lovely meal before I run over to Byrdie's to help her with breakfast. Louise said to get to the chapel a half hour before the service begins. The choir likes to run through their hymn at least once before people start coming."

"You don't have to rush," Jane said. "Alice went to Byrdie's and took her some breakfast."

"Oh, that was kind of her," Gracie said. "Now I can savor every bite of your yummy specialty." She was glad that she wouldn't have to squeeze in a trip to Byrdie's house but a little guilty that someone else was taking care of her friend.

She had a leisurely second cup of tea and was ready to walk to the chapel with Louise when it was time to go.

"I hope I don't let you down," Gracie said as they approached the chapel.

"I'm sure you won't. I can't thank you enough for directing this morning."

The choir members arrived early and seemed pleased to be singing in church again. Gracie lost the butterflies in her stomach when the quick practice went well. By the time the choir joined the congregation in singing the opening hymn,

she was confident that she wouldn't disappoint Louise or the
rest of the choir.

Louise was relieved and pleased when Gracie did a lovely
job. Several members of the congregation told her how happy
they were to have the choir back, and the choir members
seemed buoyed up by the encouragement.

Florence was the exception. She was waiting for Louise
and Gracie when they went to hang up their robes.

"I want you to look at this," Florence said, holding a robe
for Louise to see. "The gold trim is a disgrace. Look how
frayed it is."

Instead of answering, Louise slipped out of the robe she
was wearing and examined its trim.

"There does seem to be some wear on yours," Louise
said, "but mine looks as fresh as the day it was put there."

"It's not just on this robe," Florence said a bit petulantly.
"I've noticed several that are the worse for wear. Look at the
one Gracie is wearing. You can see the fraying."

Gracie took off her robe and examined the collar trim.

"I think you've just had a wonderful idea, Florence," she
said.

Florence looked as surprised as Louise felt.

"You've said that the robes should show off the choir to advantage, and no one wants the members' outfits to look drab."

"You agree that we need new robes?" Florence said with
a stunned look on her face.

"I'm reminded of a song we used to sing when I was a
child," Gracie said. "'Make new friends but keep the old/
One is silver and the other gold.' I'm afraid I don't know the
origin, but I've always liked it."

"I've heard that," Louise said, although she didn't know
what it had to do with choir robes.

"But what—" Florence began.

"The trim on your robe and several others is unraveling," Gracie said. "It's the perfect opportunity to keep the robes the choir members are attached to, but change the look by replacing the old gold trim with fresh silver-colored trim. That way there won't be a problem trying to match the old gold with new, and the choir will have an impressive new look overall. They'll have the tradition of the old, and the excitement of the new."

"And the members will be so grateful to you for your idea," Louise said, seizing the advantage provided by Gracie's clever diplomacy.

"How wonderful! Would you be willing to head up a group to replace the old trim, Florence?" Gracie asked.

"Well, I don't know." She was obviously caught off guard by Gracie's suggestion but pleased that she was receiving credit.

"We need someone with good taste to choose the trim," Louise said in her most persuasive voice.

"Someone who will ensure that the alterations will be made carefully," Gracie added.

"You know which women in the congregation are skillful with a needle," Louise said.

"Well, yes, but—"

"It's fortunate that you noticed the fraying," Gracie said. "No one wants her choir to look shabby."

"I guess new silver trim would be okay," Florence said doubtfully.

"Only if it meets your approval," Louise reminded her. "A wrong choice would look tacky. None of us would want that."

"Maybe we should take it to the church board," Florence suggested.

"I think not," Louise said decisively. "The choir robes are our responsibility. The board has too many other things to take care of."

"Still—"

"Can we count on you?" Louise asked.

"I wouldn't want to let the choir down," Florence said without enthusiasm.

"Wonderful! I'll ask Rev. Thompson for some funds from the choir's budget, and you can start looking for new trim as soon as the robes are sorted and you know how much you'll need."

"That won't be necessary," Florence said. "Ronald won't object a bit if I use our donation to buy the new trim myself. I'm sure Rev. Thompson will find a use for any money that is left over."

"That is awfully generous of you, Florence," said Louise.

Gracie patted Florence's hand as she said, "You are a blessing to the choir."

A transformed Florence glowed with the compliment.

Louise couldn't help smiling as she walked back to the inn with Gracie. *Some new friends*, she reflected, *are far more precious than silver.*

Alice hadn't intended to stay so long at Byrdie's. She was breathless when she arrived at the chapel and didn't settle down until the congregation and choir had finished the opening hymn.

She and Byrdie had been nodding acquaintances for many years, and she blamed herself for never taking the time to get to know her better. Byrdie's sprained ankle had given her an opportunity to visit, but she hadn't expected it to be such an enriching experience. Alice had formerly thought of Byrdie as distant, but now she realized that in reality she was simply reserved and a bit shy.

Although it had always seemed that she and Byrdie had little in common, their visit allowed them to enjoy mutual interests. They spoke only briefly of Byrdie's husband and

Alice's father, but they reached out to each other in sympathy and in soothing words and in prayer. Alice, who knew that she sometimes prided herself on giving comfort, had received it from an unlikely source.

This morning at Grace Chapel, Alice appreciated the fine job done by the choir. However, she had a hard time concentrating on Rev. Thompson's sermon, but not because he wasn't a skillful and convincing preacher. Her mind was just too full of new thoughts.

Although she served people by working at the hospital, sponsoring her ANGELs and helping at the inn, she hadn't really reached out to someone new in a long time. She walked with Vera Humbert at least three times a week and filled her life with activity, but lately she'd felt a need for more. She had a comfortable circle of friends in Acorn Hill and at the hospital, but it had been a long time since she had added anyone to that circle, and, as strange as it seemed, she was now eager to have that be Byrdie. With startling clarity, she realized that she needed to expand her opportunities for fellowship, exactly what Louise and Jane had been doing when they enthusiastically accepted Gracie into their affections.

When the service ended, she went outside the chapel where people gathered to visit. Today Alice made a special effort to greet people she knew only by sight or hardly at all. Many were younger than she was; some were older. All, she realized, were potential friends.

She found Jane talking to Elma Grayson, one of the older members of Grace Chapel Inn. Alice knew her, of course, but only as a church-door acquaintance. She walked over to them.

Jane was so engrossed in talking to Elma that she didn't notice Alice at first.

"Good morning, Elma," Alice said. "It's nice to see you."

"Good morning, Alice. Your sister and I have been having a lovely conversation about gardens."

"It's a topic she's rather fond of," Alice said with a light laugh.

"Elma has invited me for tea this afternoon," Jane said. "She's going to show me more of her garden."

"Is three o'clock all right with you?" Elma asked. "You're welcome to come too, Alice."

"No thank you," Alice said. "I plan to visit a friend who's laid up with a sprained ankle."

Jane looked at her in puzzlement. The only person she knew who had a sprained ankle was Byrdie. Alice had never referred to her as a friend before, but perhaps she was using the term loosely.

Elma bid the sisters good-bye, and they walked back to the inn together.

They talked about the return of the choir and the sermon, although Alice seemed a little vague in her comments.

"It was nice to have the choir in church again," Jane said.

"Yes," Alice agreed. "The choir adds so much to the service."

"You're going to visit Byrdie this afternoon?" Jane asked.

"Yes, we had a nice talk when I delivered her breakfast. She said to be sure to thank you for it."

"I never thought you were more than casual acquaintances," Jane said, still wondering why Alice had referred to her as a friend.

For several moments Alice didn't answer, and Jane wondered if she'd brought up a touchy subject.

"The truth is," Alice said, taking a deep breath, "I've been thinking about friendship."

"In what way?"

"You and Louise both left Acorn Hill. When you moved back, you set about renewing old friendships and making new ones. Except for college, I've always lived here. Many of my friends are lifelong friends. I haven't thought about making new friends in a long time."

"The whole town admires you," Jane said. "You're always helping people."

"Thank you, but I'm not talking about service. I mean reaching out and forming special attachments."

"Bonding," Jane said.

"Yes, bonding. I haven't bonded with anyone new in a long time."

"You make new friends with patients and staff at the hospital. At the inn too, for that matter." Jane still wasn't sure where this conversation was going.

"You're going to Elma's for tea."

"Well, yes."

"Are you looking forward to it?" Alice asked.

"Yes, I can't wait to hear more about her garden."

"So even though Elma is someone you've known from church, you could say she's a new friend."

"Yes, I guess so."

"That's what I haven't been doing, reaching out to new people in friendship. I've become too complacent in my relationships. I depend too much on you, Louise, Aunt Ethel and Vera for friendship."

"I think you're underestimating how many people care for you," Jane said seriously. "Your ANGELs adore you."

"And I adore them, but they grow up. They're more like Louise's pupils, children we can help on the way to becoming adults."

"I guess friendship is something different," Jane admitted.

"Anyway, I'm going to see Byrdie again this afternoon," Alice said.

The inn was a busy place after church. Louise and Alice checked out guests, and Jane prepared lunch for her sisters and Ethel.

Jane had planned to make extra for Gracie to take for her

lunch and Byrdie's, but their guest had hurried away right after church.

Sharing a meal with Ethel was often a lengthy process, and their aunt was especially chatty today, relating in some detail the highlights of her visit to the dentist and of a movie she'd seen that week.

"Is your guest still here, the lady with the red hair?" Ethel asked.

She was never thrilled to see bright red hair on other women, somehow believing that it was her private trademark.

"She's probably at Byrdie's house," Louise said. "She sprained her ankle."

"Your guest sprained her ankle?" Ethel was notoriously absentminded when it came to remembering the names of people who didn't have her stamp of approval.

"No, Byrdie did," Alice said.

"Oh, the poor thing. Maybe I should drop by and cheer her up."

"Alice is going over this afternoon," Jane said. "Why don't you wait until tomorrow?"

"Well, if you say so." Their aunt sniffed a little to let Jane know she felt rejected.

Jane suspected that Ethel was relieved. She wasn't keen on visiting the sick, but Jane was too tactful to mention that. She did believe that Alice would prefer to go alone to strengthen her budding friendship with Byrdie.

When lunch was over and the table cleared, Jane had just enough time to bake raisin cookies from dough she'd stored in the freezer. As soon as they were cool, she arranged some on a plate to take to Elma's. They would go nicely with tea, sweet but not too rich for midafternoon snacking.

Jane went to the trouble of changing clothes, deciding that her long green, gold and white skirt with the parrot design would add a festive touch to Elma's tea party. She wore it with beige suede sandals with wide straps, and a sleeveless knit top that matched the gold in the skirt. She decided to drive, more to avoid walking in the hot afternoon sun than because the distance was too great. She covered the cookies with a forest-green napkin she'd embroidered in the spring with colorful little elves that seemed perfect for this occasion.

A few minutes later she arrived at Elma's door with the cookies resting on one palm and her woven, fawn-colored handbag hanging from her other hand.

"Jane, I'm so glad you came," Elma said, welcoming her with a delightful little grin. "I've set out my china cups in the breakfast nook. It has the best view of my back garden."

Elma led her through a small living room filled with a jumble of antique furniture, including a walnut Victorian loveseat with carved grapes hanging in bunches from each arm. Just off the kitchen a small table, just big enough to serve two, was set beside a bay window that looked out over the back of Elma's property.

Jane was speechless. The front and side of the yard were laid out like crazy quilts, and the fenced-in back area was a jumble of contrasts. She couldn't begin to take in the many different plants. There was more color than she'd ever seen in one garden at one time.

"It was so nice of you to bring cookies," Elma said. "I never thought to get any."

"Oh, the napkin is yours to keep," Jane said remembering that she was there for tea, not just to gape. "I embroidered it to give to someone special."

"Thank you very much, Jane. It's the perfect size to put under a vase of flowers. Would you like to go out and see my garden before we have our tea and cookies?"

"Oh yes," Jane said thankfully, not sure she could sit still until she got a close-up view of the spectacularly unusual garden.

"I call it my friendship garden," Elma said as she led the way through the maze of flowerbeds and bushes. "Everything that grows here was given to me by people dear to me. Look, there's a lily that a girlhood friend planted after I lost my husband, and that rose bush was a gift from a neighbor to celebrate my . . . a special birthday."

"Lovely," Jane murmured, marveling at the sheer volume of plants.

The lily didn't have a bloom, but she could imagine how the roof-high stalk would look when it did. The roses were smaller than her carefully tended ones, but the plants were heavy with flowers in shades from brilliant red to snow white. One especially beautiful rose was the shade of a ripe peach, and another was so buttery yellow it made Jane sigh with appreciation.

"My husband built the little windmill," Elma said as they passed a weathered wooden structure no higher than Jane's knee. "I suppose it could do with a coat of paint, but I like leaving it just as it is. He wasn't a gardener himself, but he liked to add little things for me. My early spring bed looks much nicer when the tulips and daffodils are in full bloom. The tulip bulbs came from a second cousin in Holland, Michigan. They have a marvelous tulip festival there every year. She and I were such good friends before she passed on."

"Everything in your garden must remind you of someone or something special," Jane said, awed by how much there was to see.

"Oh yes. Every flower is a memory, and I cherish them all. As people gave me more and more, it felt like cheating to buy plants myself."

Jane didn't know what to say. Elma's garden was disorderly in an absolutely charming way. Except for stone paths, it was a sea of greenery and brilliant colors with no apparent rhyme or reason to the arrangement. Jane guessed that the area was easily twice the size of her garden. There were traces of a wooden fence with long horizontal slats, but it had long ago been swallowed up by a profusion of bushes and vines.

"My Harry was fond of rocks," Elma was saying. "He brought that big pinkish stone from his grandparents' farm before it was sold. He had to hire a truck and get his two brothers and a cousin to help him. His cousin's wife gave me cuttings for the plants that surround it. We were so close. I was heartbroken when she and her husband moved to Florida, because I never got to see her again."

"Doesn't your garden make you sad, remembering people you've lost?" Jane asked. She was feeling a little weepy herself and couldn't refrain from inquiring.

"Oh no, dear. All my happy memories are here. That's why I cherish it so much. I've been blessed with wonderful people in my life, and they seem to talk to me when I'm in my garden."

Jane didn't want to leave the friendship garden. She could see that her napkin wasn't gift enough for the pleasure of seeing this beauty. She mentally went through her own plantings, wondering what she could possibly give the elderly woman that would add to her fantastic array of flowers.

"Shall we have tea now?" Elma said, interrupting Jane's thoughts.

"Oh yes, of course," Jane agreed, trying to cover her reluctance to go inside.

Jane enjoyed talking with Elma over tea, although later she couldn't remember the flavor of the beverage or whether she'd eaten a cookie. Elma had wonderful memories of friends who'd contributed to her garden, helping with the labor as well as giving her things to plant. It was a tremendous undertaking to keep it from becoming a wild space, but Elma didn't seem short of friends and relatives who were willing to help out.

"I can't thank you enough for sharing your garden with me," Jane said. "I hope you'll come to Grace Chapel Inn sometime soon. We can have lunch, and I'll show you my garden."

She left promising to call Elma soon and thanking her profusely for inviting her.

Much to Jane's surprise, it was well past five when she got home. The afternoon had passed more quickly and pleasurably than she could have imagined. Elma's friendship garden had given her a great deal to think about.

Chapter ♪♪ Twelve

On Monday morning Alice left by the front entrance to meet Vera Humbert for an early morning walk. As she went down the porch steps, Jane called to her from the garden, "Alice, you're starting out early."

"Vera and I want to beat the heat. We haven't been able to get together in a couple of days, so we're planning a long walk."

"Good idea," her sister agreed. "No wonder you look so fit."

"Do I?" Alice asked in surprise

"You could pass for ten years younger," Jane said, only half teasing.

"Oh, I doubt that," Alice said, self-consciously patting her short reddish-brown hair only lightly sprinkled with gray strands. "Every time I look in the mirror there's a new wrinkle."

"It doesn't matter when they're all smile lines," Jane said, smiling broadly herself. "While you're walking, keep an eye out for spectacular gardens. Let me know if you see anything unusual."

"This is the week the botanical society comes to judge, isn't it?"

"Yes, and I don't know what to expect."

"I'm sure you'll get high marks," Alice reassured her. "You've done a wonderful job restoring the garden and adding your own unique touches."

"I've done the best I can," Jane said, not sounding at all confident.

"The results are splendid, but Louise and I will be glad when the judging is over. You've worked so hard."

"Hardly," Jane said, laughing off her sister's concern. "The more I work, the more energy I have. But I won't keep you from your walk."

"Vera is meeting me at the hardware store, so I had better get going."

Alice left her sister and hurried toward Vera and Fred's store. Fred wanted to go in early to work on his accounts, so Vera had walked that far with him.

In a matter of minutes, Alice and Vera were walking down Chapel Road at a brisk pace. Vera was younger by ten years and shorter than Alice's five feet six. Still, they had been walking together for so many years that they easily fell into their usual, comfortable rhythm.

"Do you have the whole day off?" Vera asked as they passed Berry Lane and headed toward a country road that was a favorite route.

"No, I'm working the three-to-eleven shift in emergency. I'm covering for nurses who are on vacation, so this is actually my busy season. How did your quilting class go?"

"I had a few really enthusiastic people. We're done for this session, but several have expressed interest in another class. I think I'll teach an advanced one. So much for my summer of home improvement. By the time I get around to doing anything with the house, it will be time to go back to school."

Alice smiled, knowing her friend had good intentions about keeping her house shipshape, but something always distracted her. Fortunately her husband was good-natured and contributed a lot to keeping things straightened.

"Are you teaching fifth grade again this year?" Alice asked.

"Yes, the children in fifth are my favorite age group. Although from what I've seen of last year's fourth graders, I'll have my hands full in September."

Their walking time passed quickly as they shared news of their families and the village. "Have you heard that Byrdie Hutchinson sprained her ankle?" Alice asked when they'd fully caught up on their families.

"Someone mentioned it to Fred at the store. You know how news travels in this town. How is she doing?"

"She has to stay off it as much as possible, but she's cheerful about it. I went over yesterday, and we had a nice visit."

"I don't know her very well," Vera admitted. "She always seemed a little distant to me."

"She's just reserved," Alice said, wanting to present Byrdie in the best possible light. "You should meet her friend, Gracie Parks. She has quite a reputation as an amateur sleuth."

"A grown-up Nancy Drew?" Vera asked with a chuckle. "Fred told me about the problem in Byrdie's attic."

Alice knew that Vera loved the fictional teenage detective as much as she did. In fact, they both were avid readers of cozy mysteries.

"Fred helped a lot, especially by giving them a lead. Because of his tip, Gracie and Byrdie went to Potterston and talked with Matilda Singleton. They're convinced the same man swindled her. I just wish there was something I could do to help."

"Maybe her crooked contractor will fall off a ladder or something and come to the emergency room," Vera suggested jokingly. "It must be easy to get hurt working in the building trades."

Alice didn't take her friend's suggestion seriously, but it

did make her wonder. So many people came to Potterston Hospital. Had Eustace Sims ever been a patient there?

If he was using a false name, it would be futile to try tracking down his medical records. Much as she wanted to help, she didn't see any possibility of finding him through the hospital. Still, Vera had given her something to think about.

Alice went into the hospital to begin her shift at three o'clock. She felt refreshed by her long walk and talk with Vera, and breakfast they'd enjoyed at the Coffee Shop afterward. Although Jane's breakfasts were the tastiest in town, it was still fun to eat out, not because of the food, but because of the friendship, Alice realized.

Alice was a willing worker, and she found that her shift went much faster when she was busy. Still, when she worked in the emergency room, she always prayed for a quiet day. Too many serious illnesses and injuries came first to emergency services. She would gladly stand by idly if it meant no one would be suffering enough to come there that day.

In fact, it was a quiet day. There were even a few lulls in routine patient care that typically kept the staff busy. Alice had time for a dinner break, something she sacrificed when the workload was heavy.

She was nearing the end of her shift when a mother brought her eight-year-old son to the emergency room. Alice remembered him because a year or so ago he'd fallen into a bonfire and badly burned one leg. Fortunately this time he was only there because of a reaction to a bee sting. It proved not to be serious, and he was easily treated. However, the shorts he wore during his stay allowed Alice to see that the scar on his leg would remain with him the rest of his life.

Alice felt sad for him, but seeing him also provided her with a promising idea.

Just as her shift was ending, Alice had to assist with a

possible heart-attack victim. By the time she left the hospital
and drove home to Acorn Hill, Grace Chapel Inn was dark
except for the porch light and the light that stayed on all
night in the foyer.

The yellow bug bulb gave an eerie glow to the familiar
porch that ran across the front of the house. Alice was used
to nighttime darkness because her work could keep her out
at all hours, but it always felt lonesome to return to a sleeping household. Little night sounds assailed her. A chorus of
insects, the distant bark of a dog and the hum of a car motor
coming down Chapel Road all reminded her of spooky
scenes in the mysteries she loved to read.

She let herself into the house with her key and locked the
door behind her, hoping one of her sisters was still up. It
wasn't fear of the night that made her wish for companionship. Instead, she was bursting to tell someone the idea that
had come to her that afternoon in the emergency room.

Switching on the light in the big, empty kitchen, she set
about finding a bedtime snack. Some cookies and milk would
still hunger pangs until morning.

She slowly munched on oatmeal cookies, dunking them
in her milk from time to time, but her mind wasn't on her
snack. She couldn't wait to try out her idea on her sisters and
Gracie. The wonder was why she hadn't thought of it sooner.

Monday passed slowly for Gracie. She picked up cinnamon
bread from the bakery to toast and serve with Byrdie's breakfast and used ingredients in her fridge to prepare salad and
sandwiches for lunch. Byrdie was very appreciative of her
efforts but chafed at being confined to the couch.

Gracie understood her restlessness. It was difficult to sit
by idly while someone else worked in your kitchen. No doubt
she would feel the same way if their positions were reversed.
In fact, she was certain of it.

"I think the swelling is going down, don't you?" Byrdie asked after Gracie had cleared away their lunch dishes. "It looks better than it did this morning."

In truth, Gracie couldn't see any difference. Her friend's ankle was still puffed up like a party balloon. She tried to reassure Byrdie while at the same time discouraging her from hopping around on crutches. Byrdie could get around on the old wooden devices, but she was more impatient with them than she was cautious.

"Would you like to watch some television?" Gracie asked as a last resort.

She remembered how hard it was to entertain her son, Arlen, when he'd been sick as a child, and Byrdie wasn't much easier.

"Oh dear, no. I've never been one to watch much TV."

"We could play a game of canasta or—"

"I'm really not much of a game player," Byrdie said apologetically. "You surely don't have to stay here all day, Gracie, if you have other things you'd like to do. I know I'm not very good company with this ankle."

"I wouldn't think of leaving you alone all day when you can't get around," Gracie said, her conscience taking precedence over her own restlessness.

Somewhere out there, Eustace Sims was scheming to defraud another innocent person, maybe a widow or elderly person who could ill afford his scams. Gracie couldn't do anything about it sitting here with Byrdie, but then, she wasn't sure what to do about it anyway.

"If I could get up the stairs, I could finish the curtains I'm making for the spare bedroom. I do wish it were ready now. You could be staying here," Byrdie lamented.

Gracie didn't think it was the time to tell Byrdie that she was having a lovely time at Grace Chapel Inn or that getting to know the Howard sisters was an unexpected bonus in her visit to Acorn Hill.

"Oh, there's the phone," Byrdie said, responding instantly to a ring coming from the kitchen.

"I'll get it," Gracie said, hurrying to the portable phone and carrying it to Byrdie on the couch.

"Oh, hello, Florence," Byrdie said in a surprised voice.

Gracie had been on her way back to the kitchen so that it wouldn't seem she was eavesdropping, but mention of Florence's name stopped her.

Most of the conversation came from the other end of the connection. Byrdie nodded and occasionally got in a word or two of agreement. Florence obviously wasn't calling to console Byrdie, because her friend was given no opportunity to relate the details of her fall.

"Yes, that would be all right," Byrdie said, agreeing to whatever Florence had said.

She hung up looking a little taken aback.

"It was Florence Simpson. You must have met her in the choir."

"Oh yes."

"She promised to do some work on the choir robes. She tried to get a group together to change the trim on some of the robes, but so far no one has agreed to help. She thought that since I'm laid up, I might have time to pick out old stitching."

"And you agreed?" Gracie asked, knowing the answer.

"I guess I did. Turning down Florence is like saying no to a tornado. She's on her way over."

When Gracie came up with the idea of changing the trim, she'd never thought the robes would end up in Byrdie's lap. At least her friend didn't object to the job. It would give her something to do, although carefully pulling out old stitching was likely to be a tedious job.

They didn't have to wait long for Florence to arrive. She came to the front door loaded with choir robes and looking a bit harassed. A lock of brown hair had escaped from her usual neat twist and a light sheen of perspiration showed on her broad forehead. She was wearing a white pleated skirt with a red polka-dot blouse escaping from the waistband on one side. She took tiny steps in her high-heeled white pumps, and rightly so, because she could hardly see where she was walking given the pile of robes she was carrying.

"There are more," she said, dropping them on a wing-back chair opposite the couch.

"Would you like me to help you?" Gracie asked politely.

"Yes. I never realized those things are so heavy." Florence headed back for another load without saying anything to Byrdie.

When they'd hauled all the robes to the living room, the pile was impressive.

"The frayed trim was put on by machine," Florence said, "so it's going to be a nasty job to pick out the stitches."

"Is there any hurry about getting them done?" Byrdie asked.

"Unless there's a problem, the choir will sing at Grace Chapel next Sunday," Florence said, dropping onto an antique walnut chair and fanning herself with a magazine that had been lying on the table beside it.

"I wouldn't want to rush and damage the cloth," Byrdie said pensively.

Gracie was more than willing to help Byrdie, but she hesitated to volunteer. The robes were Florence's responsibility, and she didn't want to intrude.

"I do appreciate your help," Florence said.

"It's a bigger job than I thought," Byrdie said.

"I was planning to shop for new trim this afternoon," Florence said with obvious reluctance, "but I guess I wouldn't be much of a friend if I just dumped them all on you and left."

Gracie wanted to say the more hands the better, but she restrained herself. This was between Byrdie and Florence.

"I can probably get three or four done today," Byrdie said, sliding to the edge of the couch and reaching for her crutches.

"Oh, your ankle is really swollen, isn't it?" Florence said as if noticing it for the first time. "Does it hurt?"

"Not too much as long as I keep it elevated."

"Can you work there on the couch?" Florence asked with concern, whether for Byrdie's pain or her ability to finish the job Gracie wasn't sure.

"I'll try," Byrdie said in a weak little voice that made Gracie smile behind her hand. "I'll have to get my sewing box."

"I'll get it," Gracie offered, leaving the room to fetch it from the sewing room upstairs.

When she returned, Florence had taken off her shoes and pulled her chair closer to the couch. She and Byrdie were bent over one of the robes talking about the best way to remove the stitches.

"If we turn the collar up like this"—Byrdie demonstrated—"we can work from the back side. I hope we don't snag the material, but if we do, it won't show."

"Good idea," Florence said. "I probably would have picked at the side with the trim."

Gracie caught the most important word, *we.* Apparently Florence had realized that it would be unfair to leave the whole job to Byrdie. Before long, the three of them were picking away the stitches. Later, Gracie appointed herself to make a pot of tea and serve it in the living room, but she didn't hurry. Much to her surprise, Florence and Byrdie were finding a lot to talk about as they worked. Byrdie related all her problems with the attic, and Florence matched her story with several about incompetent workmen and garage mechanics.

Nor did the two of them spend all their time complaining. Florence loved to travel, and she encouraged Byrdie to talk about the trips she'd made with her husband, some with

Gracie and El. The afternoon passed, and a whole pile of frayed trim accumulated beside the couch.

"The last two," Florence finally announced, giving one to Byrdie and keeping one herself.

Gracie didn't feel slighted. She was pleased that the two women were enjoying their task. Was it possible that Florence needed Byrdie's companionship as much or more than her assistance in removing the trim?

Gracie hoped it was the beginning of a new friendship for Byrdie. She and Jake had been so close that having women friends in town probably hadn't seemed terribly important to her before his death. Her sprained ankle could be a blessing in disguise if it brought her attention and new friends like Alice and Florence.

"I don't know what I would have done without you, Byrdie," Florence said when the last bit of trim had been plucked free of its robe. "And you too, Gracie. I really appreciate your help." Florence spoke with sincerity.

She started to make a pile of robes to carry back to her car.

"Why don't you leave them here?" Byrdie suggested. "And when you have the trim, I wouldn't mind sewing it on."

"Are you sure?" Florence asked, obviously unused to enthusiasm for one of her projects.

"We can make a day of it, have lunch here, then stitch on the new trim by hand. That will make it much easier to remove if it ever needs to be changed again. If you wouldn't mind making lunch for three, Gracie?" Byrdie asked.

"I'd be happy to," Gracie agreed.

"Wait, why don't I bring my famous tortellini salad? Ronald doesn't care for it, but I absolutely adore it. I use pasta stuffed with cheese, then add thin-sliced red onions, fresh mushrooms and three kinds of peppers. It's the red, yellow and green peppers that really make it look special. And I make my own Italian dressing."

"That sounds wonderful," Byrdie agreed. "Just let me know when you want to come. I won't be going anywhere for a few days, I'm sure."

Gracie helped Florence make a neat pile of robes on the dining-room table while they talked about the peculiar eating habits of their husbands.

"My husband wouldn't touch green gelatin," Gracie said. "In fact, he didn't like bright food coloring of any kind, not even my Halloween cake with orange frosting."

"Ronald has a thing for ketchup," Florence said. "I think he would put it on bananas if I let him."

"Jake always used to put it on eggs," Byrdie said. "We didn't do that in my family. And he only liked pancakes made with buckwheat flour."

Gracie laughed with the other two and decided that Florence's obsession with choir robes had started something good. She couldn't help thinking that God does indeed work in mysterious ways.

Chapter ♪ Thirteen

Tuesday, Jane prepared the makings for a breakfast of scrambled eggs and honey-cured bacon along with hot biscuits and homemade raspberry jam. The two salesmen who'd stayed the night before ate early and checked out before her sisters and Gracie came downstairs.

Louise came first but ate only toast and coffee because she was having lunch in Potterston with an old friend and just wanted something light for breakfast. After having coffee, she went over to the chapel to ready herself for that evening's choir practice.

At the inn Gracie and Alice, chatting happily, arrived together for breakfast. "Good morning, Jane. Preparing another basic diet breakfast?" Gracie teased.

"Hi, Gracie, Alice." Jane laughed in response to Gracie's question. "I've planned things so that you'll receive just enough calories to keep up your strength. By the way, how is Byrdie doing?"

"Her ankle was still swollen yesterday, but she's had several visitors to cheer her up," Gracie said. "Alice went over on Sunday, and yesterday Florence was there for most of the afternoon. She surprised me a bit. She enlisted Byrdie to rip stitches out of the old trim on the choir robes. I thought that she was going to drop them there and leave, but she helped until the day's work was finished. I believe they both enjoyed socializing while they worked."

"She was probably glad to have something to keep her hands busy. It can be irksome to be laid up," Alice commented. She yawned. "I'm sorry if I'm a sleepyhead this morning."

"Our male guests checked out, and Louise went over to the chapel, but you're hardly a sleepyhead," her sister assured her. "You should sleep late when you have to work until eleven in the evening."

"Actually, I couldn't get to sleep right away. Yesterday at the hospital I had an idea about the man who swindled Byrdie, and I couldn't get it out of my mind."

"I'm desperate for new leads," Gracie said. "Do you know some way to find him?"

"Not exactly, but my friend Vera started me thinking when we walked yesterday morning. She suggested that men in the building trades are prone to injury. It's not impossible that your man . . ."

"Eustace Sims," Gracie said.

"He may have been in Potterston Hospital at some time."

"Unfortunately, we don't know his real name," Gracie pointed out.

"No, but I had another thought. A little boy who suffered a bad burn about a year ago came to the emergency room yesterday. I couldn't help noticing how scarred his leg is. He'll have the marks of his accident for the rest of his life. A workman like Sims could very possibly have identifying scars of some kind. That might prove significant in searching for him."

"That's true, Alice. What a clever thought! We've only described him to the building suppliers as having a beard and wearing a Detroit Tigers cap," Gracie said thoughtfully. "Unlike scars, those are both things that are easy to change. Maybe he shaves the beard from time to time to make himself harder to identify."

"He could wear the Tigers cap around his victims but another when he deals with suppliers," Jane said as she served breakfast to Gracie and Alice and fixed a cup of coffee for herself. "In fact, if he's smart enough to cheat people for a living, he probably has all kinds of ways to change the way he looks."

"Byrdie and Matilda Singleton agree that he's average height and weight with no remarkable features," Gracie said. "Nothing about him struck them as distinctive."

"In the art classes I've taken," Jane said, "the teachers always emphasize the way you look at things. Take the color white, for instance. To render it effectively on canvas, you have to use subtle shadings of other colors. People are really complicated. The more you look at a person, the more details you see."

"Doctors are really good at noticing details," Alice said. "The more observant they are, the more accurate their diagnoses."

"I wonder if any of us really look at the people who perform services for us. I know that I tend to forget a waitress' face so quickly that sometimes I don't know which one is responsible for bringing the check at the end of a meal," Gracie said, her fork poised above her diminishing serving of eggs.

Alice smiled at Jane and rubbed her tummy in appreciation for the biscuits her younger sister had fixed. "I see so many different people at the hospital that I rely on charts to identify them," Alice said. "Only a few patients stand out so much that I can remember them years or even months later."

"Thank you so much, Alice. You've certainly given me a lot to think about," Gracie said. "I'm going to talk to Byrdie. Maybe she can search her memory and come up with some characteristic that she didn't remember when she first described him to me."

Brushing aside pleas for her to relax, she joined Alice in

clearing the table as they thanked Jane for her wonderful, filling breakfast. Jane welcomed the help and relaxed over the rest of her coffee.

Louise used the key reserved for the choir director to open the church door, then stepped into the serene interior glowing with the morning light. She didn't have any physical tasks to perform to get ready for choir practice that evening, but she needed a quiet interlude for prayer and thought. She sat in a front pew silently praying for the wisdom and patience to lead the choir to the best of her ability for as long as the responsibility was hers.

She lost track of time as peace came to her spirit. Her prayers became ones of thanks. She thanked God for the love and support of her daughter and sisters, and she expressed gratitude for the help He had sent in the person of Gracie Parks.

"And please, Lord, help me to love Florence, one of Your dear children, and to work with her in harmony."

It lightened her spirit to know that God would give her strength for any tasks He set before her, but Louise knew it was still up to her to forge a working relationship with Florence.

She walked home pondering a host of notions. The choir had shown notably less resistance to the new music for "Amazing Grace" at the last rehearsal, and she sincerely hoped that they would grow to love it. As for the problem of new choir robes, that issue had been put to rest, and now Florence had turned her considerable energy to the task of supplying new trim for the old robes. There was still the knotty problem of Florence's solo. Should Louise tell her outright that her voice, pleasant as it was, wasn't adequate for the hymn she wanted to sing? Or should she let her try it, even though the congregation would surely know that she was doing a poor job?

Louise felt an obligation as choir director to protect all the members from making themselves look bad. She had prayed for help in accepting Florence as a child of God. If she abandoned her to the scorn of the congregation for a poor performance, she wouldn't be treating her in a loving way.

The answer was far from simple, because Florence had her own ideas. She'd deluded herself into thinking that she had the strongest voice in the choir. If she were a really bad singer, it would be easier to take the solo away from her. As it was, Louise had a dilemma. Maybe Gracie would have some thoughts about it. After all, her idea about the trim on the robes was brilliant.

Gracie hurried off to Byrdie's with Gooseberry at her heels. They both needed a good walk, and Gracie's head was so full of questions to ask Byrdie that they arrived before she realized it.

Byrdie must have been watching for them, because she opened the front door as soon as they got to the porch steps.

"Good morning, Gracie," she said, swaying slightly on her crutches. "I see you have a friend with you."

"I hope Gooseberry won't be a problem. I was beginning to feel guilty for leaving him at the inn so much. I'll settle him down in your sunroom. Then we have to talk."

"Talk about what?" Byrdie asked, her curiosity aroused by the urgency in Gracie's voice.

"Eustace Sims."

Gracie didn't intend to sound abrupt, but her inability to locate the swindler was more than annoying. She felt a heavy responsibility to find and stop the man because the police were unable or unwilling to do anything. Gooseberry was tired after his walk and made himself at home for a long nap. Byrdie went to the kitchen and put on the kettle for tea, apologizing for the dishes in the sink when Gracie joined her.

"You fixed your own breakfast," Gracie said. "I would've been glad to do it for you."

"You're a wonderful friend, and you've done so much for me. I'm grateful, and I do thank you, but it's time I started doing for myself."

"Does your ankle feel better?"

"Yes, quite a bit better. See, the swelling has gone down noticeably."

She stuck out her foot, wobbling enough on the crutches to make Gracie hover close.

"I'll just put the cups on the table then," Gracie said.

"I'll simmer some ginseng in the pot," Byrdie said, reaching into the cupboard where she kept her tea.

Gracie wished she'd anticipated Byrdie's choice of teas by suggesting a nice orange pekoe, but her mind was too full of what Alice had suggested about Sims. Even though Gracie was convinced that she could peel a chunk of bark from a tree in the yard and make a tastier drink, she was too eager to talk about the contractor to fret about tea. She carried the teapot to the table and did the honors, filling her own cup a scant half full.

Byrdie noticed the half-full cup.

"I thought you loved tea," she said.

Gracie opened her mouth to say that she'd had her fill at the inn, then paused. She'd begun to say something deceitful to Byrdie and didn't like herself for it.

"I'm afraid ginseng isn't quite to my taste," she explained weakly.

"Gracie Parks! Why didn't you say so sooner? We've been friends a long time. You can speak your mind with me."

"I didn't mean to be dishonest," Gracie said. "It just seemed the polite thing to do."

"I should've given you a choice of flavors," Byrdie said matter-of-factly. "Now let me fix a cup you'll enjoy. I have several different kinds. You can pick what you like."

Byrdie insisted on dumping out the ginseng in Gracie's cup and heating more hot water to pour over a bag of mint tea that Gracie chose from her assortment. She hobbled on her ankle without the crutch but wouldn't allow Gracie to help.

"I'm ninety percent better," she said. "I've been sitting around my house too much recently. Florence's project made me realize I need to get involved more. I'm thinking of volunteering at a school or the library when my ankle is back to normal. They always need extra help, and I especially like to read to children."

"Maybe the teachers at the elementary could use your help at read-alouds," Gracie suggested.

"I'll ask Alice. She's a good friend of Vera's, so it would be easy for her to find out. I think I'll ask her about being a volunteer at the hospital too. I could manage a trip to Potterston once a week or so."

"That's a wonderful idea," Gracie said. "Your helping out could be a blessing for many."

Byrdie smiled. "You are such a dear person. My whole life seems brighter since you came. I'll be sorry to see you go home."

"I think you're going to have plenty of new friends," Gracie said with conviction.

"Yes, that would be nice," Byrdie agreed. "Now what were you going to tell me about Eustace Sims?"

"It's more a matter of what you can tell me," Gracie said.

"Now you're being mysterious."

Gracie chuckled and explained Alice's theory.

"I had an uncle who was a carpenter," Byrdie said thoughtfully. "He lost the tip of his finger on a power saw, but I'm pretty sure Eustace Sims wasn't missing any of his."

"Think hard," Gracie softly urged. "Did you ever watch him working?"

"No, I didn't go up to the attic while he was doing the work. I didn't really like being that close to him. I'm afraid he wasn't careful about his hygiene."

"What about when you signed the contract? You must have been close to him then."

"Yes, he had me sign it in the kitchen. I remember asking if he wanted coffee or tea, but he declined. Now that I know how dishonest he is, I think he was in a hurry to get my signature and check."

"You sat at the table to sign it?" Gracie probed.

"Yes."

"Did he sit too?"

"Let me think. Yes, I believe he did because he laid it in front of me and indicated where I should sign. But of course I insisted on reading all the pages first. Jake taught me to always do that."

"Now think hard, Byrdie. Was there anything unusual about the way he looked?"

"He had dirt under his fingernails. I know he works with his hands, but I remember thinking that he should clean them before meeting with a client. I've always hated dirty nails."

"What was he wearing?" Gracie asked, still hoping Byrdie would remember something significant.

"A black winter jacket. He didn't want to take it off, I remember, but when he reached for the contract the sleeve rode up. Oh my!"

"What?"

"That's when I was thinking about his dirty nails, but I caught a glimpse of his wrist and arm. He has a scar. I'd completely forgotten about it."

"You're sure?"

"Yes, I think so. It was a nasty-looking one on top of his

wrist. I only had a quick look before he pulled his coat sleeve over it."

"Which arm?"

"Oh, it must have been the right, because he was reaching for the signed contract. I would've remembered if he were left-handed, because my Jake was. I usually notice when people are left-handed, because it reminds me of him."

"You never noticed the scar while he was working at your house?"

"Now that you mention it, he usually showed up for work with a faded plaid shirt or a denim jacket over his T-shirt. He left them at the bottom of the attic steps when he went up to work, but I never followed him. I don't know why I didn't remember sooner."

"We both thought his beard and Tiger's baseball cap were enough to identify him. Alice made me realize that we need some distinguishing characteristic that can't be changed."

"Do you think we'll be able to find him now?" Byrdie asked hopefully.

"I think it would be worthwhile to check with some of the building-supply companies again and mention the scar. We need to think of a good excuse for wanting to get in touch with him."

"We could pretend that we want to hire him," Byrdie suggested. "I guess that wouldn't be very honest, though."

Gracie frowned. If they didn't find Eustace Sims, there was no way to stop him. "I think we'll have to treat it as a theatrical production," she said thoughtfully. "We'll set the stage and write the dialogue, then hope our villain will show up. At least now we have a distinguishing scar to describe him. We can get started right away."

"Oh dear, there's something I forgot to tell you," Byrdie said. "Florence called first thing this morning. She's buying the trim at Sylvia's Buttons, a little shop right here in Acorn

Hill. She made her tortellini salad last night so we could have the lunch she promised and work on the robes today."

"When do you expect her?" Gracie asked.

"Any time now. She seemed in a hurry to get the robes done, so I told her to come as soon as she liked. We may not have much time to call suppliers until this evening, and they may not be open then."

"I promised Louise that I'll go to choir practice tonight," Gracie said.

"At least we'll get all of those robes off my table and back to the church," Byrdie said. "It should be fun for the three of us to work on them together."

Gracie was tempted to beg off and go back to the inn, but the new round of phone calls could wait until morning. Byrdie was practically bubbling with enthusiasm about the little sewing bee, and Gracie didn't want to let her down.

True to her word, Florence arrived within the hour with a big shopping bag full of new silver trim. She made a second trip to her car to retrieve an insulated bag that contained the salad she'd promised to bring.

"I picked up some cloverleaf rolls at the bakery. They're just the thing to go with my salad," she said, making herself at home in Byrdie's kitchen.

She put a big, apple-shaped glass bowl into the fridge and chatted about the trim she'd chosen for the robes.

"It's a tiny bit wider than the old," she said, "but the other choice was much too narrow. Can we sit around the table and work? Or do you still have to keep your ankle elevated, Byrdie?"

"Sitting at the table might be better. We need a flat surface to pin the trim before we tack it down. I can keep my foot on a stool."

Gracie fetched a stool from the kitchen and positioned it as a footrest under the table.

"Would you like some tea before we get started, Florence?" asked Byrdie. "Gracie and I just had a cup."

"Well, I don't know. What kind do you have?"

"Herbal—but that's best for bedtime—orange pekoe, mint and my favorite, ginseng."

"I would love a cup of ginseng," Florence said decisively. "I hear it's very good for you."

Byrdie, looking immensely pleased, sneaked a look at Gracie and giggled without drawing Florence's attention.

"I'll make it while you two get started," Gracie said, narrowing her eyes in feigned indignation at her friend's amusement.

She went into the kitchen and put a kettle of water on to boil. Something was different about Florence today, but Gracie couldn't quite put her finger on it. It wasn't what she was wearing, although this was the first time she'd seen her in flat sandals instead of heels. She was wearing a pink-and-white flowered dress that was a bit too fussy for daytime wear and, unfortunately, made Florence look even pudgier than she was. Maybe it was her attitude that had changed. She didn't seem so determined to express her opinions. Whatever the difference, it was a pleasant change.

Gracie poured two cups of tea, deciding to pass on another for herself. Still musing about the change in Florence, Gracie tried to think of a reason why she wasn't behaving at all like the abrasive woman who came to choir practice. She seemed happy. Byrdie seemed to bring out the best in her. Gracie carried out the tea and saw evidence that Florence was indeed enjoying herself. Her plucked and penciled eyebrows weren't arched so high, and her gray eyes were as lively as her tongue. She and Byrdie were talking a mile a minute as they measured, snipped and pinned trim on the robes.

"My Ronald would starve before he would cook for himself," Florence said. "If I'm not there to fix his lunch or dinner, I have to arrange for the cleaning woman to take care of it. And he wouldn't settle for a dish of my tortellini salad. He likes something hot like soup or a grilled-cheese sandwich. I used to try sending a cold lunch to work with him, but it didn't work. He would carry it home when he came looking for something hot. Men can be so set in their ways."

"Jake liked to grill outside," Byrdie said, "but he wouldn't think of cooking with the oven broiler. Actually, it was easier for me to make the whole meal. I never knew when he would start the meat, and I'd have to rush like mad to get the rest of the meal done on time."

"I'll go check on Gooseberry," Gracie said when there was a moment's pause in the conversation.

"Thank you for making the tea," Byrdie said, still looking pleased that Florence had asked for ginseng.

"Yes, thank you. That was sweet of you." Florence smiled.

"My pleasure," Gracie said, turning away satisfied.

She had a feeling it was going to take a long time to do the robes. Projects always took longer when friends got together.

Chapter ♪♪ Fourteen

I can't thank Alice enough," Gracie said, bubbling with enthusiasm as she told Louise about Eustace Sims's scar. "We were relying on the beard and baseball cap to describe him. Without Alice's suggestion, Byrdie might not have remembered his most significant characteristic."

Louise couldn't help smiling as they walked toward the chapel. She'd been preoccupied with thoughts about the choir all day, so Gracie's news was a welcome diversion.

"What are you going to do now?" Louise asked.

"Tomorrow we'll check with building-supply places again. It may help that we have a better way of describing him. We were too busy to start calling today."

"Oh, did you go somewhere?" Louise asked.

"No, Florence came with the new trim. She brought tortellini salad for lunch, and the three of us sewed the trim on the choir robes."

"I've had her tortellini salad," Louise said. "She often brings it to church potlucks. It's really very good."

"Yes, it was part of a very pleasant day. Florence and Byrdie are discovering they have more in common than they ever thought."

"I'm so grateful for your idea of new trim on the robes,"

Louise said. "I sincerely hope that after the alterations we won't hear about changing them again."

"I don't think you will. Florence seems to find the trim solution quite to her liking."

Louise breathed a sigh of relief.

"Now if I can think of a way to discourage her from singing a solo part, it will be quite a relief," Louise said as they reached the double front doors of the chapel.

Before Gracie could respond, Louise heard their names called out.

"Louise, Gracie, can you help me carry the robes?"

Florence was waving at them from her sedan, which she had just parked on Chapel Road.

"I'm glad I caught you," she said, gathering a bundle of robes from the back seat. "My bunion is giving me fits. I wasn't looking forward to making three trips."

"Gracie said you finished all the trim this afternoon. That's wonderful," Louise said, trying to muster enthusiasm as Florence loaded her arms with the surprisingly heavy robes.

"Many hands make light work, I always say," Florence said as she handed out more robes for Gracie to carry.

Inside the church Louise hung the robes she was carrying in the closet, then helped hang Gracie's load.

Louise had carefully planned the rehearsal, opting to begin with familiar hymns, then go on to "Amazing Grace." "I Love to Tell the Story" would be the last hymn of the evening. She had a vague hope that Florence would go home early or forget about her solo if she delayed tackling it until the last, but Louise wasn't optimistic.

Louise remembered her moments of quiet prayer that morning. She renewed her resolve to treat Florence with love, and she added a prayer that the evening's practice would go smoothly.

When the choir members arrived, Louise was pleased by

the good turnout. Only Jack O'Hara was missing, and he came in twenty minutes or so after they began, apologizing because he'd had to work late. Better still, the group had renewed enthusiasm after their success at last Sunday's service.

"All my friends were really happy to have the choir back," Toni Glendenning said. "And it's wonderful to rely on the ANGELs for babysitting. Are we going to have a second practice this week?"

Louise left it up to the choir members, and they were vocal in wanting to have a second practice.

"It's my favorite night of the week," one of them called out.

Much to Louise's relief, Florence went along with the schedule. She didn't insist that they do her solo early in the practice, but any hope that she could be put off was dashed after they finished "Amazing Grace."

"I've been practicing my solo at home. Ronald says I've improved a lot," she said.

Louise lifted her baton, suddenly as heavy as a lead pipe in her hand. It was soon obvious that, far from improving, Florence's voice was just too weak for the part she'd assigned herself. The interval was too high, and she could never hope to master it.

"Can we try it one more time?" Florence asked.

Louise couldn't take the solo away from her in front of the whole choir. She wanted to let her down easily, not humiliate her. She reluctantly ran through it one more time, but her heart wasn't in it.

She made up her mind to talk to Florence as soon as the practice was over, but she was thwarted. No one seemed in a hurry to leave except Florence. She was the first one out the door, and Louise didn't have a chance to say anything to her.

On the walk back to the inn, Gracie was sympathetic but couldn't think of a way to help with the Florence situation.

"Her feelings will be terribly hurt," Gracie said.

"I know," Louise said bleakly. "Maybe I'll have to let her sing the solo. I've never known her to take no for an answer."

Gracie was surprised to find that singing with the Grace Chapel choir had made her a bit homesick. She missed being part of the choir at Eternal Hope, and she missed her friends in Willow Bend. Much as she enjoyed visiting with Byrdie and her new friends at the inn, it would be good to get home.

She resolutely put all nostalgic thoughts out of her mind. If Eustace Sims could be found, she would find him. She could only do it with the Lord's help, and she trusted that He would show her the way. After all, she already had wonderful people ready to help stop Sims. The biggest problem was to find him, and the scar on his wrist might be his undoing, even though he obviously tried hard to keep it concealed.

"There's a light on in the kitchen," Louise said as they entered the inn. "Let's see what's going on."

Gracie followed her to the pleasantly bright room where Jane worked her culinary miracles. Not surprisingly, the chef herself was still busy with the next day's menu. Alice was with her, peeling apples over a stainless steel bowl.

"You had a long practice," Jane said when she saw them. "Did it go well?"

She was rolling pie dough, something Gracie hadn't done in quite some time, as it was so easy to use frozen crusts. Her mouth watered at the thought of homemade apple pie, giving her another reason not to stay too much longer in Acorn Hill. She was enjoying the food a little bit too much.

"Fairly well. You're ambitious tonight," Louise said to Jane.

"I have to keep busy, or I'll get the jitters," Jane said. "The botanical society starts inspecting gardens tomorrow."

"What time are they coming here?" Louise asked.

"I don't know. They'll be out tomorrow through Friday, and no one knows when they'll visit. They don't want the gardeners around during their inspection. I guess they don't want to be swayed by persuasive owners."

"Your garden is sure to be among the best," Gracie said.

"Yes," Alice agreed. "You really don't need to worry. It should stand up to the most critical inspection."

Jane flipped the second of two crusts into a waiting pan, then rolled and cut the remainder of the dough into strips to top the pies.

"Did Florence give you any trouble tonight?" Jane asked as she washed the flour off her hands.

"She's given up on new choir robes, thanks to Gracie. Attaching the trim worked out well thanks to quite a lot of help from Byrdie and Gracie. They ripped off the old and sewed on the new. It was quite a project."

"Florence did her share and then some," Gracie said. "And she was right about the gold trim. Some of it was really in sad shape."

"How did her solo go?" Alice asked as she finished slicing the last apple.

"Not well, but she's still determined to do it. I don't know how to stop her, but let's forget about the choir for now. Gracie has some good news."

"Thanks to you, Alice," Gracie said.

"What is it?" Alice asked.

"You gave me the idea to question Byrdie again. She had forgotten something. Sims was very careful to keep his arms covered when he was around her. He always wore a jacket or a long-sleeved shirt, but he did slip up one time. When he reached out to take the signed contract from Byrdie at her kitchen table, his sleeve rode up. She saw quite a nasty scar on his right wrist."

"Will that help you find him?" Jane asked.

"It could. We're going to call the same businesses that sell builders' supplies again and mention the scar. What we need now is a good excuse for wanting to find him."

"You could let them think you want to hire him," Alice suggested.

"Because he did such remarkable work for a friend," Louise said with a tone of derision.

"That could work," Gracie agreed, "but after that it gets tricky. The man goes to so much trouble to disguise his real identity, it's unlikely we can get his real name and address."

"He's probably very suspicious." Jane sprinkled lemon juice over the peeled apples and picked up her tin of cinnamon.

"He's a slippery one, all right," Louise agreed. "Otherwise he wouldn't be so hard to find."

"I have an idea, if all of you agree," Alice said nodding at her sisters.

"If it's your idea, it's probably a sensible one," Jane said with a little laugh.

"I'm open to any suggestion," Gracie said.

"Maybe you can get a supplier to give him a message. Perhaps he'll call if he thinks he has a good prospect," Alice said.

"The job would have to promise to be a lucrative one to smoke him out," her older sister agreed.

"Exactly," Alice said. "A big job in a big house."

"I see what you're getting at," Jane said, reading her sister well.

"Grace Chapel Inn," Louise said.

"You're volunteering to lure him here?" Gracie asked, not at all sure the sisters should let him anywhere near their home.

"It's perfect," Alice agreed. "The house is old, and the attic will tempt him to pull another scam."

"You would have to let him come here to size up the job." Gracie still harbored some doubts.

"We're used to having people in and out. That's the beauty of it," Alice said. "There will be more than one person here to deal with him. I'm not sure exactly how to handle it, but you're clever, Gracie. You'll come up with a plan."

Gracie was afraid that Alice was giving her more credit

than she deserved, but she could see the potential in using Grace Chapel Inn as a lure.

"If you're sure you want him to come here, it's probably our best possibility. You won't have to deal with him on the phone," Gracie said. "I plan to use my cell phone number. I'll leave it with the building suppliers so he can call me if he takes the bait."

"We'll do it then," Jane said. "Let's have a cup of tea to celebrate. It's just the thing after a busy day."

"I can't thank all of you enough," Gracie said. "Especially you, Alice. Without your detective's imagination, I might be ready to give up on Sims and go home."

Alice felt ready to settle into bed for an undisturbed sleep after their late-evening tea. Jane had served some wonderful little lemon cookies she had baked, but it wasn't that treat or the tea that made Alice feel so relaxed.

She prepared for bed, then turned to the Lord in prayer: *Dear Lord, thank You for having so richly blessed my life and for forgiving me for my doubts. I really have been silly. I felt left out of my sisters' friendship with Gracie when I should have felt blessed by her presence among us. You've shown me that I need to embrace new friends and cherish the old.*

She went on to pray for her patients at the hospital, and she asked God's blessings on all those with special needs. Soon Alice fell asleep beneath the gentle covering of the Lord's grace.

Gracie awoke Wednesday morning feeling energized and ready to resume the search for Eustace Sims. She was the first guest down for breakfast, and only Jane was in the kitchen.

"You're early this morning," Jane said. "I was just

chopping pecans to put in my waffles. We have two couples from Cleveland staying until Saturday."

"I won't trouble you for a big breakfast," Gracie said. "If you don't mind, I'll just have a muffin and tea here in the kitchen. I had more than my share of cookies last night, and I want to get to Byrdie's as soon as possible."

"It's really no trouble to make a waffle for you," Jane assured her.

"You're very kind, but no thank you," Gracie said. "But would you mind keeping Gooseberry here today? He meanders so much when we walk that it will take me twice as long to get to Byrdie's if he comes with me."

"I missed him yesterday," Jane said pushing the chopped pecans from the cutting board into a bowl. "So did Wendell, I suspect. He was prowling around the house all day. You can leave Gooseberry here as often as you like."

"I appreciate that. I haven't told Byrdie about your offer to use the inn as bait. We have a lot of phone calls to make today."

"I won't hold you up," Jane said, placing a warm cranberry muffin alongside a cup of tea for Gracie. I'd like to get out for a walk myself."

"Jane, I need your grocery receipts this morning if I'm going to keep our books up to date," Louise said as she came into the kitchen. "I hope you've circled the items purchased for guest breakfasts. It's such a help if I know the deductible expenses every week."

"Good morning, Louise," Gracie said as she hurriedly finished her muffin.

"Oh, Gracie, good morning to you. I didn't see you there. You're up early."

"I'm eager to get to Byrdie's and start making calls."

"Well, good luck," Louise said, turning her attention back to Jane's kitchen expenses as Gracie prepared to leave.

Gracie checked that her cell phone was in her purse, then began walking briskly through the quiet town. She didn't know whether to make all the calls herself or share the job with Byrdie. Her friend was eager to help, but she didn't think quickly on the phone. Or maybe she just wasn't a very good actress. It was going to be tricky persuading business people to put them in touch with Sims. She just hoped someone would remember seeing his scarred wrist.

Byrdie was dressed in a yellow housedress with pale-blue flowers when Gracie arrived at her house, but she'd abandoned the crutches in favor of a walking stick that usually rested by the back door. She moved stiffly, favoring her sprained ankle, but it was good to see her improvement.

As soon as she was in the house, Gracie sprang her news.

"Thanks to you for remembering the scar, we have another chance to find Sims. We can tell the suppliers that we want to find a man with a scar on his wrist because he did such a good job at a friend's house. The good news is that we can use Grace Chapel Inn as bait. Alice, Jane and Louise all agree that we can lure him to their attic on the pretense of wanting him to build a cedar closet to store out-of-season garments."

"Oh my," Byrdie said, sounding amazed by the news. "We can say the job is in the attic of the inn? Even after the disaster in my attic?"

"Yes. I thought I should write out what we need to say, sort of a script. Sometimes it's hard to think while on the phone."

"I don't know, Gracie. What if the person who answers the phone wants details about the job? What if he's reluctant to pass a message to Eustace Sims? I'm afraid I'll be too nervous to be convincing."

"I'll tell you what," Gracie said. "It will be confusing with two of us calling. I would hate to have both of us contacting the same supplier. That would look suspicious. Why don't you find the list from the library phone books and keep a record of the ones I call. If they say anything significant, you can write it down. That way we'll be sure to cover as many as possible without repeat calls to the same place."

"Yes, that's a good plan," Byrdie readily agreed. "Why don't I start by making us a nice pot of tea? Not ginseng."

They laughed together and got to work.

Several hours later, Gracie was discouraged. Some building suppliers were courteous, but a few were rude or indifferent. One remembered that she'd called before and impatiently cut her off. Telephone canvassing was definitely tedious work. For a moment she felt sympathy for all those telemarketers who called her at home—but only for a moment.

She punched in another number, this one belonging to a large lumber-and-supply yard north of Potterston. A woman answered, and Gracie quickly explained the reason for her call.

"You say he had a scar on his right wrist?" the woman asked.

"Yes, quite a noticeable one."

"I remember him. He's been in quite a few times, but I don't know his name. I seem to remember he paid cash."

"Do you have any idea how to reach him?"

"No, but if he comes in again, I can have him call you. I won't mention his scar, of course. I'll just ask him if he's interested in a project that a lady I know has in mind."

"That would be wonderful," Gracie said. "Tell him we have a large older home with an attic. We'd like to have a cedar closet built in it."

"I'll do that," the helpful woman said. "Let me write down your number."

Gracie enthusiastically thanked the woman, then literally danced around Byrdie, who was conscientiously making notes on every call.

"At last someone is willing to pass on our message."

"If he goes into that place again," Byrdie said.

"We'll keep calling and hope for the best. Eustace Sims can't hide forever."

Chapter ♫ Fifteen

Gracie continued making calls through the afternoon without getting more leads. No one else remembered a man with a scar on his wrist.

"Maybe he buys all his material at one place," Byrdie suggested.

"I hope that's true." Gracie was weary after so many phone calls.

Byrdie decided to bake a pizza from her freezer for dinner, and Gracie—despite the likelihood of a forgettable repast—welcomed the change from making calls. The activity could really take the energy out of a person. She'd done it many times for church projects, but it was much harder to talk to strangers who might or might not care what she had to say.

The pizza was dry and skimpy on toppings, but Gracie chose to eat enough to keep up her strength.

She wondered if Eustace Sims would get their message. If he did, would he call? He might be suspicious. On the other hand, he might be greedy enough to risk contacting her.

How long could she stay in Acorn Hill waiting for him to take the bait? Her son Arlen, his wife Wendy and their darling little Elmo were coming to visit "Gram" for a week over the Fourth of July. Gracie wanted to get home and put her house in tip-top shape before their visit.

She was catering a wedding at the end of July. Even though it was weeks away, she would have to spend some serious time on the planning. Also, she'd promised to organize a cleanup day at the church. She would have to end her visit soon.

Gracie did have some mixed feelings about leaving. She'd grown close to the sisters at Grace Chapel Inn during her visit. She wondered how Jane's garden would fare in the competition and how Louise would cope with Florence's solo. She and Alice had only begun to be friends, but she admired the nurse's common sense and caring nature.

At least she felt very good about Byrdie. Her sprained ankle had been a blessing in disguise, bringing her visits from acquaintances who she hoped would become more than that. True, Florence had originally come for help with alterations, but the two of them hit it off surprisingly well. Alice had visited because she was a kind, caring person, but there was potential for a deeper friendship there too. Best of all, Gracie knew that Byrdie realized she had to put aside her grief and contribute to the community. She was full of plans for volunteer work and seemed much more cheerful than when Gracie had arrived.

"I think I'll go back to the inn now," Gracie said after washing up the few dishes that they'd used for dinner. "All that calling wore me out."

"I never realized that there's so much hard work involved in sleuthing," Byrdie said. "I'll never be able to thank you enough for all you're doing."

"We're friends," Gracie said with a smile.

She walked slowly back to the inn, enjoying the leisurely pace of the town. Strangers said hello when they passed on the sidewalk or waved from their yards. Gracie could understand why Louise and Jane had returned to Acorn Hill when they were left on their own and why Alice had chosen to stay. It was a town she might choose as home if Willow Bend didn't suit her so well.

It was still daylight when Gracie reached the inn. The long days were one of the many things she loved about this time of year. A light wind blew warm air against her face, causing a pleasant sensation, never mind that her bright-red curls were blown into an unruly tangle. She tried to pat her hair into some semblance of order as she walked onto the porch of the inn.

The foyer was deserted when she got inside, but she could hear voices in the kitchen. She decided to go up to her room without intruding on the gathering in the rear of the inn. Even though all three sisters had made her feel more than welcome, she didn't want to take advantage by making herself part of everything that happened at the inn.

Her foot was on the first step to the second floor when the cell phone sounded in her purse. She paused to fish it out, then said hello.

"You the lady that wants some work done?" a rough male voice asked.

"Who is this?" Gracie asked with heart-thumping excitement.

"The name's Sims. Brenda at the lumberyard gave me your number. You got a job for me?"

"Yes, Mr. Sims. I certainly do have some work for you, if you do carpentry. We want a cedar closet built in our attic." Gracie's mind was racing. "We're in Acorn Hill. Maybe you could come by sometime and give us an estimate."

"I can come tomorrow morning. What time do you want me?"

"Oh," Gracie said, a bit breathless because her plan to get in touch with him had actually worked. "I really do need to check the calendar. This is an inn, Grace Chapel Inn. It's a big old house, and I need to check whether any new guests are due to arrive. Can I call you back in a few minutes after I've checked tomorrow's schedule?"

"I'll call you back," he said, abruptly ending the call.

Gracie looked at the caller ID on her phone and made a mental note of the number, then quickly found a pad of paper in her purse to write it down.

Her sleepiness forgotten, she had to speak to one of the sisters right away. She was only a guest. She couldn't make an appointment with Eustace Sims without checking with at least one of them.

She hurried to the kitchen, realizing that one of the voices there was only vaguely familiar. All three sisters were there along with the red-haired older woman she'd met while using the fax machine. She didn't know whether to mention the call from Sims in front of her, so she stood in the doorway until Louise noticed her.

"Gracie, come in," Louise said warmly. "I think you've met our aunt, Ethel Buckley? She lives right next door."

"We met when I tried to chase her away from your fax machine," Ethel said with a little snort of laughter. "The way the door is always unlocked here, it's hard to know who's a guest and who isn't. I didn't know whether she had your permission to use it." Ethel smiled at Gracie.

"Come have a cup of tea with us, Gracie," Jane invited. "Aunt Ethel was just telling us about plans to do some renovations at the town hall."

"They're still in the talking stage," Ethel quickly said. "Nothing has been decided for sure. I only know because I'm friends with the mayor. I wouldn't want it to get around that I was telling secrets."

"Your secret is safe with Gracie," Alice assured her.

"I just got a phone call," Gracie said, too agitated to hold back her news. "I need to—"

To her surprise, Jane was vigorously shaking her head from a position behind her aunt.

Alice must have picked up on Jane's signal, because she stood and spoke directly to Ethel.

"Aunt Ethel, have you seen what Jane has done with the garden?"

"I walked through it a few days ago. You've done a nice job, Jane. My brother would be proud of the way it looks." She turned toward Gracie who was on edge, needing to set a time for Eustace Sims to come before he called back, but it was obvious that Ethel was inclined to visit with anyone who would listen.

"Acorn Hill is a very nice community," Gracie agreed. "I'm a widow, so I can imagine how lonely it was living out in the country."

"That and the work," Ethel said emphatically. "I leased the land, but there was still a house to keep up. It got to be too much, so I'm really grateful to be living here. The girls are wonderful to me, not that I don't miss Daniel terribly. He couldn't have been a better brother. I don't drive, but he was always willing to take me to Potterston when I needed to go to the doctor or dentist. Now my nieces are too. Fortunately, I do have all my own teeth, and they don't give me too much trouble. I can't tell you how unusual that was in my parents' day."

Perhaps it was a result of Ethel's references to teeth, but as she listened—and listened—Gracie realized that she had been grinding her own.

"I can remember my grandfather keeping his false teeth in a glass beside the bed at night. I thought it was funny then, but I think they were awfully uncomfortable."

Gracie didn't know what to do. She needed to talk to one of the sisters without further delay, but she couldn't be rude to their aunt. Ethel was probably a sweet and caring woman, but she did enjoy talking. It wouldn't be good if she spread the word about Eustace Sims coming to the inn. Nor was it likely that she would buy the story about building a cedar closet in the attic without a great many questions.

"I thought I would walk over to the chapel before it gets dark," Louise said. "We're having another choir practice tomorrow night, and I want to sort out some music. Why don't you come with me, Aunt Ethel? I'll show you the new trim on the choir robes. It was Florence's idea to replace it, and Byrdie Hutchinson and Gracie helped her remove the old and sew on the new."

"I'd like to see the results," Ethel said.

"Well, come along then. I want to hear more about the plans for renovating the town hall. I didn't read anything about it in the newspaper."

"Oh, it won't be in the paper for a while," Ethel said, lowering her voice. "You might say that it's insider information. I'm trusting all of you not to breathe a word."

"You know you can trust us, Aunt Ethel," Alice said with a smile.

"Of course," Jane agreed, speaking for the rest of them.

Ethel made something of a production of carrying her cup to the sink and rinsing out the last of the tea.

"I always like to clean up after myself," she said. "Jane has way too much work to do without following after me."

"I'm happy to do things for you, Auntie. You're never any trouble," Jane said.

Gracie was still holding her purse in one hand and her cell phone in the other as she tried to keep from wincing. She expected Eustace Sims to call back at any moment, and she didn't know how to put him off a second time without losing him.

Louise and Ethel walked past Gracie as they headed toward the front door of the inn. Gracie opened her mouth to tell Jane and Alice her news about the call just as Ethel scurried back to the kitchen.

"I wanted to tell you that it was nice visiting with you, Gracie," she said. "If you ever have a few spare minutes, you're welcome to have tea with me at the carriage house. No need to call ahead. I'm there quite a bit, although I do try to get out and about every day."

"Thank you, Ethel," Gracie said as sweetly as she could, knowing it wasn't the aunt's fault that she was on pins and needles waiting for a call.

As soon as she was sure Louise and her aunt had left, she spilled out her news.

"He called!"

"Eustace Sims called?" Alice asked.

"Yes, he wants to come here tomorrow morning. I couldn't give him a time without asking you. He's going to call back." She was still clutching her phone, waving it for emphasis.

"Thank you for not saying anything in front of Aunt Ethel," Jane said. "She's a dear, but she can be something of a gossip. It seems like a bad idea to spread the word about Sims all over the town."

"Yes, it's possible that he has friends or relatives in Acorn Hill," Gracie said. "What should I tell him when he calls? If he does, that is."

"It sounds like he's interested," Alice said.

"Yes, interested in swindling another homeowner," Jane said, sounding unusually harsh.

"Unfortunately, I have to work at the hospital tomorrow," her sister said, "so I won't be here in the morning. But you definitely shouldn't be alone with him. Whatever he says, you want a witness."

"I don't know what Louise's plans are," Jane said, "but I'm free after breakfast. If you could get him to come around ten o'clock, that would be perfect for me."

Gracie started to agree to the time when her phone sounded again.

"Hello," Gracie said a bit apprehensively.

"Sims here. What time do you want me to come?"

"Ten o'clock. You take Chapel Road—"

"Yeah, I'll find it," he said abruptly. "Ten tomorrow."

The phone went dead in Gracie's hand. For better or worse, the corrupt contractor would be there in the morning.

"What should we do when he gets here?" Jane asked, sounding a bit worried.

"Let him look around in the attic," Gracie said. "He gave Byrdie and Mattie rough estimates, then came back later with a contract for them to sign. We can't do anything until he does something fraudulent."

"Are you sure he will?"

"Pretty sure," Gracie assured her. "I don't know if he'll pull the woodworm scam again, but a leopard can't change its spots. He'll come up with something."

"I'm not sure I should sign a contract," Jane said. "I wouldn't want the inn to be liable for whatever he plans to charge."

"No, you shouldn't sign," Gracie agreed. "I'll come up with a plan. I've been so busy trying to find him that I haven't worked out the details yet. But we have one big advantage."

"What's that?"

"We know he's a criminal."

Gracie smiled to show Jane that she was confident of success, but it was bravado on her part. She was as nervous as Jane was or more so. She would need strength from the Lord to face down Eustace Sims.

Dear Lord, she silently prayed, *help me to be clever and courageous. Help me to use the gifts You have given me so that others won't be hurt by this man.*

"We'll have quite a morning then," Jane said with a smile. "This is the first time I've played Watson to a real Sherlock. I hope I don't let you down."

"I don't know that I deserve that comparison, but I'm sure you'll be a big help in trapping Sims."

Gracie said good night and gratefully went up to the comfortable bed waiting for her.

⚭

Jane said good night to Gracie, but she didn't feel at all like sleeping herself. Her brain seemed to be humming with too many thoughts, and she needed time alone to sort out things in her mind.

She stepped out into her garden, the place that brought her the most peace. It was fully dark now, but she knew the pathways so well that she didn't need to turn on lights to wander among the fragrant plants.

It wasn't Gracie's plan to trap the crooked contractor that was foremost in her mind, although she was a bit nervous about taking him up to the attic. At least Gracie would be with her, and Louise too if she wanted to join them. Although she didn't look forward to meeting Sims, she put the encounter out of her mind.

Something else was troubling her, something she didn't want to discuss with her sisters. Alice would tell her to pray about it. Louise would dismiss Jane's worries in her usual practical way. They would both be right, but what worked for her sisters didn't always work for her.

Jane had prayed, but God's answer seemed very different from what she wanted, and she was not inclined to emulate her oldest sister and let events run their own course.

For a brief moment Jane wished that she'd never restored the inn's garden. Maybe she should have planted grass or made it into a patio for outdoor meals, anything but the garden with which she had nearly been obsessed the last few months.

But she quickly changed her mind about that, for the garden was a memorial to the mother she'd never known, and it also satisfied her own longing to bring beauty into her life. Once she'd finished decorating the inn's rooms, she felt at loose ends, not quite sure what her goals and aspirations should be. The garden had given her a focus for all her excess energy. It completed her in ways she didn't quite understand.

Should she have entered the botanical society's competition? Wasn't it enough to have created something lovely? Did she need the approval of strangers? Would it be more beautiful if the garden won first place or less beautiful if it didn't? Was a competitive nature a bad thing? Was there a pitfall in trying too hard to do her best? She had many questions but no answers. Maybe Alice and Louise were right about her expending too much energy on her garden, working herself beyond reason to make it perfect.

She wandered carefully to avoid stepping off the path and damaging a flower. Whatever the effort to create it had cost her, she knew the garden was as lovely as it had ever been. She was happier being here than any other place, much as she enjoyed ruling over the kitchen and putting her training as a chef to good use.

Her doubts had set in when she saw Elma Grayson's garden. It was a hodgepodge of plants in no particular order, but each and every one had been planted in friendship and love. Elma's garden was unique. Jane's was only beautiful.

Jane was beside the roses, remembering all the lovely shades of color and the perfection of the large blooms even though it was too dark to see them. She bent to touch her cheek on a velvety petal, careful not to harm the flower. When she reached out to keep the stem from bending under her caress, she jerked back with a start. She'd stabbed her finger on a sharp thorn.

Chapter ♪ Sixteen

Gracie rolled over in bed and reached for her travel alarm on the bedside table. To her surprise, it was only a little after five, much too early to consider getting up. She replaced the clock, being careful not to turn off the alarm, and settled down for another couple hours of slumber.

The house was silent, and no street noises filtered up to the snug second-floor bedroom. Gooseberry had staked out territory on the foot of the bed, and Gracie's movement hadn't disturbed him. There was no reason not to go back to sleep.

Seven minutes later she checked the clock again. She couldn't be more wide-awake, but if she didn't nod off again, she would be terribly sleepy all day. Determined to get back to sleep, she rolled into a comfortable position on her left side, then changed her mind and tried the right.

A half hour later she accepted defeat and picked up a paperback mystery novel that had lain neglected since she arrived in Acorn Hill. Sometimes reading made her sleepy, but not this morning. In fact, the exploits of a fictional sleuth only reminded her of what lay ahead.

Whether she was ready or not, Eustace Sims was coming to the inn. She couldn't shake a vague feeling of dread. She felt like an actress on opening night who hasn't memorized her part.

When she was quite young, maybe ten or so, her beloved Grandpa Bob had taught her how to fish. She learned not to yank hard on the line when she had a bite. If she wanted to catch her fish, she had to set the hook carefully and reel the line in slowly. She tried to think of Sims as a much bigger fish. The advantage was hers because he had no idea that she was a friend of Byrdie's. Nor was there any way he could know she'd spoken to Matilda Singleton. All she had to do was be pleasant, ask a few foolish questions and hang on his answers. If he planned to cheat the Howard sisters, she would help make it easy for him.

She picked up her clock one more time and turned off the alarm, planning to read a chapter of her book before she got up. She'd already guessed the guilty party in the story and was reading to find out whether she was right.

A soft knocking sound caught her attention, and she sat up in surprise.

"Gracie, are you awake?" Jane's pleasant voice called through the door.

Gracie glanced at her clock. It was past nine-thirty.

"Ohmyohmyohmy!" she exclaimed, jumping out of bed.

She opened the door wide enough to speak to Jane, and Gooseberry stalked out of the room.

"I hate to disturb you," Jane said apologetically, "but Sims will be here soon. I don't want to face him alone."

"I turned off my alarm thinking I couldn't possibly go back to sleep, then fell asleep reading," Gracie said, giving her a hurried explanation. "Let me get some clothes on, and I'll be right down."

She grabbed clothes from the neat pile of laundry she'd washed at Byrdie's and didn't notice until she was dressed that she was wearing her yellow striped top with blue striped slacks. Well, no matter. Sims was interested in money, not her fashion sense.

By the time she got down to the foyer, Jane was pacing nervously.

"I didn't expect to get all jittery about this," Jane said with a light laugh.

"I was awake before dawn worrying about it," Gracie admitted. "I certainly didn't expect to go back to sleep."

"He could be here any minute. Would you like some tea while we wait? I'll fix something for your breakfast when he leaves."

"I imagine your other guests ate ages ago. I would love some tea, but after Sims goes, I'll drive over to Byrdie's and have a bite there. Otherwise, she'll be on pins and needles wondering what happened."

Jane headed for the kitchen but didn't get far: There was a sharp rap on the front door that sent both women hurrying to answer it.

Gracie didn't feel at all ready for this encounter with Sims, but she took a deep breath and silently prayed for courage. Jane opened the door.

"You the folks that want an estimate?" a shabbily dressed man asked gruffly.

"Yes, I'm Jane Howard, and this is my friend Gracie Parks," Jane said. "Come in, please."

Gracie decided that Byrdie and Matilda had done a good job describing him, but there was something about him that couldn't easily be put into words. His eyes seemed small for his face, and he didn't look directly at them. He might be called shifty looking, but that didn't quite cover it. He seemed overly alert, almost defensive. Of course, a criminal had to have a suspicious nature to keep out of trouble with the law, but he radiated distrust.

She glanced beyond him through the open doorway and

saw the back of a battered pickup truck. There appeared to be mud splashes on the rear license plate. No matter how early she might have gotten up, she still would have been at a loss for words, something that rarely happened to her. She was thankful that Jane was doing the talking.

"I'll show you the attic," Jane said. "Since we turned the house into a bed-and-breakfast, we're really short on storage space for clothing and linens. A cedar closet seems like an ideal solution."

She led the way to the stairs, and Gracie noticed that she'd dressed appropriately for showing an attic. Jane's slim, neat figure managed to look dignified in worn jeans and a loose-fitting green shirt with rolled-up sleeves. The dark-brown hair in her ponytail bobbed confidently.

Sims, who hadn't bothered to introduce himself, followed, and Gracie brought up the rear. Gracie was glad his attention was focused on Jane. It gave her a chance to observe him without attracting his attention. She had an instinct for recognizing lies, and she expected to hear some big ones from him.

They walked across the second floor toward the stairs to the third story. Sims was a few yards behind Jane when a dark form raced between them.

Gracie saw immediately that it was Wendell, but she didn't anticipate the contractor's reaction. He let out a loud yelp and stopped dead in his tracks. Jane turned to see what was wrong.

"Oh, Wendell," she said as the gray-and-black striped tabby bounded down to the first floor on four white paws.

"You have a cat," Sims said in an accusing voice as though she'd deliberately withheld that information from him.

"Yes, actually we have two at the moment. Wendell has a visitor."

"Well, I guess that's okay as long as they don't leap out like that," Sims said grudgingly. "Do you have a dog?"

"No dogs," Jane said as they reached the third floor

"Good. I don't work where they have dogs."

"You don't like them?" Gracie asked.

"I can't stand mutts," he said bitterly. "I used to be a delivery man. Quit because I got tired of being fresh meat for walking fleabags."

"Oh, that's a shame," Jane said. "Most dogs have sweet natures, but I guess there are always a few exceptions. I had one howl at me something fierce when I was out walking last week. Of course, I did step into his yard to look at a garden, so he was only doing his job."

Apparently her sympathy reminded him of all the times he'd been harassed by canines. His face contorted with anger.

"I got no use for any of them," he snarled.

"The attic is up here," Jane said leading the way up a steep flight of stairs.

"Good thing I'm handy at building things," Sims said as if remembering that he was there to sell his services. "I sure don't miss that delivery job with dogs always nipping at me."

Gracie decided it was a good idea for her to keep quiet. Jane had introduced her as a friend, and a friend wouldn't ordinarily have any say in home renovations. Because she wasn't obligated to say anything, she could keep a wary eye on Sims. His reaction to Wendell and his avowed hatred of dogs were interesting. She would have to think about that.

He was wearing a New York Yankees baseball cap, a departure from his Tiger's cap. Did one of the building-supply people tell him about her original inquiries? If so, he might have been warned off wearing the same cap he'd worn at Byrdie's and Matilda's.

She couldn't see the scar on his wrist. Just as Byrdie had said, he kept it covered. Today he was wearing a plaid flannel shirt so faded that it was difficult to tell the original colors. It was a warm garment for a hot summer day, and attics tended to have especially high temperatures at this time of year. He certainly hadn't dressed sensibly for the job, but it confirmed that he wanted to keep his scar hidden.

The three of them entered the attic, an unfinished space crowded with the castoffs of what appeared to be several generations. Gracie saw an old dresser with a block of wood substituting for a missing leg and a clothes-drying rack with rungs darkened from long usage. A chair with shredded upholstery was pushed back into a rear corner beside a steamer trunk and dress form.

Like Byrdie's attic, this one was unfinished with bare boards on the floor and exposed joists. Also like Byrdie's, it had pads of pink insulation blanketing the walls. It also had windows the size of those on lower floors with views of the town center in front and a wooded area in back. It was well lit, so it wasn't at all forbidding or spooky, which was fine with Gracie. She'd had quite enough of poking around inhospitable places like Byrdie's attic and basement.

"*Humph*," Sims grunted as he looked around.

"We'll have to clear out some of the items up here to make room for a closet," Jane said, playing her part to perfection in Gracie's opinion.

"How big do you want it?" Sims asked. "You can never have too much storage space. If it was my place, I'd have it line one wall."

Gracie very much wanted to let him know that they were on to his scams, but this wasn't the time. Their job today was to gain his confidence and set up the Howards to be swindled. She was glad his back was toward her so he wouldn't detect the scorn on her face.

"We don't want to spend a fortune on it," Jane said as though she'd rehearsed the claim a hundred times. "Can you give me an idea of how much it will cost?"

"That's why I'm here," Sims said, sounding almost jovial now, probably because he sniffed the possibility of a successful swindle. "Course, I got to do some measuring, then figure things out at my place before I can talk dollars and cents."

"Do you live near here, Mr. Sims?" Gracie asked.

"Near enough," he said. "While I'm at it, you may want me to figure in some more insulation. You're losing a lot of heat through the roof. Heat rises, you know."

"It rises? I'm afraid I don't know much about that sort of thing," Jane said, making Gracie wonder if she'd had any acting experience. "I'd have to talk to my sisters before I could agree to having any work done. The three of us own the house together."

"No problem." Sims had completely put aside his dour demeanor. "I'll work out the figures. Then we can go to contract."

"Oh, would I have to sign something?" Jane asked.

"Just a formality. You and your sisters have to sign. You wanna know what you're gettin' for your money, don't you?"

"Well, yes." Jane was hesitant just to make it seem that she was considering it.

"I'll get to work then," he said, pulling a steel measuring tape out of the side pocket of his baggy jeans. "No need for you ladies to stay up here in all this dust if you got other things to do."

"Oh, I'm fascinated to see how you go about measuring," Gracie said.

She hoped she hadn't overplayed her hand, but there was no way she was going to let that man stay up here alone. She wanted to see everything he did, and Jane seemed to feel the same way.

"I don't have anything that has to be done right now," Jane said.

Gracie had to admit that Sims put on a good show. He flipped his metal tape around like it was alive, getting numbers for the height, length and width of the space that seemed best for a closet. When he was done with that, he poked the end of the tape up to the highest part of the ceiling and tried again to convince them that the house was losing heat through the attic. After every measurement he jotted numbers in a shabby little notebook he carried in his shirt pocket.

Just when she thought he was done, he took a small screwdriver out of the same pocket and started tapping boards wherever he could reach. When Jane asked what he was doing, he avoided answering.

"Just technical things, little lady."

Gracie cringed. Did he use that demeaning tone with all his prospective clients? Jane looked ready to protest, but Gracie shook her head in warning. He used the tip of the screwdriver to poke at the insulation already covering the walls. Gracie was relieved to see that he didn't rip any away.

"Not a good grade," he mumbled as though talking to himself, although plainly they could hear.

Gracie detected little pitter-patter sounds on the bare boards of the steps to the attic and looked down to see Gooseberry heading toward them. She was curious to know whether the big orange cat would spook Sims the way Wendell had, so she didn't say anything.

Gooseberry started prowling the space, no doubt sniffing out the possibility of catching a plump mouse. He padded right next to Sims before the man saw him, startling him almost as much as Wendell had. Whatever else he was, Eustace Sims obviously was not an animal lover.

"If I decide to take this job," he said, "I don't want cats around the place tripping me up."

"That's not a problem," Jane said. "They can stay outside."

"They better," he muttered.

Maybe it only seemed to take him forever because Gracie's stomach was rumbling after missing breakfast, but he seemed willing to spend the day puttering in the inn's attic.

"Do you have much more to check?" Jane said, at last losing patience with his pokey act.

"Should do it." He put the measuring tape back in the pocket of his jeans and stuck the pad and pencil in his shirt pocket.

"Can you give me a rough estimate now?" Jane asked. "So I can give my sisters an idea of what's involved."

"Wouldn't be fair to you or me to bounce around a ballpark figure. Let me work it out, and I'll get back to you real soon."

"How soon is real soon?" Gracie asked.

"Maybe by tomorrow afternoon. Let me think. Yup, Friday's clear for me. Will you folks be here?"

"Call us first," Jane said, "but it should be all right. I have to speak to my two sisters before I can say for sure."

"I'll need all three of you to sign the contract before I can start buying materials. My usual deal is fifty percent down and fifty percent when the work is done. Pretty standard in the building industry."

Pretty standard for honest contractors who intend to finish the work, Gracie thought.

After Sims had finally left the inn, Gracie hugged Jane in sheer relief at having him gone.

"He certainly was unpleasant," Jane said.

"To say the least."

"I think he bought it," Jane said with a girlish giggle.

"Hook, line and sinker." Gracie joined her in laughter.

"He acted as if he was doing us a favor. Can you imagine calling me a 'little lady'?"

"I believe he will be back," Gracie said. "Do you think Louise and Alice can be here then?"

"I'll ask. As far as I know, after today Alice is free through the weekend."

"Then I will scoot off to Byrdie's," Gracie said. "She's probably dying of curiosity."

⌒⌒

When Gracie turned down her offer of brunch, Jane retreated to the kitchen. For a change there was nothing pressing to be done, so she gravitated naturally toward her garden. She'd watered and done a bit of weeding early this morning, but she put on her straw hat and located her gardening gloves in case she saw some other way to improve it. She especially needed fresh air after being in the attic with that dreadful man.

She went through the storage room and opened the side door, then froze in her tracks. There were visitors in her garden, two people she didn't know. They could only be the judges from the botanical society. As quietly as possible, she eased the door shut, hoping they hadn't noticed her. It stated in the rules that competitors were not to be in their gardens while the judges were there. The prohibition was frustrating to Jane. She wanted to explain what she'd tried to do and tell them it had originally been her mother's garden.

All she could do now was worry. Would her color arrangements be pleasing to them? Would they see the garden as a whole rather than a collection of separate areas? How did it stack up to other gardens in their opinion? What exactly did they use as criteria for judging?

She went back to the kitchen, itching to know what they were saying and doing. There she brewed a cup of tea and decided to clean the spice cupboard, not exactly an urgent task but something to keep her busy for a short time. First she looked out the front door to see if the judges had parked an unfamiliar car near the inn. She saw a black sedan at the end of the walkway. At least she would be able to tell when they were gone.

She set her cup on the table, answered a nuisance call on the phone and completely forgot to drink her tea.

Chapter ♪♪ Seventeen

Louise felt better about going to choir practice than she had in several weeks. It was gratifying that the members had requested a second rehearsal, and she was more than willing to devote this Thursday evening to another practice.

Gracie seemed genuinely delighted to sing with the Grace Chapel choir during her visit. Her enthusiasm was catching, and Louise was pleased to meet with her at the inn after dinner.

"Byrdie and I had dinner in Potterston," Gracie said as they walked toward the chapel. "We visited Matilda Singleton first so that we could tell her the latest about Eustace Sims before he arrives tomorrow."

"That's good. She was the one who lost the most because of him," Louise recalled.

"Yes, and she's eager to confront him. Now what we need is a plan. I hope you'll sit in with Jane, Alice and me after choir practice. We have to know exactly what we want from him and how to go about getting it."

"Yes, I'll be happy to," Louise said. "The sooner he learns that he can't get away with swindling people, the better."

They talked about the meeting with Sims until they were inside the chapel. Florence was the only choir member who'd arrived ahead of them, and Louise knew she had to confront the problem of her solo. At least this evening she had an alternative for Florence to consider.

"I've been practicing my solo," Florence said a little hoarsely. "I think I'll be ready for this Sunday's service."

"I did want to talk to you about that," Louise said as Gracie discreetly moved out of hearing.

"Can we work on it at the beginning of practice?" Florence asked. "I'm a tiny bit hoarse from going over it so much at home. I may not be at my best by the end of the evening."

"Yes, we certainly can," Louise said, glad to begin the conversation on a positive note.

She fingered a strand of pearls hanging over her high-necked, blue silk blouse. Louise favored soft colors, and tonight she'd deliberately chosen one of her better blouses for choir practice. She knew it went well with her gray-white hair, and she wanted to look dignified and maybe even motherly. Florence wasn't going to like what she had to say, and it couldn't hurt Louise to bolster her own confidence by dressing well.

"Good," Florence said.

Louise took a deep breath. "I've been working on the music for 'I Love to Tell the Story' and—"

"Oh, please don't tell me we're going to have to learn new music for that too," Florence said, her face crinkling in distress.

"No, not at all. Let me show you."

Louise picked up the folder she'd left on top of the piano earlier in the day.

"You're going to like this," Louise said, mustering an optimistic expression.

Florence frowned and took the sheet of music that Louise had had copied.

"It doesn't seem much different."

"I just made a few small changes in your solo," Louise said.

She was hoping that Florence would accept them without explanations. How could she tell her that she'd followed Jane's casual advice and rewritten the solo part to make it easier for Florence?

"I guess it's all right," Florence said doubtfully.

"If all goes smoothly with the rest of the choir, we'll be able to sing it in church," Louise said. "Oh, Gracie," she called out, "would you mind passing out those music sheets when the rest of the choir gets here?"

"I'll be happy to," Gracie agreed. "Florence, I wanted to tell you how much Byrdie enjoyed working on the robes. It was just the tonic she needed to get over her sprained ankle."

"It was rather fun, the three of us stitching together." Florence smiled. "Maybe we can do it again sometime without the sewing."

"That would be a nice treat on another visit here," Gracie said.

The choir members were arriving, and when it was time to start, all but one person was in attendance and ready to sing.

Louise noted that Jack O'Hara was missing, but most likely he'd had to work overtime.

They started with Florence's solo, and it seemed that she would be able to handle the new arrangement a little bit better. Her voice did sound scratchy, but that was likely a result from practicing a lot that day.

They finished that hymn and went through "Amazing Grace" before Louise noticed Rev. Thompson standing at the back.

"If you don't mind, I'll interrupt your practice for just a minute or so," he said, walking toward the group.

When he was in front of the choir, he smiled broadly and complimented them on how they sounded.

"I have an opportunity for you, but it's up to the choir

and Louise whether you want to participate. You probably know about the interfaith service at the Methodist church this Sunday."

Several choir members murmured assent.

"A choir from the Baptist church in Potterston was scheduled to participate, but I'm sad to say they've had to cancel because of the death of one of their members. They haven't been able to practice, and they've decided to withdraw from the service."

"Oh, what a shame!" Loueda Ullman said in a soft, sympathetic voice.

Several other people expressed their regrets as well. Then they quieted down to hear the rest of what the pastor had to say.

"They've asked if our choir would be willing to take their place."

Louise had seen the offer coming, but the rest of the choir buzzed with surprise and questioned whether they were ready.

"I listened to you sing 'I Love to Tell the Story' and 'Amazing Grace,' and both would fit into their program very nicely. Assuming you're willing to participate, that is," Rev. Thompson said.

Louise heard only positive comments and thought that it would be good for the choir to spread their wings a bit. She wasn't sure about including Florence's solo in their selections, but Florence didn't give her a chance to consider alternatives.

"That's absolutely wonderful," Florence said in a voice that was sounding more and more strained.

"You're sounding a bit hoarse," Louise said sympathetically. "Are you sure you'll be up to it?"

"It's only Thursday," Florence reassured her. "By Sunday I'll be in top form. You can rely on me."

"Does everyone agree that we should participate?" Louise asked, calling for a show of hands.

No one voted against it, although one member did question whether they were quite ready. She went along with the group when she saw the confidence of the others.

"It's settled then," Rev. Thompson said. "I'll let their worship committee know. I think it's a good opportunity for Christian fellowship and cooperation."

"What is?" asked a voice from the back of the church.

Louise was happy to see Jack O'Hara even though his late arrival did mean Rev. Thompson had to explain about the interfaith service a second time.

"Sounds great to me," Jack said after he'd heard the explanation. "Sorry I'm so late. A farmer out on Hornsbee Road had a stray mongrel trapped in his barn. He didn't want to shoot it if he didn't have to, but he had to get into the barn. Fortunately, the pooch turned out to be all bark and no bite."

"Good job, Jack!" a member called out.

"We'll concentrate on the two hymns for the interfaith service for the rest of the evening," Louise announced.

Gracie watched with interest as Jack O'Hara took his place in the choir. He was wearing his animal-control uniform, an official-looking light-blue shirt and gray-blue trousers worn with black boots and a wide black belt. In fact, with the badge he wore above his pocket, he could easily have passed as a policeman. He had a bright-red crew cut and a luxuriant handlebar mustache that would have done a county sheriff proud. He had a commanding presence too. He was a man to be taken seriously, someone who might be just the person they needed to put Eustace Sims in his place.

Jack didn't seem in a hurry to leave after the practice was over, so Gracie had time for a whispered consultation with Louise.

"I guess we could ask him," Louise said with a doubting frown.

She walked over to Jack as soon as he was alone.

"Jack, I wonder if you have time for coffee at the inn before you go home."

"Only if it's decaf," he said in his usual good-humored voice. "And I wouldn't mind a couple of Jane's famous cookies."

"She always has a supply in the freezer," Louise assured him. "We want to talk to you about something. We need help, but we want you to be of assistance only if you're completely willing."

"Now you've got me curious," Jack said, smiling.

Gracie enjoyed chatting with Jack on the walk over to the inn. She'd been right about his bearing. He'd been in the marines and was proud of it. He was even prouder of his wife Alison and their three sons.

By the time they reached the inn, Gracie was pretty sure Jack was the person they needed to pull off their sting. Her mind was whirling with ideas, but nothing would do any good unless Eustace Sims could be convinced, scared or intimidated into giving up his shady practices.

They found Jane in the kitchen with Alice, and Jack excused himself to call his wife to tell her that he would be late.

Jane was a born hostess. She didn't bat an eye when Louise asked her to produce some cookies for Jack. In a very short time she had a plate of butterscotch-walnut bars on the table, a cup of steaming decaf in front of Jack and a pot of herbal tea brewing for the rest of them.

"Now what is it you ladies want to pow-wow about?" he asked between appreciative bites.

"Gracie, you tell him about Eustace Sims," Jane prompted. "You know the most about him."

Gracie chose her words carefully, telling Jack how Byrdie had been persuaded to have unnecessary work done.

Jack shook his head at the woodworm threat, and he reacted with anger at the rest of the scam.

"There's more. Matilda Singleton in Potterston paid to

have him renovate her kitchen. He tore it apart, then insisted on full payment before he would finish the job. He took the money she'd already given him and disappeared."

"That's fraud. What are the police doing about it?"

"Basically nothing. Sims isn't his real name, and they couldn't find him."

"But Gracie did," Jane said proudly. "She's something of a sleuth."

"Good for you, Gracie," Jack said.

"I had a lot of help," Gracie said modestly. "Alice gave me the idea I needed to stimulate Byrdie's memory. He has a big scar on top of his wrist that he carefully keeps concealed under long sleeves when he's out on a job. Once we knew that, we were better able to describe him to building suppliers. One remembered him as an occasional customer and gave him our message."

"What was in that message? I hope you ladies aren't playing with fire. You're dealing with a criminal here."

"We told him that we have a job for him here at the inn. He's been here once to look at the attic. He's coming back tomorrow with a contract to build a cedar closet, but I suspect he'll try to sell us on adding some insulation too. That seems to be his specialty, talking victims into having unnecessary insulation installed," Gracie said.

Jack frowned and forgot about his drink. "I don't like the sound of that. What are you planning to do about it?"

"I know we're asking a lot, but we were hoping you might be here when he comes," Gracie said.

"In uniform," Louise added.

"I can only take animals into custody," Jack said with a chuckle.

"From what Byrdie and Matilda have learned, it would be hard to send him to jail. And a civil suit could be tricky. In fact, he probably would just disappear. We know for sure that he's used at least two different names."

"A slippery one, eh? What else do you know about him?"

"He drives an incredibly dirty pickup," Gracie said.

"He's quite unpleasant except when he's making his sales pitch," Jane said. "And he's no animal lover. I think he would've kicked Wendell down the stairs if we hadn't been there."

"He especially dislikes dogs," Gracie said. "He says he was a delivery man, but he quit because dogs gave him so much trouble."

"I'd say he was afraid of them." Jane refilled Jack's cup. "Maybe the scar is from a dog bite."

"Very interesting," Jack said, tapping his finger on the tabletop. "You can count me in. I can't arrest him, but I can help slow down his swindling. Tell me what your plan is so far."

Jane encouraged Jack to have another bar and heated water for another pot of tea while the rest of them threw around some ideas. Then the three Howard sisters and Jack joined Gracie in some serious planning. It was past eleven when Jack headed for home.

After Jack left, Gracie said good night and went up to her room. Her body was weary but her brain was bubbling over with the plans they'd made. She wanted to sleep but felt compelled to go over every aspect of the plan they'd put together with Jack's wholehearted help.

Dear Lord, please help us to stop the evil that Eustace Sims has perpetrated on others. Help us not to judge but to act with wisdom to protect the innocents he preys upon. Help him to come to an understanding of Your ways. Lord, I'm scared of what might happen tomorrow. Give me courage and faith to follow through.

She prayed a long time, then gently fell into an untroubled slumber.

Chapter ♪♪ Eighteen

F riday morning Alice came home from her walk with Vera feeling energized and ready to tackle jobs around the inn. They'd treated themselves to a leisurely breakfast at the Coffee Shop, so it was midmorning before she returned.

As she entered the foyer, she heard piano music and assumed Louise was giving a lesson. Alice's first job of the day was to check upcoming reservations to see if there had been any cancellations. Sometimes they had a waiting list of people who wanted a few days of vacation at the inn and were willing to come on short notice. She was pleased to see that they were full from Monday through Sunday, so her next responsibility was to make the laundry and cleaning schedule.

Absorbed as she was in her duties, she couldn't get the afternoon appointment with Eustace Sims out of her mind. She was gratified that they had a plan to confront him, but she was just a tiny bit nervous too. In spite of being uneasy about having him at the inn, she was pleased to be part of what Jack O'Hara and Gracie called "the sting."

The piano music stopped, and she looked up expecting to see one of the children who came for lessons. Instead Florence came toward her.

"Good morning, Alice," she said in a husky whisper.

"Goodness, Florence, what's wrong with your voice?"

"Just a little throat problem from too much singing," she whispered. "I expect it will go away by tomorrow."

"Maybe you should see a doctor," Alice suggested.

"No, that's not necessary. I thought it was better this morning, but when I started practicing my solo with Louise it got worse. I just need a day off from singing."

"Well, I hope you will feel better," Alice said, although she doubted the condition would go away very soon without medical attention. "Louise told us about the interfaith service Sunday."

"I'll certainly be in shape for that," Florence assured her. "I'm going home to gargle with warm water and molasses. My mother always swore by it."

"Well, good luck," Alice said as Florence walked to the front door.

Louise came into the foyer just as the door was closing behind Florence.

"Florence certainly sounded hoarse," Alice said. "I wonder if she'll be able to sing Sunday."

"So do I," Louise said, "but you know Florence. She's determined to do her solo. It's possible that she just strained her voice. She promised not to use it today and tomorrow unless it's absolutely necessary."

"True. I'll be glad when this business with Eustace Sims is over," Alice said. "It's hard to know what a criminal will do when he's cornered."

"I'm really glad Jack is going to help us," Louise admitted. "I wasn't sure we should ask him, but he certainly is enthusiastic. I felt as if we were planning a military campaign last night."

"Once a marine, always a marine," Alice said with a broad smile. Whatever happened, it was good to be sharing the encounter with her sisters and Gracie.

Gracie called Byrdie after breakfast to explain their "sting." They hadn't given her a role to play in their plan, and Gracie couldn't think of any reason for her to be there. They had more than enough people to pull it off, and her ankle still wasn't up to attic excursions.

"I do feel a bit guilty leaving it all up to you," Byrdie said toward the end of their phone conversation.

"It will be too congested in the attic for all of us. There's not much standing room with the family's stored items up there."

"I do feel I should be there."

"You could come over and wait out of sight," Gracie suggested.

"I would have to drive, and Sims has probably seen my car."

"If he sees it parked anywhere near the inn, it might scare him away," Gracie agreed. "Why don't you wait at home, and I'll call you as soon as it's over."

Byrdie agreed to stay away, and Gracie thought she heard a sigh of relief at the decision. Crime busting wasn't for everyone. Gracie had fears of her own, but it was too late to back out.

With time on her hands before Sims was due to arrive, Gracie decided a brisk walk would do more than anything else to steady her nerves. The exercise felt good to her, and it enabled her to relax. She hoped that she would have time to freshen up before Matilda arrived from Potterston. Then she remembered that Alice had known Matilda in college and would undoubtedly keep her entertained until it was time to put their plan into action.

She was several blocks from the inn when she saw a vehicle with the animal-control logo parked on a side street. Jack was already there, his truck parked discreetly out of sight. Matilda had been advised to do the same in case Sims recognized her car. Gracie felt like a general reviewing the positions of the troops, but, of course, no one had put her in charge. It was very much a group effort spurred on by Jack's determination to give Sims his just deserts.

Gracie wasn't surprised to see that everyone was there when she got back to the inn. She greeted Matilda warmly, then turned to the one participant she hadn't met.

"This is Roscoe," Jack said, introducing her to a plump, black bull terrier that lay at his feet in the kitchen. "He and I go way back. He has the sweetest disposition of any dog I've ever come across. We've sort of stuck together ever since I rescued him."

Something was different about Jack, and Gracie quickly realized that he was armed.

"You've brought a gun," she said, surprised by the weapon in a black holster at his waist.

Jack laughed. "It's just a fancy water pistol loaded with a chemical to repel dangerous animals. I've only had to use it once. A chow over in Potterston was determined to chew my arm off."

Gracie petted Roscoe and smiled when the dog responded with the canine version of a satisfied purr.

"No one could be afraid of a gentle creature like you," she told him. Then she excused herself to go upstairs to wash her face.

In her room she was assailed by doubt. It was easy to feel confident surrounded by helpful, caring people like the Howard sisters and Jack, but as soon as she was alone her misgivings returned. El always said she suffered from an overactive imagination. She could think of all kinds of things that could go wrong. What if Sims carried a gun? It wouldn't be hard to conceal it if he left his shirt hanging out. What if he simply didn't come? Their trap depended on his showing up. If he postponed or came very late, all their plans could be for nothing.

"Dear Lord," Gracie prayed softly in the sanctuary of her

room, "the closer we come to confronting Eustace Sims, the less sure I feel about what we're doing. Whatever happens, please let no one be hurt because of our actions. Please give me courage and wisdom to see this through."

Soon she felt better about putting their plan into action.

When she went back to the kitchen, she found a quiet group. They seemed to feel as subdued as she did by the plan that would unfold at any moment. Gracie felt compelled to go over the logistics one more time.

"Jane, Louise and Alice, you'll meet him at the door. He may want you to sign the contract without going up to the attic, but you'll insist on going up there first."

"Yes, Louise and I want him to point out exactly what he plans to do," Alice said, looking a little flushed with anticipation. "We'll pretend to disagree with each other about exactly where the closet should be."

"Matilda, Jack and I will stay out of sight in the kitchen," Gracie said. "I'll watch you go up the stairs. It won't matter too much if he sees me since he's already met me. Then I'll carefully time three minutes, and the rest of us will start up."

"That's the part that makes me nervous," Jane said. "Do you think we can ask enough questions to keep him up there that long?"

"Indeed we can," Louise said, absentmindedly petting Roscoe, who seemed to adore everyone who gave him the least bit of attention. "If he wants us to pay an exorbitant price for his work, he'll answer our questions no matter how silly they may seem."

"We can get him to present the contract. Legal language is always complicated. We'll ask him to explain every word if necessary," Alice said.

"It won't be," Gracie assured her. "Remember not to look at your watches. He's a sly one, and it might make him skittish."

"When the time is up, we'll all be sure to remain close to

the stairs while we have Sims check out the back of the attic," Louise said. "That way we can retreat down the stairs before Gracie comes up ahead of Jack and Roscoe. Gracie can distract him for a few moments to give Jack space to put his part of the plan into action."

"Yes, and I want to get up there after Jack so Sims can have a good look at me," Matilda said emphatically. "I want him to know that I helped bring him down."

"I do wonder about one thing," Gracie admitted. "Where are Gooseberry and Wendell?"

"They're off somewhere doing their own thing," Jane said. "I haven't seen them in hours. I wanted to put them in the basement in case Roscoe isn't fond of cats, but the little rascals are nowhere to be found."

"No worry about that," Jack assured them, patting Roscoe's head. "Roscoe gets along with two- and four-footed critters, but we've practiced his growl. He can sound fierce when I give him our secret signal."

"I made sure to lock the front door," Alice said. "We don't want any surprise visitors wandering through the inn."

"Sims is cheeky enough to walk right in," Matilda said.

She looked flamboyant in bright-red walking shorts and a white halter top, but her expression was grim. The group had debated whether to include her. Alice was worried that she was too impulsive, but Gracie was sure Matilda understood the plan and would support it successfully.

The doorbell sounded, and the room went instantly silent. Without a word, the three sisters moved to answer it.

Gracie listened at the kitchen door to be sure it was Sims.

"It's him," she whispered softly to Jack and Matilda.

Jack was stroking Roscoe's head to keep him calm and quiet. Matilda looked as if she were holding her breath in anticipation. Jack was relaxed with a little grin on his face.

As soon as she was sure that Sims and the sisters had climbed to the second floor out of sight, Gracie began timing.

Three minutes had never passed so slowly, but they'd all agreed that they needed to have Sims present the contract and give his spiel.

At last she gave the signal for the rest of the team to creep up the stairs.

Gracie went first. Jack had called her the "point man" when they were making the plan until Jane suggested that "point person" was a better way to put it. Gracie didn't bother to muffle the sound of her feet on the attic stairs, but behind her Matilda and Jack were moving as silently as possible. Roscoe snorted a little but didn't bark.

When Gracie stepped into the attic, Sims was gesturing at the beams overhead with a roll of paper that she took to be the contract. Louise and Jane were near the top of the steps without blocking them. Alice was a few steps away from them apparently having a heated discussion with him.

"Gracie, you're just the person we need," Alice said, wisely backing closer to the stairs. "Gracie's niece is an attorney. I would feel better if Gracie reads the contract before we sign it, Mr. Sims."

Sims was wearing a long-sleeved maroon shirt hanging out over his jeans. It was open in front to reveal a black T-shirt. Gracie remembered her apprehension about a gun but didn't see any suspicious bulges. He didn't need to be armed to swindle unsuspecting women.

"It's a standard contract, same as builders everywhere use. One half down on signing, the rest when the work is done," he said in a patronizing tone.

"There are an awful lot of words just to say that," Jane pointed out. "I would feel better if Gracie looked at the contract too."

"It's the part about the insect infestation that I don't understand," Louise said. "Are you sure you can take care of woodworms yourself?"

"No problem," Sims said. "You can call an exterminator

if you want, but it'll cost you double what I'm charging. I made the package deal as easy on you as I could."

"Well, we appreciate that," Louise said with an edge in her voice, "but it still seems odd to me that we have internal damage in the beams. This house has stood for many years without any sign of termites or carpenter ants."

"Woodworm is different," Sims said in a cajoling voice that made Gracie want to interrupt.

She didn't, but she did move to keep the contractor's attention focused away from the stairwell. Louise and Alice were doing just fine pinning him down, but it was time for the sisters to leave to make room for Jack.

"What is the scientific name for what we have?" Louise asked in a stern voice.

"Can't say that I know." Sims didn't quite manage to keep a surly undertone out of his voice, suggesting that he wasn't used to having his word questioned. "My pa called them woodworms, and that's good enough for me."

"I have one question," Gracie said, keeping her voice as bland as possible. "What did you use to get rid of the wood-worms at Mrs. Hutchinson's house?"

"What do you mean?" Sims asked in a belligerent voice. "I used what I needed to use to do the job."

It was the sisters' cue to retreat, and they did so quietly without attracting attention. Sims was too intent on arguing with Gracie.

"Is that so?" Matilda's voice came up the stairs before she was visible from the attic.

His face contorted with anger when her head appeared at floor level and he recognized her.

"What is this?" he demanded, stepping toward the stairs.

For a minute Gracie was afraid he would try to rush past Matilda and possibly push her down the stairs. She had jumped the gun and gone ahead of Jack in her eagerness to confront the contractor. Then Sims looked beyond her and froze.

"Well, Roscoe," Jack said in a conversational tone. "I guess these ladies have cornered a rat for us."

"Keep that dog away from me!" Sims yelled. "You got no right to come at me with a dog."

Matilda stepped aside to let Jack and Roscoe move closer to Sims, crowding him toward the furniture-strewn rear of the attic and blocking the escape route down the stairs.

"I've had some serious complaints about you, Mr. Sims," Jack said in a commanding voice.

"Let me out of here!"

Roscoe growled on cue, and Sims grabbed an old kitchen chair to use as a shield.

"Don't even think of swinging that chair, Sims. I've put tougher curs than you into custody."

Roscoe made an especially menacing sound, although Gracie couldn't see what Jack had done to trigger it.

The contractor's eyes flickered over Jack's uniform, which in Gracie's opinion looked very much like that of a deputy sheriff in her county at home. But it was the dog that riveted his attention.

"Get that mutt away from me!"

"I can't do that, Mr. Sims. You might say Fang here is my partner. He might take offense if I didn't include him. He likes to snack on a felon from time to time. Now let go of that chair. Pronto!"

"You got no right to threaten me." Sims released his hold on the chair, but he was still trying to back away from Roscoe.

"Some serious charges have been made against you, Sims," Jack said, letting anger show in his voice as he let Roscoe advance a step and give another menacing growl.

"You can't take the word of that woman," he said, pointing

at Matilda. "She's a loony. Had me buy materials, then refused to use them. I gave her every chance, but she wouldn't work with me."

"Do you admit that you insisted on full payment, then failed to do the work?" Jack seemed larger than life in the confines of the attic and a whole lot more intimidating than he had sitting at the kitchen table.

"No, I don't admit to anything. Get that mutt away from me. I know my rights. I want a lawyer."

"We're not quite at that point," Jack said in a harsh voice. "First, I want to know who you really are."

"Eustace Sims." He looked at Matilda and realized his mistake. "That is, I sometimes go by the name of Houston."

"Let me see your driver's license," Jack demanded.

"What right—"

Roscoe barked furiously, a menacing sound that would've unnerved Gracie if she hadn't known he was a sweetie.

Jack moved a step closer to Sims with Roscoe right beside him.

"Okay, okay, just keep that dog away from me."

He slowly reached into his rear pocket, pulled out his billfold and handed the license to Jack.

"Sam Dustin," Jack read. "You ladies heard that name before?"

They all indicated that they hadn't, although Gracie was quick to point out that it fit with their theory that he picked names using many of the letters in his real name.

"Now about the complaints we've had about you," Jack said, playing out Roscoe's leash so the dog could edge a couple of inches closer to the culprit.

Jack pulled out a small notebook and pretended to read from it.

"Mrs. Byrdie Hutchinson alleges that you fraudulently replaced insulation that didn't need replacing."

"She wanted it done!"

"Only because you frightened her into believing the old insulation was dangerous," Gracie said.

"I never said it was asbestos."

"Whatever she believed, you replaced it just to make a profit," Jack continued. "Then you invented the presence of woodworms."

"I treated the attic for that." His voice wavered between fear and nastiness.

"You spilled a little oil or something so there was a nasty smell. You didn't treat for woodworms in my friend's attic because there were none there," Gracie said, speaking for Byrdie as they'd agreed in their plan.

"You face fraud charges for your work at Mrs. Hutchinson's," Jack said, "but that's only the beginning."

"I want my money back," Matilda said. "It cost me a bundle to have another contractor come in and renovate the kitchen after you tore it apart and ran off with the money."

"You hafta prove it," Dustin said angrily, eyes still riveted on the dog.

"Oh, these ladies have a very strong case," Jack said in a firm voice.

Roscoe growled again. Gracie wondered how Jack prompted him to do it. Possibly he just didn't like the contractor.

Dustin nervously rubbed his scarred wrist as though it had started itching. He tried to shield himself behind a stack of old suitcases.

"It was your scar that gave you away," Gracie said, unable to resist bringing it up. "Mrs. Hutchinson remembered seeing it. It's from a dog bite, isn't it?"

He looked at her, and the fear in his face gave way to a repellent look of cunning.

"I was a delivery man. A rottweiler practically took my arm off when I tried to toss a package on a porch," he said, whining a bit to gain sympathy. "Drove me out of the delivery business. I had to do something, so I set up as a handyman. Couldn't make a living at it until I got into insulation work."

"I would like to see you in jail," Matilda said, "but first I want my money back."

"I don't have it. I gotta live, you know."

"Does your wife know what you do for a living?" Gracie asked, playing a hunch.

"No." He barely whispered.

"I'd like to think we could settle this here and now," Jack said in an official-sounding voice.

"Nothing to settle."

Dustin sounded sullen and belligerent, not what any of them wanted.

"I say take him to jail," Matilda said with unrehearsed anger.

"Do you have children, Mr. Dustin?" Gracie asked in a kind voice.

He gave her an angry scowl, then nodded.

"It would be very hard on children to see their father in jail. I wonder if there's any way we can work this out," she suggested.

"He should have thought of his family when he started swindling people," Matilda said.

"Kids gotta have food, clothes, school supplies. They need something new all the time." His eyes never left Roscoe, and Jack let the dog edge closer.

Gracie took a deep breath and prayed that he was softening. There was, of course, no way that Jack could actually arrest him. He could only frighten him into making some restitution and, possibly, running his business honestly in the future.

Then, unexpectedly, Roscoe yanked the leash from Jack's hand and started toward the contractor with a threatening bark. Dustin tried to bolt, but there was no way past the dog. He scrambled for safety, putting Gracie between the dog and him, then cowered in terror as Jack quickly subdued Roscoe. Jack looked as surprised as Gracie felt at his dog's surprising hostility toward Dustin. She could only guess that the contractor's manner had triggered an intense, instinctive reaction in the usually placid Roscoe.

"I think," Gracie said, trying to speak in a calm, resolute voice, "that we should continue this conversation in the kitchen."

Jack gestured for Dustin to step from behind Gracie and proceed down the stairs.

"Just remember, Fang can move a whole lot faster than you can," Jack said in a voice that was almost as menacing as Roscoe's bark. "And he hasn't had breakfast."

Well, this wasn't part of our plan, Gracie thought as she followed the others from the attic. *Not even Jack could have predicted that Roscoe would take such a dislike to Dustin. He must be a magnet for canine hostility. I hope he won't do any real harm to Dustin. That isn't at all what any of us wants, and it could cause a lot of trouble for Jack.*

She needn't have worried. Jack had Roscoe under control as he escorted Dustin, who glanced frequently over his shoulder to be sure the dog was restrained.

"Well now, why don't we all sit down and have a glass of lemonade," Jane suggested as they rejoined the sisters in the kitchen.

She put out a plate of assorted cookies and poured glasses of homemade lemonade for everyone. At first Dustin looked like he would refuse it, but he gave in and downed his in a few large swallows.

Roscoe sat by Jack's knee, distracted by a sugar cookie that Jack fed him in small bites. His opaque brown eyes never seemed to leave Dustin, and Gracie was glad he wasn't giving her that intense look.

"I won't press charges if I get my money back," Matilda said evenly.

Dustin glared at her but said nothing.

"Can you pay any part of it?" Jack asked.

"Yeah, maybe."

"Maybe isn't good enough. You don't know what I've been through since you tore my kitchen apart and left," Matilda said slapping a hand on the table. "I need a new garage too. Fat chance of that, now that you've conned me out of all that insurance money."

"Maybe there's a way to settle this," Gracie suggested. "Matilda, if Mr. Dustin builds you a new garage without charging for his labor, would that wipe the slate clean?"

"I guess. Well, it would certainly be better than nothing. But he should buy the lumber."

"Are you willing to do that, Dustin?" Jack was leaning to the side, the better to allow the contractor to see the "gun" he wore.

"Yeah, but I'll have to borrow cash from my brother. I don't want my wife to know."

His driver's license was still in Jack's pocket. Jack took it out and made a production of writing down the address in his little notebook.

"There's still Mrs. Hutchinson," Gracie said. "You do admit, don't you, that her attic didn't need new insulation and there were no woodworms."

"Nor are there in ours," Louise said.

"I put time and new insulation in that attic," Dustin protested.

"And charged her triple what it was worth if that contract you brought for us is any indication," Jane said.

Somehow she'd thought to retrieve it from the attic floor and was keeping it firmly in her possession.

"I think I can speak for Byrdie," Gracie said. "She isn't expecting to get any money back, but she badly needs someone to clean out her attic and cellar and haul away the things she no longer wants. Is that something you would be willing to do as restitution, Mr. Dustin?"

Roscoe whimpered for another cookie, but it was reminder enough to Dustin.

"Yeah, I guess."

"That's settled then," Jack said with satisfaction, helping himself to another cookie and sharing it with Roscoe.

"There is one other thing," Alice said. "Have you pulled this scam on any other innocent victims?"

Dustin wasn't a big man, and he seemed to have shrunk since confronting all of them.

"No," he denied vehemently.

Gracie didn't exactly believe him, but she didn't have evidence to the contrary.

"If I hear of you pulling this stunt again anywhere in this county, you'll get another visit from me and Fang," Jack said. "Remember, I know your real name and where you live."

"I'll expect you tomorrow to start tearing down the old garage. I want a two-car garage with a new cement floor," Matilda said.

Dustin looked decidedly ill. Gracie suspected that his punishment would begin when he started working for Matilda again, but difficult or not, she didn't deserve to have her money stolen.

"Byrdie won't be in a hurry to get her jobs done. You can clear her attic and basement when the garage is finished."

"Fang and I will be dropping by from time to time to see the work is done right," Jack assured him. "I'd as soon put you in a pen myself, but if the ladies are satisfied, I'll go along with their wishes. You owe them thanks for being so reasonable."

Dustin muttered something, and Gracie was pretty sure it was a thank you.

When everyone had left the kitchen except Jane, Gracie gratefully slumped in a chair. She didn't feel at all triumphant.

Instead it was a relief to have things settled, but she felt sorry for Dustin's family. He had two sons, he admitted before he left, one in middle school and one in high school. Both were old enough to help him with the job at Byrdie's, he said, if that was okay with her.

The women didn't have a guarantee that the contractor wouldn't go back to swindling people, but at least he knew that someone was watching. It was amazing how fast information spread from one small town to another. And she didn't think he would risk another encounter with "Fang."

She went up to her room to call Byrdie and treat herself to a short nap. Cornering criminals was an exhausting business.

Chapter ♪ Nineteen

Jane awoke in the hazy light of dawn and lay for a while enjoying the room that wholly reflected her decorating taste. The eggplant-purple paint and contemporary blond furniture were completely different from anything else in the inn, and she'd covered the walls with her own paintings. Each one represented a period of her life. She wondered what scene would best represent the present, and a vision of her garden immediately came to mind.

It was much too early to start breakfast, but she was too keyed up to go back to sleep. Her garden had been judged. She was sure of that, but how had it fared in the judges' opinions? Did it deserve to be the winner?

She couldn't help thinking about Elma's friendship garden. It was totally different from Jane's, yet so sweet in its own unique way.

At least it was finally Saturday. The judges would announce their decision at a garden party this afternoon. All those who had submitted entries were invited to the home of Angelina and Peter Whitney for the occasion. Angelina was the chairman of the judging committee and a woman regarded by some to be rather intimidating. Jane knew her only by sight, and this would be the first time she'd been invited to the Whitneys' historic federalist home. It sat on rolling acres south of Acorn Hill on Village Road and had been built by Peter's ancestors, pioneers in the area.

If Acorn Hill had nobility, it would be the Whitneys. Jane smiled as she imagined Peter and Angelina riding through the town on high-strutting chestnut horses while the humble townsfolk lined the street. Peter had served in the state legislature for many years, and Angelina was well known in Pennsylvania as an activist on environmental issues. Jane wasn't easily intimidated by successful people, but she did admire this couple's accomplishments.

It was no use staying in bed. She couldn't quiet her thoughts by lying still, so she decided to get in motion.

By ten o'clock Jane's morning duties were done. Their guests and her sisters had eaten breakfast, and Jane had put the kitchen in order.

Alice and Gracie bubbled with enthusiasm over the success of their "sting," but Louise was quiet. No doubt she was worried about the interfaith service tomorrow. Jane had no idea what Louise would do if Florence couldn't sing her solo, but it was obviously bothering her sister. Tone deaf herself and unable to sing on key, Jane had a hard time understanding most choir problems, but she hated to see her sister upset. Louise was the unflappable Howard, the one they relied on for common sense and balance in their lives.

Jane was distracted too, but she had a different kind of dilemma. She couldn't get Elma's garden out of her mind, and her conscience told her that something had to be done.

The botanical society's rules were clear. No one was allowed to influence the judges' decision by discussing his or her garden with them.

Rules were made to be broken, Jane thought decisively.

Jane had something on her mind, and she wasn't going to be intimidated by rules or judges. She knew what she had to do.

An hour later she carefully navigated the long, winding driveway to the Whitney home. She'd borrowed Louise's aging Cadillac because her own little compact had been decidedly cranky lately. She'd dressed in a smart outfit, a light-beige pantsuit with a chocolate-brown silk blouse and high-heeled pumps. With her usual dark ponytail pinned up in a bun she felt like a different person, but this visit seemed to demand formality.

The original Whitney homestead had been enlarged with one-story additions on either side, rather like white angel wings nestled up against the dark-red brick facade of the old house. Even in her agitated state, Jane noticed the many trees in the yard. She identified black walnuts, a cherry tree and what she thought was a Chinese elm. Dogwood flanked the house, and all manner of smaller shrubs gave warmth to the otherwise austere, early nineteenth-century house. She was curious about the garden, but she would see it this afternoon unless she was disqualified for coming ahead of time.

Jane was tall and slender, but the woman who opened the front door was even taller and rail-thin. Her white hair was close-cropped, and the network of wrinkles on her tanned face marked her love of the outdoors.

"Mrs. Whitney, I'm Jane Howard, one of the entries in the garden competition."

"Of course, Jane. You're one of Daniel Howard's daughters. I was very fond of your father. The whole community misses him."

"Thank you," Jane said. "It's nice of you to say so."

She'd rehearsed what she wanted to say on the drive to the Whitneys, but actually getting the words out was going to be more difficult than she'd planned.

"I just put the kettle on for tea. Will you join me?"

"That would be very nice," Jane said.

She followed the older woman into a large, sunny kitchen with aged beams, rough-plastered white walls and worn gray flagstones. Bundles of herbs were suspended from hooks in the ceiling, and the blended fragrances of rosemary and sage in the room delighted Jane.

The modern appliances had flat gray surfaces that didn't conflict with the period ambiance, and there were no built-in cupboards, only freestanding storage pieces including a large walnut dresser with blue-and-white chinaware on display. Jane fell in love with the charm of the room and could easily imagine working in it.

She also couldn't help noticing covered platters on every available surface, stacks of plates and cups and a large portable cooler. The Whitneys were obviously prepared for the afternoon reception.

"There," Mrs. Whitney said, pouring tea into two white ironware cups without saucers.

"Thank you. Perhaps I shouldn't have come, Mrs. Whitney—"

"Please call me Angelina."

"Angelina." Jane tried the name but felt awkward using it. "I know I'm not supposed to have contact with any of the judges before the competition."

"I think we can overlook that since the judging has been completed," Angelina said. "You must have a very good reason for coming now."

"Yes, I do," Jane said resolutely. "I have something to tell you."

"The judges were very impressed with your garden, myself included."

"Oh, I'm not here about my garden," Jane quickly explained. "It's Elma Grayson's."

Angelina looked puzzled but didn't comment.

"It's just that I've never seen a garden like hers. I know she wasn't allowed to tell you about it, but I think you should know that it isn't an ordinary garden like mine."

"What do you mean?"

"I only improved on what my mother did years ago. I went to nurseries, bought good plants, read a lot of books."

"All your preparation certainly showed," Angelina said.

"Anyone could do what I did. That's what makes Elma's friendship garden so special. Every plant, every flower, every little garden ornament is a symbol of friendship."

"Whatever do you mean?" Angelina sat across from Jane at a scrubbed pine table, her cup of tea untouched.

Jane explained, growing passionate when she related the kindness lavished on Elma's garden by her friends.

"I know Elma wasn't allowed to explain it to you, but it is unique."

Angelina nodded.

"Well, I just thought you should know," Jane said lamely.

She'd said all she could about Elma's garden. She didn't know what she'd expected from Angelina Whitney, but the woman's only response was silence.

"I should be going," Jane said.

In fact, she couldn't wait to leave.

"I will see you at the reception this afternoon, won't I?" Angelina asked.

Jane tried to think of an excuse for not coming, but her imagination failed her.

"Yes, of course," she said, practically stammering.

"Good, I want you to be sure to come. We'll announce the winners promptly at three o'clock."

"Yes, I won't be late." Jane felt a bit childish as though she were promising a teacher to do her homework on time.

"Thank you for coming, Jane. I'll see you this afternoon."

It was one thing to promise to be there and quite another to get through the hours until the reception was scheduled to begin. Jane changed her mind a dozen times about what to wear, finally settling on a favorite long skirt in shades of bronze and green. She put on a little green vest over a short-sleeved beige knit top and decided the outfit was fine. No doubt her pantsuit and silk blouse would have been more appropriate, but she wanted to feel like herself.

Alice and Louise both made a point of wishing her good luck and seeing her off. It was much too complicated to explain why she didn't want to go. She wasn't exactly sure herself, but her earlier trip to the Whitneys' had left her feeling awkward. No doubt a sophisticated woman like Angelina would think she was naive.

Jane made sure that she wasn't the first to arrive. In fact, she was one of the last.

People were wandering around the spacious patio and garden in back of the house. Jane noticed that the Whitneys seemed to love trees more than flowers, although they did have a small but attractive garden with white-shell paths and a water fixture in the form of a swan.

She looked around for the hostess, then made sure to avoid her. She'd said her piece, and it had elicited no enthusiastic response. Angelina hadn't given her a clue what she thought about her impassioned description of Elma's garden.

For a short while Jane carried around a plate with a finger sandwich and a spritz cookie, but she was too nervous to eat. She knew some but not all of the people there. Elma was among them, surrounded by several women, but Jane didn't approach them. She wasn't at all sure Elma would approve of what she had done.

After what seemed like ages, Angelina called for everyone to gather under the canvas awning that shaded a good part of the patio. She introduced the other two judges, but Jane was too edgy to remember their names for long.

"I can't tell you how pleased the judges were with this year's entries," Angelina began. "Every garden we saw was a winner, lovingly tended by people who care about nature."

Jane made sure she was at the back of the crowd of fifty

or more people. She was poised for a quick retreat, still uncomfortable about her attempt to sway the judges.

"Today we did something that we've never done before in all the years I've been associated with the botanical society," Angelina said. "We held an emergency meeting before the reception and changed our mind about one garden. Before doing so, we consulted with those who would have received second and third places. Both were enthusiastic in agreeing with our final decision although it means a lesser award for them. For that reason we'll also have a fourth-place winner this year."

Jane listened with new alertness. Was it possible that she'd had some influence on the final decision?

"The fourth-place award this year belongs to Rachel and Joseph Holzmann."

Jane didn't totally agree, remembering that their garden had seemed crowded to her, but Angelina went on to explain that the award was earned by their use of some unusual plants that were difficult to grow in Pennsylvania.

"Our second runner-up this year is the Bentley garden. Kathy and Hart have been winners before, and they didn't disappoint us this year. Like the Holzmanns, they very graciously agreed to accept a lesser prize this year."

Jane was disappointed. The Bentleys' garden was lovely with all the statuary, but they hired a gardener to do the work. It didn't have the personal touch of a garden like Elma's. Of course, she'd hoped to be a runner-up if not the winner herself. Possibly Angelina had disqualified her for trying to influence the judges' decision. She knew herself well enough to know that she would go on to some other project, but she badly wanted Elma to get the recognition her garden deserved.

"Our first runner-up award goes to Jane Howard," Angelina said, startling Jane. "Please come up, Jane."

Jane walked in a daze, not sure what to do with her plate of goodies, but some kind soul took it from her before she reached Angelina.

"I have to tell you something about Jane," Angelina said with delight in her voice. "Her garden was slated to be this year's winner, but she convinced me to award it to another garden. If we had an award for kindness and fairness, it would go to Jane. The judges also plan to review the criteria that don't allow people to be present during judging. It seems that sometimes there's more to a garden than meets the eye."

Jane held her breath in disbelief.

"This year's winner is Elma Grayson, for the wonderful plot she calls her friendship garden," Angelina said. "Elma entered other years, but she never had a spokesperson like Jane Howard. I'm very pleased to congratulate you, Elma."

Angelina walked over to the tearful winner and hugged her as the crowd broke into hearty applause.

Jane's eyes filled with tears too. She'd never felt more like a winner herself.

Chapter ♪ Twenty

Louise liked the picturesque appearance of the Methodist church. The brick walls and tall, graceful steeple reminded her of a village scene that used to hang in her father's bedroom. She was pleased to be at the church this Sunday morning.

She was the first Grace Chapel member to arrive, but the Methodist church's organist was there for the short practice they'd scheduled before the interfaith service.

Warm sun streamed into the white interior of the church and gave a pleasing glow to the dark wood of the pews, but the serenity of the nave wasn't enough to dispel her worries. She didn't know what to do if Florence was unable to handle her solo. Or worse, Florence might insist on singing even though her voice wasn't up to it.

There was nothing Louise disliked more than a scene, and Florence was fully capable of creating one if a temporary director tried to tell her she couldn't sing.

The week had gone well for her sisters and Gracie. Louise admired Jane for explaining Elma's special garden to Angelina and gaining first place for the lovely old woman. She was even prouder of her younger sister because of the pleasure she took in Elma's win. Jane had put aside her own competitiveness to do what she thought was right. They'd both had tears in their eyes when Elma came to the inn last evening and gave Jane a lovely plant to begin a friendship garden of her own.

Alice was well satisfied with the "sting" that exposed Sam Dustin although she insisted her role had been minimal. All involved admired Gracie's persistence and sleuthing abilities, while Gracie, in turn, gave credit to Jack O'Hara and Roscoe for the success of the plan.

Louise prayed during the few minutes that she was alone, thanking the Lord for the many blessings she enjoyed, especially the special bond with her sisters.

Toni Glendenning was the next to arrive, and Louise hoped her husband would be coming too. "I have to tell you something," the younger woman said with an air of embarrassment.

"What is it?" Louise asked, a little concerned that the couple might be planning to leave the choir.

"I made a mistake. I complained about the new music for 'Amazing Grace' in front of my mother. She can be awfully overprotective. Well, to be truthful, she does like to micromanage."

"I don't think I've met your mother," Louise said.

"She lives in Potterston, so you probably haven't. The thing is, she did a really bad thing. She thought she was helping me. I only found out about it this week, and I feel terrible. The new music is really nice once you get used to it."

Louise had a feeling that she knew where this was going, but she kept still.

"She called you and complained without giving her name," Toni said.

"Ah." Louise was relieved to know the identity of her anonymous caller and grateful to know it wasn't one of the choir members.

"I'm terribly sorry," Toni said contritely.

"It's forgotten," Louise assured her with a smile. "Mothers get carried away trying to make things easier for their children. It happens sometimes with my piano students."

Soon the other choir members arrived ready for a short rehearsal with the church organist. Florence took her place but, as far as Louise could see, she hadn't said anything to anyone.

They went through "Amazing Grace" first, and Louise was very pleased that they'd mastered the new music so quickly and so well. However, it soon became obvious that Florence wasn't singing with the rest of the choir. Then it was time for "I Love to Tell the Story."

Again Louise couldn't help noticing that Florence still wasn't singing. She was standing between Gracie and Loueda Ullman, whose strong soprano voice compensated for Florence's silence, but Louise had a bad feeling about the solo.

Florence started to sing, then her voice wavered and a hoarse cough broke off her effort.

"I'm not going to be able to do it," Florence croaked unhappily. "I was sure if I rested my voice, it would come back for the solo. I can't let people hear me like this. I've let all of you down."

"Oh dear, don't be concerned. It's not a difficult part. I'm sure one of us can take over for you," Loueda Ullman said.

Several choir members looked at her in surprise, and Louise shared their feelings. Loueda was a quiet little woman with salt-and-pepper hair who'd been with the choir for over a year without making any close personal friends. She and her husband had retired to Acorn Hill, where he still ran a small computer-based home business. Loueda seemed to keep to herself, and no one had gotten to know her well, an omission Louise regretted now.

In fact, everything about Loueda was quiet and understated. She tended to wear rather subdued colors that made her complexion look sallow, and the pale lavender dress she was wearing under her open robe was no exception. It was only lately that she'd spoken up at all during choir practices.

"Can you sing it?" Louise asked, trying not to sound skeptical.

"Oh yes, I sang the same solo as part of a program my church in Philadelphia did a few years ago." She said it matter-of-factly.

"Would you be willing to try it now?"

"Why yes, I guess I could." Loueda said in a calm voice.

Louise had known that Loueda had a good voice, but she wasn't prepared for the wave of emotion that she experienced as Loueda sang the solo. Her rendition was beautiful.

"That was lovely, Loueda," she said when the hymn was over. "I hope you'll sing the solo part for today's service."

"Thank you, Louise. I'll be happy to."

"Oh, I'm so relieved," Florence said in a whisper as she slipped out of her robe. "I could hardly sleep last night because I was so worried about letting the choir down. And Loueda can sing it so beautifully."

Louise enjoyed the service more than she would have believed possible. The choir did indeed look handsome in the newly trimmed robes. Loueda's solo mesmerized the congregation, and Louise was full of questions about her musical background. She was going to invite Loueda and her husband to the inn for dinner as soon as possible.

Florence was waiting for her when she left the building, and Louise didn't know what to expect from her. Did she resent the wonderful job Loueda had done?

"I'm sorry about your solo," Louise said.

"It couldn't be helped. It was a very moving service," Florence said in her raspy voice. "I'm glad I was here. We're so lucky to have Loueda in the choir."

"Yes, it was good of her to fill in on such short notice."

"She did a wonderful job, better than I could do even if

my voice was at it's best," Florence admitted. "I was so proud of the choir today."

"It's very much a group effort," Louise said, impulsively hugging Florence. "I hope your voice is better for our next rehearsal."

"I feel bad that I didn't take time to get to know Loueda better," Louise confided to Gracie when they were back at the inn. "She's lived here for over a year, and I haven't made any gesture of friendship."

"It's hard to include everyone in a friendship circle," Gracie consoled. "I've been guilty of being too wrapped up in my own life to reach out to newcomers. But it's never too late to make new friends. Look what happened to me in Acorn Hill. I met the three of you and had an adventure."

"Is that what you call it?" Byrdie asked. She'd come to the inn for a luncheon Jane had prepared to say good-bye to Gracie. "I was worried sick about your meeting with Sims. I mean Dustin. Do you really think he'll come to clean my attic and basement?"

"I think you can rely on Jack and Roscoe to see that he does," Gracie assured her.

She joined her friend in helping herself to the buffet, which included Jane's luscious Normandy cheese puffs and a particularly tempting dish of egg noodles and beef Stroganoff served with fresh baguettes and whipped country butter. The tossed salad was a delicious blend of romaine lettuce, grape tomatoes, shredded carrots, croutons and a sprinkling of walnuts. An antique cut-glass bowl was filled with melon balls, and the blackberry cobbler was hot from the oven.

It was a meal made for lingering, and the friends ate slowly, wanting to delay the time when Gracie had to depart.

Gracie was sad to leave the Howard sisters and Grace Chapel Inn, but it couldn't have been a more successful visit. She had indeed made new friends, and so had Byrdie. Alice and Byrdie had chatted over lunch and made plans to see a movie together. After the interfaith service, Florence commended Gracie and Byrdie for the handsome results of their efforts to adorn the choir robes. She promised to call Byrdie and set a time to visit at the Simpsons' house as soon as her voice returned to normal.

Louise thanked Gracie profusely for her help with the choir, although Gracie said that her participation had been more pleasure than work. Louise still felt bad about not taking the time to get to know Loueda Ullman better before her stunning solo, but she was sure their common love of music would make them closer in the future.

Jane gave Gracie some cuttings from her garden, carefully potting them to survive the drive home.

"I learned more from Elma's friendship garden than I did from all the gardening books I've read," she admitted to Gracie. "I can't wait to visit it again and to share my garden with her."

Gracie hugged them all on the front porch of the inn and hurried down to her car, packed and ready for the trip home. She waved as she drove away, and a heartfelt prayer came to her lips. *Thank You, Lord, for friends old and new. They are truly living reminders of Your love and grace.*

Jane's Lasagna

SERVES SIX TO EIGHT

1 pound ground beef
2 cups canned diced tomatoes
18 ounces tomato paste
3 tablespoons parsley flakes, separated
1 tablespoon dried basil
10 ounces lasagna noodles, cooked according
   to package directions
3 cups ricotta cheese
½ cup grated parmesan
2 beaten eggs
1 pound thinly sliced mozzarella

Preheat oven to 375 degrees. Lightly spray a 9" x 13" pan and set aside.

Brown ground beef and drain. Add tomatoes, paste, basil and one tablespoon parsley. Simmer thirty minutes.

Combine the ricotta cheese, parmesan, eggs and two tablespoons parsley.

Layer ingredients in the pan in this order: noodles, ricotta cheese mixture, mozzarella, meat sauce. There should be at least two layers of each.

Bake for forty-five minutes or until bubbly. Let set fifteen minutes before serving.

About the Authors

Pam Hanson and Barbara Andrews are a daughter-mother writing team. They began working together in the early 1990s and have had twenty books published, including fifteen under the pseudonym Jennifer Drew.

Pam has taught reporting courses at West Virginia University and is now director of advising for the School of Journalism. She has presented writing workshops and has been involved in school and church activities. She lives with her husband, a professor, and their two sons in West Virginia, where she shares her home with her mother.

Previous to their partnership, Barbara had twenty-one novels published under her own name. She began her career writing Sunday-school stories and contributing to antiques publications. Currently she writes a column and articles about collectible postcards. For twenty years she has sponsored a mail postcard auction with all proceeds going to world hunger relief. She is the mother of four and the grandmother of seven.

A Note from the Editors

This original book was created by the Books and Inspirational Media Division of Guideposts, the world's leading inspirational publisher. Founded in 1945 by Dr. Norman Vincent Peale and his wife Ruth Stafford Peale, Guideposts helps people from all walks of life achieve their maximum personal and spiritual potential. Guideposts is committed to communicating positive faith-filled principles for people everywhere to use in successful daily living.

Our publications include award-winning magazines such as *Guideposts*, *Angels on Earth*, *Sweet 16* and *Positive Thinking*, best-selling books, and outreach services that demonstrate what can happen when faith and positive thinking are applied to day-to-day life.

For more information, visit us online at www.guideposts.org, call (800) 431-2344 or write Guideposts, 39 Seminary Hill Road, Carmel, New York 10512.